WELCOME TO THE 31ST CENTURY, WHERE:

If you're bored with your own life, you can relive the lives of famous people, either real or fictional. Just beware the consequences of getting too caught up in the experience. . . .

Sightseeing can take you anywhere in the known universe—except home. . . .

When men and women can each have worlds of their own, what will happen to the human race . . . ?

These are some of the thirteen fascinating journeys into the future you will find when you venture into the pages of—

MILLENNIUM 3001

MILLENNIUM

EDITED BY

Martin H. Greenberg
& Russell Davis

DAW BOOKS, INC.

DONALD A. WOLLHEIM, FOUNDER

375 Hudson Street, New York, NY 10014

ELIZABETH R. WOLLHEIM
SHEILA E. GILBERT
PUBLISHERS
www.dawbooks.com

First Printing, February 2006
1 2 3 4 5 6 7 8 9

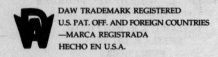

DAW TRADEMARK REGISTERED
U.S. PAT. OFF. AND FOREIGN COUNTRIES
—MARCA REGISTRADA
HECHO EN U.S.A.

PRINTED IN THE U.S.A.

CONTENTS

CONTENTS

INTRODUCTION

by Russell Davis

YOU KNOW WHAT I'd love to be able to do? I'd love to be able to write this introduction and tell you that when I was in high school and college, I kicked some serious intellectual ass in the hard sciences. That I reveled in biology and chemistry and physics, and was often taken aside by professors and encouraged in a career involving NASA or cutting edge medical research. The truth, however, is quite a bit less glamorous than that. In fact, let's put it this way: I took astronomy—a lot. And I avoided every other hard science course like the plague.

On the other hand, I read a lot of science *fiction*. I have little doubt that I learned more from reading all those novels than I ever would have bothered with in a classroom. Hard science was never my cup of tea. Even from a writing perspective, when I write SF, I usually use a soft science approach—sociology, psychology, human development—areas, basically, where it's harder to prove I screwed it up. It's not that the hard sciences don't interest me, it's just that there seem to be actual right and wrong answers. My BA is in BS for a *reason*.

I got to thinking about that a little, and it occurred to me that part of my fear of getting the science wrong was because what seemed incredibly fantastic and far-off when I was a teenager, didn't seem nearly so out of reach as an adult. The speed of technology was so fast that new developments were coming faster than you could say "handheld computer." Think about the technological developments in recent years: cloning, tiny computers, electronic books, the Internet, hybrid cars, and so much more. In many ways, the visions and imaginings of writers in the 50s and 60s (even the 70s and 80s) have come true— and then some.

But I do love well-realized science fiction. Especially when I get it. You know what I mean, don't you? Have you ever picked up a science fiction book that's *waay* more science than fiction, and found yourself wondering if the cover shouldn't have warned you that a PhD was required to understand it? It's happened to me, anyway, and more often than I care to admit. That said, I've read hundreds of science fiction novels and stories where I got it. The science was explained in a way that made sense, and the fiction took me away to another world or another time.

To one degree or another, that's what *Millennium* is all about. I asked twelve of today's finest writers of science fiction to imagine the future—but not just any future. Our future—1,000 years from now. That, my friends, is a long, long time. Think about 1,000 years ago—the year would be 1005 AD. How far have we come since then? What would the people of that time make of our time? At a guess, it would probably scare the wits out of them.

I wanted these talented authors to imagine the year 3005 and share their vision. Far enough out that the technology wasn't going to catch us with our predictions down. Far enough out that it might be unrecognizable to those of us here in 2005. Far enough out that it might be scary. And, I'm pleased to say, that every single one of them came through in a way I hadn't thought of myself.

Their voices—from renowned names that need no introduction like Brian Stableford, Jack Williamson and Kevin Anderson to newer authors like Sarah Hoyt and Jim Fiscus—have imagined our far distant future in a unique and enjoyable way. It's been a real pleasure putting together this anthology, but I have to tell you one more thing before I take my cue and exit stage left.

The best part was that in reading these science fiction stories, I got it. Every story, every time. And man was it fun to get swept away. I hope you do, too. Enjoy!

AFTERWARD

by John Helfers

THE BLUE, WHITE, AND BROWN planet is quiet now.

It still continues in its orbit, whirling around the G2 star it has circled for the past 4.6 billion years, the third of nine planets held in that massive, fiery, red-golden orb's inexorable gravity. The energy thrown off by this star, that takes the form of light that is essential for all known life, still takes about seven minutes to traverse the ninety-three million miles to the planet's surface, always revealing oceans and continents on one half of the world, and leaving the other half shrouded in darkness.

The third planet is still orbited by its own satellite, a round, white rock that is visible due to the star's reflected light off its desolate terrain. Its airless, cratered surface is littered with debris, including a sun-bleached piece of cloth on a stick upon which can still be seen rows of white stars against what might have once been a dark-colored field. Several vehicles also rest motionless there, and a cluster of cold silvered domes near several holes dug into the surface give evidence that at some point some kind of creatures had walked on its surface, and perhaps delved under its crust for some long-forgotten reason.

Three hundred eighty-four thousand kilometers away, beneath black space that has been wiped clean of all artificial satellites long ago, clouds still form in the blue planet's atmosphere, growing, swelling, scudding across the bright blue sky, sometimes releasing violent storms that rage across continents and oceans, sometimes fading back into the rain cycle without shedding a single drop of moisture, just as they have for millions of years, and will do for millions more.

Once an innumerable number of species of animals roamed over this planet, from lowly yet almost indestructible insects; cockroaches, blowflies, and their ilk, to higher forms of life, including reptiles, mammals of both the air and the land, and sea creatures tiny and large. Now all of the animal species on the entire planet number in the thousands; mostly insect life, the hardy cockroach, seasonal cicadas, and flies. There always seem to be flies. The oceans are nearly dead, containing only single-celled animal life, carrying on as it has for millennia. It is rare to see warm-blooded mammals anywhere on the northern half of the planet; anything left with fur or feathers is born, lives, and dies near the equator. Looking north, it is obvious why.

As the blue planet rotates, part of it always turning into the bright sunlight, continents come into view, most of them unchanged for thousands of years. Except one. This irregular mass, pocketed with hundreds of inlets, bays, rivers, and lakes, with a small peninsula jutting from the southeastern corner into an ocean, and a large swath of land bulging from the northwestern corner that seems to reach out with a scattering of broken islands to almost touch the enormous continent nearby, at first seems just like the rest of the land masses around it. But closer examination reveals a different story.

What used to be a broad, high, unbroken chain of mountains that stretched from the ice caps of the frozen sea at the top of the world to the banana-shaped land-mass bridging the ocean between this continent and the next one is now shattered into pieces. What had once been hundreds of lofty, snow-capped mountain peaks in the middle of this once-mighty range is now a huge crater, more that two hundred kilometers wide. The crater would be visible from this planet's moon, if there was anyone there to see it.

As the star's light shines more fully on this vast

terrain, it reveals that this land is not like the others. Every one of the other continents has spots of green, small ones, no doubt, but pockets of vegetation, nevertheless. This land, however, has not a speck of green to be seen. Instead, it is swathed in a thick layer of gray-brown ash stretching from the western coast to a cluster of five large, still, dead lakes that lie directly below a huge bay in the northeast quadrant of the continent. It reaches from the frozen tundra in the north to the end of that mountain chain in the south, and covers everything it touches. The huge canyon to the southwest of the mountain range. The thick, once-verdant forests that ranged the entire length of the west coast, now only dead branches caked in a thick, hardened coating of ash. The remains of a long suspension bridge, its girders and foundation now twisted and buckled by a long-ago earthquake, have turned a dull gray as well. And the buildings.

The hundreds of thousands of houses, skyscrapers, farms, churches, businesses, and every other building dotting the planet are all still and quiet. Ornate spires are choked in dark dust. Mirrored windows, those that were still intact, obscured by a coating of gritty soot, hardened by years of rainfall that had turned them into a solid coating. Nothing living moves throughout the breadth of the land.

The planet turns, as it always has, and reveals more of what has been left behind by those that once lived here. Tall clock towers are now silent, pointed hour and minute hands stilled centuries ago. Here and there natural wildfires have destroyed what was once dozens of communities, incinerating acre after acre of cities, towns, and forest. Several pyramid-shaped structures near a large sea are slowly being both eroded away by the constant desert wind and buried by the ever-drifting sands. A large lump that might once have been a strange, sculpted amalgam of man and crouching animal is now little more than an eroded hill of featureless stone.

On other continents, nature is reclaiming the land that had once belonged to it long ago. Thick jungle advances over tall buildings, disintegrating roads and foundations, slowly bringing down what were once monuments to the race that had thrived here. Rivers swollen by melting runoff from the mountains over-flow their banks and flood tens of thousands of miles of landscape, altering it each time. In other areas, the desert sands inch forward, covering earth and grass and water and buildings. The unstoppable ocean occasionally builds and releases its fury on the coast-lines of the world, destroying, reshaping, renewing. Seasons pass, thick, heavy snow drifting down to cover the once-magnificent cities that were the pride of the race that had built them so long ago.

Once, the beings that had erected these buildings had teemed on this planet, spreading over the land and water in multitudes. Ever-curious, they traversed almost every inch of the world they had inherited, scaling the highest mountain, descending to the bottom of the ocean, and even splitting the very ·atoms that comprised existence itself. They conquered disease, joined the world together in technology, and almost destroyed themselves more than once. They split the sky with their vehicles, always seeking to go farther, faster, and eventually slipped the surly bonds of earth to explore the near reaches of space. They even took enough of an interest in the galaxies beyond their own to send out a signal, hoping for a response from another life form somewhere in the universe. But, as with all cycles, their time had to come to an end eventually, leaving only the scattered monuments to their legacy behind.

Now, the remains of the vast transportation system lies in abandoned rows near what were once centers of civilization. The once-vibrant communications systems that used light itself to carry information around the globe in the blink of an eye are long gone. The artificial space stations that had orbited this planet have long since streaked across the sky in a fiery blaze as they reentered the atmosphere. The history of this race, preserved first in clay and stone, then later on paper, in steel and silicon and electrons, is now dormant, the buildings erected to house their story stolen by time.

Perhaps someday, hundreds or thousands of years in the future, another race will evolve on this planet that will discover the remains of this civilization, and will wonder at those who came before them. Perhaps it will be visitors from a distant star, who have received a signal broadcast into space centuries before, or who have recovered an ancient probe launched into space before any of them were alive, and who have journeyed across space to locate the source of this strange technology. Perhaps they will unlock the mysteries of this race in the sealed technology hidden inside a mountain, or uncover records that reveal the history of this race, and what eventually happened to it.

Or perhaps, in about nine billion years, the star that this blue, white, and brown planet orbits around will swell into an immense red ball of flaring helium, incinerating the two smaller planets closer to it, and yes, this planet as well. After a few million more years, having exhausted its fuel, it will collapse into a dense core of tightly-packed atoms, forming a white ball about the size of the third planet it had destroyed those many years ago.

And in the end, except for those scattered bits of technology which may have survived their endless journey, and centuries of radio and television signals that have been broadcast throughout the universe, it will be as if that race that had briefly held dominion over that third planet all those billions of years ago had never existed at all.

RIVER

by Keith Ferrell and Jack Dann

EVEN THE SHOCK of the water when Tom knocked me from the raft wasn't enough to wake me completely. I shouldn't have been awake at all, not then, not that soon . . . shouldn't have been aware of myself not yet fully formed and formatted. Tom should never have seen me until I was all there, and the end of that long rafting pole should never have found flesh to strike. I should've had more time and I should not have been aware of so much as an instant of that time's passage.

Should in one hand, shit in the other and one of your hands will fill up: words of wisdom. Both my hands were filled with muddy water and nothing more as I flailed against the current and splashed against drowning, the river trying its best to drag me down. But I was also still swimming in the stream of dreams, and its tug may have been the strongest of all. For an instant I was tempted to let that river take me and take me where it would—no telling what I would see: I'd never heard of anyone waking up during a lifeload. It was a technical impossibility, so we had been told. If I let myself go with the dreamstream's flow, no telling where it would take me and what tales I would bring back from wherever I went. All I had to do was relax and be borne away.

But there are times when the body has a logic that's stronger than the mind's, no matter how many minds you have put in your body. This was one of those times, and that's the God's truth, mostly.

The water had pulled me down far enough that what light there was above had moved nearer to darkness before my body began the effort of dragging me back toward the dimness of the surface . . . and not the surface of my dreams.

The surface of the river was what my body wanted and I had no choice but to follow my body's lead.

The body was Huckleberry Finn's.

The water was dark but not all that deep—how deep could it be if Tom was poling a raft? My bare toes touched cold mud, but only for an instant, and then I went up fast, lungs burning, diaphragm heav-

ing, heart stuttering, ears filled with a rhythmic chut-
tering that I assumed was the pulse of my
bloodstream echoing but was not.

I broke surface into a dusk not that much brighter
than the water itself, but filled nonetheless with lights.

The lights were lanterns and lamps strung along
the decks and railings of a steamboat churning its
way upriver—that rhythmic pulse in my ears had
been the steamer's paddles taking bites of the river.

I worked on such a boat, when I had been Mark
Twain.

The boat was close, passing me no more than
thirty feet away. I could see passengers in rough
finery for a twilight promenade, couples holding
hands, con men and grifters seeking marks, the
boat's deckhands going about their labors, servants
and possibly slaves attending to the needs and de-
mands of their betters.

The boat moved in a stately manner, its paddles
dripping river water like diamonds in the near-night.
Beyond its wake I could see Tom on the raft, just a
shadow in the distance, the raft bobbing in the steamer's turbulence, Tom bobbing, too, furious to keep
his balance, steadying himself with the same pole
he'd used to bash me.

The steamer's wake was tossing me as well, but I
had my anger to keep me steady, and raised an arm
to begin swimming toward the raft and my revenge

when my attention was seized by a sudden motion on the boat's top deck.

If she had waited a moment, or hesitated, I would never have seen her—the sternwheeler was moving too steadily beyond me.

But she picked that moment, and I saw a flash of her and then lost her behind a group of shocked passengers, then saw her again as she raced toward the end of the boat.

She was nude and that may have worked to her advantage. It had before.

Now her nakedness served to shock the passengers and deckhands long enough for her to get by them, to reach the railing at the stern of the boat and vault up onto it like the athlete she had never been, launching herself up and outward in arc whose form was as immaculate as her own.

I forgot about Tom and what he had done to me, forgot that only seconds before I had been close to drowning, forgot that I was remembering things that I should never have been able to, forgot everything except her perfection and the perfection of her transit across the evening sky, wide out over the spin of the paddlewheels, out just far enough to miss their swipe as she at last plummeted and pierced the roiled breast of the river where the steamer had churned it.

I did not blink once during her flight and her fall. I never had been able to take my eyes from her.

Her name was Simonetta Vespucci, and I had painted her when I was Botticelli.

She disappeared beneath those turbulent waters and had not resurfaced a full moment later when the steamboat's foghorn began to sound. The boat had traveled a ways already and it would go a ways farther before it could slow enough to lower a boating party to search for Simonetta, much less to stop or reverse course.

If its captain permitted any of those actions.

Suicides were no less uncommon from the prows and sterns and promenade decks of paddlewheelers than any other vessel on waters deep enough to drown in. By the time any of those actions were inaugurated, the jumper was likeliest long dead: best if you're the captain to keep going.

Besides, there was already a rescuer in the water and while I thought for a moment that it was me, I realized quick enough that it was Tom and his raft that would come to Simonetta's service.

I had no energy to swim faster than a sluggish crawl, and that pace was slowed by the residue of the steamboat's passage.

You try to make good time through waters of heavy chop—can't be done even if you were Johnny Weismuller or Buster Crabbe or Mark Spitz, and I had in my time been at least one and possibly two of them during those not infrequent seasons when Olympiad loads are the fashion.

I swam as hard as I could but couldn't swim that hard for long, by which time it was too late. I kept my mouth and chin high above water and not just to breathe. I wanted to save Simonetta, sure, but I also wanted to keep my eye on Tom and that raft. As a result, I saw him save her.

He was always a hard worker, that Tom, and he threw himself and his pole into the work of saving Simonetta as completely as any task he ever undertook. He poled furiously until he saw something, or so I assumed by his movements, Tom swung that rafting pole—whose effect on my left cheek and jaw, shoulder and arm, came back to me now in one solid wave of aching—over his head and then lengthwise down the fore of the raft, himself kneeling there at the very front.

When he did that the raft gave a sudden violent lurch, its stern rising up dripping water the way the steamboat's paddles had dripped, only these drops didn't look any more like diamonds than Tom did. They looked like gobbets of river water and nothing more than that. Tom knelt lower and I heard him shouting words of encouragement.

The raft shimmied then and there was more splashing, then it settled belly-level on the river again, slewing a bit toward the far shore for a moment.

The raft gave its most violent lurch yet, and another violent shudder immediately thereafter and I had a moment's hope that Tom had gone overboard.

But things settled down after that, the raft bellying flat on the finally flattening surface of the river and I could see that Simonetta had been rescued, was on the raft, was kneeling right there naked with Tom standing over her.

The only time I had pulled people from the water they were dead, when I had been Ernest Hemingway cruising the Florida Keys for the bloated bodies of veterans after the Labor Day Hurricane.

I made a couple of strong strokes; then my energy was gone again, and I could only watch.

Tom had plenty of energy. He saw to Simonetta first, draping a rough blanket around her shoulders and settling her down against the rucksack that had his and maybe my belongings in it while he went back to work.

And he went back with a vengeance, standing tall and using the pole to steady and stabilize the raft, set it on course again. He was as good at that as he had been at striking me from the deck, or rescuing my Simonetta, and even more purposeful as he made his way to the stern.

I found the energy to lift my arms high and wave them madly, certain that he could see me even as dusk deepened.

The sight of his victim on the surface rather than beneath it gave him no pause. He probed with the pole for river bottom.

"Hey!" I called. "You bastard, hey!" My voice was hoarse and weaker than I wished. My left jaw and throat ached from where the pole had struck me.

Tom heaved his weight into the pole and levered the raft forward, away from me, angling it slightly toward the closer shore. He stared at me—I know he did—for a second before turning his back.

"Hey!" I called again, but my voice was weaker than before.

My eyes were strong, though, and sharp that night, sharp enough to see what happened after Tom's next stroke.

She stood up and let the blanket fall from her shoulders, and walked in her nakedness, unsteady if not unashamed, to be closer to him and watch admiringly as he worked the river.

That was enough. I moved my arms in the water, working my body the way Tom was working the raft, only not so well. But I began to make progress at a rate a little better than the current alone would provide. I could feel my strength returning, rejoining and reinvigorating the anger that had not gone away.

I would chase them down and take back Simonetta, who was mine, who had always been mine, and give Tom some things that were mine as well.

I knew more than a bit about revenge, for I had been Hamlet and Heathcliff and Ahab . . . Ahab more than once.

But revenge takes energy and I had less than a little of that. The raft began to move away from me, Tom propelling it with the pole and Simonetta expressing her delight at each levering display of skill as a raftsman.

The sight of them pulling away from me—of Tom pushing them away from me and Simonetta applauding him as he did so—was almost enough to reinvigorate me. I raised my arms again and I called after them:

"Hey! You bastard, hey!"

My voice was hoarse, and weaker than I would have wished. Neither of them looked in my direction.

They left me behind, Simonetta standing next to Tom as naked as ever she had been when she posed for me, and perhaps even lovelier.

I forced myself to relax and began making steady, easy strokes with my arms. I would catch them no matter how much time it took.

I understood time and what it could take: once, I was Rip van Winkle.

* * *

Not that I could have remembered that, then, or should have remembered it or any of it then, though I did. My should hand remained empty, but as I began to swim steadily at perhaps a third the rate of the pace Tom set for the raft I had my first moment to think about all the people I had been, and even more, about the fact that I could remember them at all.

I had paid for a pure lifeload, nothing but my own me and the persona I had purchased, historical and geographic context to match Huck's, common language for all participants whetever their native lingua, with a margin or randomization and anachronism allowed for *frisson*, hence fifteenth-century Simonetta leaping from a nineteenth-century paddlewheeler.

That's what I paid for—that and the required surcharge for a dampener to hide all access to any memories of all earlier loads while the current load was in process. None of my other pasts should have been available to me, not even as the vaguest of *deja* views.

Should've been just me as Huck, with Tom on the raft.

My should hand was emptier than ever, while the other was filling up fast.

But I was alive and I was by the moment more and more alive with anger, all of it aimed at Tom. That fury propelled at a better clip along the river.

He thought that he had killed me, that I had

drowned, but I would have a surprise for him. My anger would propel me until I caught up with them..

Not that drowning was all that frightening to me. I had drowned before, when I was Percy Shelley.

Anger, it turned out, can fuel a journey so far and no farther. Huck's body gave me another dozen good strokes, half a dozen beyond that of diminishing effect, and then no more. I was drained, and more fully than before.

I took a slow breath and floated, letting the current do Huck's work for me.

The current was sluggish and Tom's raft work was expert. They moved farther ahead of me by the minute.

I worried when the raft pulled ahead and I lost it round a bend. It was nearly full dark now and I would have to get out of the water soon. I should have gotten out a while ago, should have made for shore as soon as I broke the surface after managing not to drown. The should hand remained empty, though, however full the other was becoming.

I kept on. I had the river to myself—no sign or sound of any search or rescue party from the steamboat. I knew there wouldn't be. I was the only one who could rescue Simonetta, and that thought overtook all others. For now, there was only Simonetta and my desire to be with her again. That was stronger than my urge to break Tom's jaw.

I could do both, but I would have to catch them; and I would need good fortune for that.

I had both: this was one of my lucky loads evidently. When I drifted around the bend, I saw a shadow on the shoreline not far ahead of me. It was the raft. Tom had good luck, too, and he had it first—the raft sat on a wide sandy beach that sloped up gently to a broad stretch of grassy bottomland, rimmed with willows.

I caught a glimpse of them, Simonetta once more blanket-wrapped, accompanying Tom up the slope and away from the beach.

I waited until they had disappeared behind the willows before I swam toward the raft and the shore, quietly and slowly. I wanted surprise on my side: surprise to delight my Simonetta as she had shown such delighted surprise when I unveiled my paintings for her the first time.

And surprise to take Tom off his guard, the way surprise had worked for me against Lincoln when I was Booth.

The muddy river bottom squished against my feet but the mud gave way quickly enough to rough sand. I came out of the water on shaky legs and sank to my knees, pressing my palms against damp sand.

It felt coarser than the sand on Crusoe's island when I had been his Friday.

* * *

Tom and Simonetta had not gone far. I was still on hands and knees, vomiting, when I heard them. I was puking from the exertion and the anger, the pain where Tom had struck me, the surges and larger surges of adrenaline, the oily river water I had drunk, bile, harsh phlegm, all of it retching out of me.

I wanted to vomit out everything I had in me—except the loads.

I could remember every load I'd ever taken, and while I had been aware of this from the instant I came to awareness, it did not sink in until that moment puking on the beach.

I *remembered*.

All of them and there were close to three hundred—as there were for anyone of my social status, economic privilege, and age. A lifeload a month is the maximum permissible by medicine, not to mention propriety; but if you've got the means, you get your monthly load.

I had the means, and then some.

I'd done a dozen loads a year for the last three decades, dropping into my docking divan as though returning home, the sweet-and-sour scent of serum in the air working me like pheromones. You can't smell the serum, the technicians say. Any more—they tell me—than you can hear the buzz and whir of the machinery that coordinates the conjugation of your identity with the replication of the historical or fictional persona you've purchased.

We all *know* we're loads, of course, when we encounter each other in this historical period or that fictional context, but we never acknowledge it. Because we cannot; the dampener sees to that, insuring discretion for the sake of illusion for the duration of the load, however much we're all eager to discuss our latest loadlives as soon as we're unloaded, even if all we've been is a paramecium.

Say what they will: I could smell their serum, and I could hear their machinery. I could remember the transit of electrons across gaps, the mingle and the merge and all of their details.

And I knew who all of me had been.

One had been Botticelli, who painted Simonetta.

And another me had been her lover, when I was Giuliano of the Medici.

There was not much moon that night, but there was enough to silhouette them as they returned to the raft. I heard them before I saw them, a twig snapping, her soft voice still familiar to me, footfalls on grass, Tom speaking softly for her to step carefully.

I got to my feet and prepared myself to greet them, wiping my mouth and brushing sand from my palms and knees. Not my knuckles, though—I wanted grit there to abrade Tom's cheeks when I pounded them.

Simonetta was slightly behind Tom when they returned to the beach, framed in my vision by two wide willows whose weeping canopy made a parted curtain from which they emerged. She had a blanket draped around her. Tom carried a load of branches, for firewood I assumed, and I wished that I had thought to grab a stick myself. The raft was not far away from me and I could have kicked myself when I thought of that. It was so close. I should have grabbed the same raft pole he'd used to beat me, but my should hand was emptier than ever.

Fine or, at least, so be it—done was done and opportunities missed are best forgotten or ignored. I would take him empty-handed and do so while I had surprise to work with.

"Get away from her, you bastard, and take what you've got coming," I said. My voice was still hoarse, but far stronger than it had been in the water.

Startled, Simonetta stepped back. Stepped away from Tom I thought, *good girl*—she would not know me as Huck but she would know a real rescuer's tone and timber when she heard it.

Tom stopped still, his arms laden with wood. "I would advise you, sir," he said, "to release that tone from your voice and identify yourself."

"You advised me, *sir*, to drown, and you did it with the wet end of your rafting pole, you son of a bitch. Now you'll pay for that." I took a step toward him but he neither flinched nor retreated.

"Is that who you are?" he asked. "That was you? Who I struck from my raft?"

I raised a hand to my bruised jaw. "Who you tried to kill."

"I assumed you were already dead," he said evenly.

"Not by way of your work. You didn't do it well enough."

He dared to chuckle. "No, you mistake my meaning, sir, as I mistook your form. Or what appeared to be your form only partially, well, *formed*, there on the river. I assumed you were not corporeal. These waters are known to be populated with those not of this world but of another."

"*Vampyri*," Simonetta said softly.

"Haints," Tom said and chuckled again. "I see now, though, that you are as real as we." Was there irony in his tone? I put myself on guard—it occurred to me that mine might not be the only glitched life-load this night. "And I will do you the goodness of assuming that you're no haint made flesh but a man same's me. In which case some hospitality is in order, and not simply as reparation for my actions. Mistress Simonetta and I were preparing to strike fire and see what can be done about a meal. You will join us?"

"I will," I said, and unclenched my fists even before my decision was fully made. I would deal with him later. After I had insured Simonetta's safety and revealed to her or reminded her that she was mine.

"Fine, sir, fine. Now I would have your name."

I stepped toward her and said nothing to him.

"Your *name*, sir! I must insist upon that. And the aversion of your eyes from my companion's *dishabille*."

She surprised Tom then, though not me, by stepping even with him and shrugging the blanket from her shoulders to stand before us revealed. "My *dishabille* is for you, Thomas, all of this that is me the least I can provide you who saved it. But it is not for you to defend. Whatever I give you of myself, I reserve that right for myself. I will decide when I wish to be modest, and when I wish it is not now." She spread her arms wide and inhaled deeply, her breasts rising as though on a slow tide itself flowing from her delta. I had no doubt that Simonetta knew what she was showing us and I knew that she was showing it to me.

Simonetta had her appetites, as I knew so well, and those hungers would allow us to feast only so long on her. "*Now*—both of you can get on with getting us fed!" Her laughter was as large as the night sky, though lovelier.

Tom stared at me as I stared at Simonetta, but he let the moment pass. "I would appreciate the courtesy of your name, sir, would you join us for supper."

I continued to look at her instead of him. "Huck," I said. "Huckleberry Finn."

"A pleasure. My name is Tom—Tom Jefferson."

Of course it was, and I had known that for a few moments, as I had known him when I was Adams and when I had been Washington, when I was Franklin and when for that matter I had been him.

We sat around the campfire Tom built, toasting our fingers and toes if not each other. Tom had started the blaze effortlessly and naked Simonetta had applauded his achievement, her palms making smacking sounds as the kindling began to crackle..

We ate catfish that we roasted on sticks. Tom caught the cats barehanded, reaching down along the riverbank to where they nestled, hauling them onto the riverbank in a single fluid movement. It was a Huck Finn skill, but not one I could make work.

"Poor Huck," Simonetta said when I raised an empty hand that should have held a fish. "Life on the Mississippi is not for you, I think." She was standing with her back to the growing blaze, her feet well apart. I had been between those legs, and given her great joy when I was there, though this did not seem the moment to remind her of that.

Nor did the opportunity arise while we dined. I held Huck's spitted fish too close to the flames and the stick Tom had whittled for me burned through, the catfish falling into the embers, lost.

Simonetta laughed when I lost my fish, though she had the courtesy to turn her head from me in an attempt to muffle her mirth.

Tom was all sympathy and solicitousness, insisting that I take his fish, while he shared Simonetta's.

She sat next to Tom and they ate from the same large fish. Her legs were spread as she ate, and she wiped grease on her breasts to clean her hands. Watching me she said, "We could adopt the boy, Thomas, and make him our child. He needs to be cared for, don't you think? He needs to be looked after."

I did not hear Tom's reply.

I was thinking without wishing to of the time I loaded Whitechapel's Jack and how, were I still he, I could rip her.

When I painted Simonetta's eyes as Botticelli, or kissed them during lovemaking as Giuliano I was never far from an awareness of their sharpness, their ability to pierce and puncture either or all of me with a gaze, a glance, a narrowing stare, a glare of anger or sullen impatient flare—her eyes were infinite in their capacity to diminish as well as nourish me. I remembered that now, the memory at least as clear as the rest or better.

True in perspective and true in profile—my painting *Young Woman In Mythological Guise* captured only her right eye but that was enough. Whatever she is looking at in that painting, she is looking at with the contempt of one born Simonetta rather than born a lesser being, mythological or not.

You could lose yourself in those eyes, but you

could also lose yourself to them, as I had, and not just me or even my own me.

I should have been her at least once; should have loaded Simonetta and seen what my other lives were like through her bitter eyes, but that had never occurred to me until now and now was too late.

I had been one of her relatives once, her cousin Amerigo Vespucci, but it was as another explorer that I had discovered this very river that brought us together.

When I was DeSoto, I found the unbesmirched Mississippi and did so two years before Simonetta was born.

By the time our meal reached its midpoint, I knew that they were pure unglitched loads or the finest actors who'd ever performed, and I did not believe they were actors.

Did they think I was one? I didn't think so—my illusion was as perfect as theirs, more perfect in fact, it being my creation, the difference lying in the fact that my dampener and my discretion came from me, invoked by decision and will and determination rather than as part of a load. I would reveal myself when I chose to, and not before.

They could not reveal themselves at all.

No, whoever they were in our own old world, they were Tom and Simonetta in this one, and no more than themselves and their two loads ever would be.

I felt a certain sudden sympathy for them and the sheer narrowness of the experience. What they saw and heard—and felt: Tom had a blatant hand on Simonetta's thigh—was all they would have of our evening together, uninformed and unenlightened by anything larger than themselves and the selves they had loaded.

So restricted a perspective, so proscribed a point of view! I could weep for them were I of a mind to.

I was not—why weep for these two alone when my tears were large enough for all the others who had been in me?

I threw the last of Tom's fish into the fire rather than choke on another bite of it.

If I constricted myself, it was because I contained multitudes.

"Why, I jumped from the steamship to be rescued by you, Thomas," Simonetta said in response to the question Tom had waited all evening to pose.

She was looking at me while she answered him. "I would never have done such a thing, such a horrible and unforgivable thing had I not known that you would be there to save me."

Her hand was busy in his lap and his in hers. I might as well have not been there at all, and so far as practical philosophy I no longer was—all of me were here now, every one of them hearing what she said, Huck the very least of me.

"I have never, you know, known a real man such as yourself, Thomas."

"My poor dear," Tom said, his tongue thick.

A moment later he had that tongue in her mouth and hers in his.

I could take all of this from them with the right word or words from any of my selves, just as when I was Savanorola I set to flame many of the paintings I had done when I had been Botticelli.

I had had enough and not just of their company. I left them to it and stepped away from the campfire.

They made no notice of my departure; but soon were making the most of it, the sounds of their love-making undampened by modesty. She cried out and it was his name she cried, not any of mine. Her cries grew louder, Tom's rough grunts playing counter-point. I headed down the riverbank.

My mind wandered while my body did, and soon enough all of us were alone with our selves. We found a spot near a willow that overhung the river and sat with our back to its bole. We had put some distance between our selves and them—but not enough. Her cries grew louder and more delighted.

For me, when I was Giuliano de Medici, her moans had been infrequent and soft. When I was Botticelli painting her on her half-shell, she broke wind more than once: what would Tom say were I to tell him that?

The waters of the river were dark and appealing as I stood beside them. They beseeched me—I could hear them.

I had heard the song of waters before, and a full chorus and a vast immersive choir chanting watersong when I drowned as Shelley.

And that drowning was easier than what followed. When my body was recovered, my friend Byron saw to its burning on a beach, the flames consuming every bit of me as him except my heart and his, which would not be consumed.

Of course, I'd been burned alive, too, and not just when I was Joan, though that immolation was by far the most memorable.

I started back not long after their moans finally subsided, their cries having climbed an auditory amorous peak that could I was sure be heard at either end of the river, and all the way to Memphis; but not the one of this river but on the other where I had been more than one Pharaoh each able to make everyone around them do what any or all of us wanted.

I was nearly back to the raft when their cries and moans resumed.

I waited until this round—larger and louder than the previous, though of lesser duration—subsided, but it was not that great challenge for me to be patient.

I had been the Buddha as well as the Christ.

When this latest bout drew to its close, I rejoined them.

They were together beside the fire, Tom holding Simonetta and each of them in a kind of a trance. They hardly acknowledged as I approached and stood over them, but I knew how to get their attention.

"You mentioned ghosts," I said as I stared at them. "Haints and *vampyri*. Would you care to hear a ghostly tale now?"

I looked away from them and stared at the embers while I waited for their answer. I knew what it would be, and I knew what I would do. I had a tale to tell them and it would not be just mostly true. I would test their discretion if not their mettle. I would tell all.

"Please," Tom said.

Simonetta sat up, her high breasts damp with perspiration. She nodded at me. "We'll be like you, Huck," she said, "children around a campfire listening to stories."

I stood and faced them.

"I was born," I said slowly, softly, and paused for another moment.

"Of man and woman no doubt. As were we all,

sir," Tom said. Simonetta laughed and made a small patter of applause for him. He bowed his head a bit, that red forelock bowing as well.

I indulged them; and at last they sat back, close together, Simonetta's hand on Tom's left knee, his own hand covering hers. Tom cocked his head at me and with his eyes urged me to tell my story. I laced my fingers together and, holding hands only with my self, began again.

I told them what it was like when I had been me.

"My name is Tiril Neame," I said. "I was born three thousand years after the birth of Christ."

Simonetta clapped her hands together again at that, but only once, her expression showing her disbelief and her hands having other work to return to almost immediately. She placed one against Tom's strong face, while the other found its familiar home in his lap where I could not see what she was doing save by the effort and exertion on Tom's face to keep me from seeing the effect her hand was having once more on him. He was inexhaustible that Tom, as much in service of a libertine as ever in service of liberty

"Which means that I was born a thousand years and more after the younger of the two of you died."

Did I have them? Did my words hold their attention? I would know soon enough, though I knew already how little it mattered.

"It means that we are of the same time and the same world, the three of us," I said, "whether you are able to admit this or not. You *know* it, which is not the same thing as admission, much less acceptance, but there are forces at work upon you which restrict those capacities within you and will restrict them for so long as you are in these bodies in this world."

Tom was staring at the fire, but Simonetta was staring at me, those eyes of her a blaze of their own. Knowing that I was watching her, she turned from me and trained her eyes on Tom, leaning forward to flutter her lashes against his earlobe. Tom grinned, and his shoulders gave a small shudder, but he did not look from the fire.

"And encased in these bodies in this world," I said, "you are also encased within a transaction that each of you and both of you made, a bargain wrought from artifice and fashioned from falsehoods, for benefit of the experiences that will recall and relate when you return to our world, and which are not experiences at all, and never were."

Tom did not look at me when he spoke. "You claim that I am not myself?"

"I make no such claim sir. I tell the truth: you—whoever you are—have purchased the opportunity to be Thomas Jefferson, just as *she*, whoever she may be, has made her bargain as well for the opportunity to pretend to be Simonetta Vespucci. Just as I have made, this transit, my purchase of Huckleberry Finn, no more real I had expected as he than any of the hundreds of other lives I loaded and led. Those lives are lies and I see that now. Yet we all do it—I no less than you."

Tom poked at the fire with a stick. "And what would you have us do with this story you tell—believe it?"

"Not now," I said. "I do not think you *can* believe it now. The conditions of purchase won't allow that. But you will remember this when these lives are ended and you are returned to your own lives, and that will be a gift. It is my gift to the two of you."

"A gift?" he said, the word sound harsh and ugly from his lips.

"The gift of an authentic experience here within the veil of . . . *haints*," I said.

Simonetta sat up and leaned forward, interposing herself between me and Tom. "You are a fool," she said.

"More than one," I could not resist saying. "But why—because I thought to convince you?"

Her laughter was feral and repellent. "Because you thought that we would *care*."

None of me had any answer for that, although all of me had expected her response. We really did know her.

And knew her well enough to know that she was not yet quite finished.

Simonetta sat back, propping herself on an elbow and after only the barest of pauses added her grace note:

"What," she said, "could be more real than this?" She opened herself and, revealed, drew Tom upon her.

One thing could be more real, I thought and thought I knew, and left them to it and left them to each other, while I returned to the river which was more real than either and meant more to me, now, than both.

I thought of what I had thought of last night, drowning, and if I was not certain that to finish that job would mean the end of me, I also had no way of knowing that it would not. Perhaps I would awaken on the docking divan as though this had been an uneventful load. Perhaps I would not awaken at all.

We shall see, I told myselves as I stepped into the river and did not linger long in the shallows.

I had unfinished business in deeper waters, a job Tom had begun for me and that I would finish for myself, beneath the surface of that river whose current I hoped and whose depths I prayed could bear me and all of everyone who had ever been me back into the ceaseless past.

LANDSCAPES

by Kevin J. Anderson

B Y THE TIME OUR CLUNKY shuttle finished two weeks in roundabout transit to the "designated wilderness" planet of Bifrost, Craig and I were more than ready to stretch our legs on the trails of a new alien world. I just hoped we weren't too out of shape for vigorous trekking.

The uniformed ranger who piloted us wasn't altogether happy with his chauffeur duties, but his gruff answers to our many questions could not diminish my exuberance. We were two hard-working guys, looking forward to having the peace and solitude of an entire world to ourselves, and determined to take the long, risky hike to see one of the greatest sights in the Galaxy. With humanity spreading across practically every habitable world, it was nearly impossible to get away from it all. Yet time and again we managed it.

Craig had filled out the sheaf of required forms, and I had paid all of the fees. We were not just tourists of the "pull over, look, then drive on" variety. We were *authorized* to be here on Bifrost. We had the best modern backpacking equipment, semisentient adventure clothing, and camp supplies—not to mention embarrassingly detailed maps. These expeditions had become an annual ritual for us.

Scenery. Solitude. Adventure. This was going to be heaven.

To minimize the impact of visitors on the environment, our ship touched down in a meadow, the single authorized landing zone for official vehicles. When the shuttle's hatch opened, Craig and I stuffed the appropriate allergen filters into our noses, then took deep breaths of the clean alien air. Ready to go.

"I have been counting down the nanoseconds until today," Craig said. "Oh, I was looking forward to this." He had looked tired and a little withdrawn during the long trip, but now he seemed to come alive again. Though he spends most of his life inside an artificially lit starship cabin, Hawaiian genes from somewhere back in Craig's bloodline endowed him with honey-tan skin, deep-brown eyes, and blue-black hair. I, on the other hand, am freckled and pale

as protoplasm; despite undergoing melanin treat-
ments and applying sunfilms, I'd probably burn beet
red before the end of the trek.

The ranger unloaded our packs from the shuttle's
cargo bin. Craig and I hoisted the heavy loads onto
our shoulders, carefully adjusted the straps and
clamps for balance, and double-checked each other's
equipment as if we were orbital construction workers
suiting up for a spacewalk.

For us, no first-person-tourist simulations would
do: no 3-D images of scenery, no implanted memories of the perfect vacation. This was the real thing.
We were going to be entirely and blissfully alone in
the wilderness of Bifrost. Making a memory.

"You've got seven days," the ranger said. "Make
sure you're back in time, or I'm gone."

Craig turned his wide face to the sky. "If you don't
see us in a week, maybe we don't want to go back!"

"Uh-huh." The ranger expressed an encyclopedia
of skepticism in those two syllables.

"How often do you really lose people out here?"
I asked him.

"About one in twelve miss the scheduled pickup
and are never found."

"Maybe they decided to turn Robinson Crusoe,"
Craig suggested.

"Probably got eaten." The ranger shrugged. "With
budget cuts, the Planetary Wilderness Bureau can't

afford to go looking for everybody. It's all in the waiver you signed."

"We can handle ourselves," I said. "We do a wilderness trip every year. Even if we get lost, we know how to find our way back."

The ranger stared at us with a grim frown, convinced this would be the last time anyone would ever see us alive. I see that look on my wife's face every time I leave on one of my outdoorsy expeditions with Craig. She never believes me when I promise to be careful, though I have survived every adventure relatively unscathed. So far.

Craig grabbed his walking stick and tossed the other one to me. "Come on, Steve, we'd better start relaxing as fast as we can. Only seven days to cure a year's worth of headaches."

We activated the staffs, which would help us navigate and could also act as cattle-prod defenses if we were harassed by wild animals—though we'd face severe fines and time on a penal planet if we dared to *hurt* any endangered alien species.

"Right," I said. "Asgaard awaits."

Bifrost vegetation had more blues and oranges than a typical chlorophyll-based ecosystem. We passed between scaly ferns and ethereal lichentrees that looked like upside-down waterfalls, and got a view of an ugly swatch of clear-cut ground where

43

loggers had managed to chop down everything before strict preservation regulations had been passed. Now, gray-white stumps thrust up from the soil like razor stubble on a giant's face.

Neither Craig nor I are foaming-at-the-mouth environmentalists, but when you're utterly alone on a wilderness planet, it changes your perspective, clears your head. The scars left by human greed or carelessness tend to look like a big steaming pile of dog shit right in the middle of a playground—*our* playground for the next week.

"I'm glad I never had to haul freight for lumberjockeys or stripminers." Craig scowled, taking the environmental damage as a personal affront. "In a beautiful place like this, what the hell were they thinking?"

"I didn't think the company gave you any choice about the cargoes you carry," I said.

"Screw the company—they've done it to me enough times. Gotta take a stand once in a while." Frowning, he stumped off, as if turning his back on the problems of his real life. "I came here to get away from all that."

Craig is a long-distance cargo hauler who flies a company-owned transport ship around five systems, picking up percentages along the way. He has always dreamed of buying his ship from the company and becoming an independent hauler—and he's gotten close—though recent months had brought a series of setbacks. I didn't know the details, but I would probably hear plenty during the long trek.

At some point each year Craig and I need to get away, escape our jobs and civilized home lives, no matter how much it costs or how far away we have to go. Forget spas and empathic massages, nightlife and interactive entertainment experiences. Sometimes a guy just wants to get sweaty, be miserable, sleep in an uncomfortable tent, eat bad-tasting food, get lost, and then find the way back again, ready to face another year of reality.

Before long the faint path descended toward the distinctive rushing-wind sound of a wide creek. We picked our way over boulders toward the cascade. Wiping perspiration off his brow, Craig climbed up onto a squarish talus slab and shook his head. "This is a *trail*?"

"It's a *route*." I flipped the filter over my right eye and turned it on so I could see the infrared cairns, little beacons invisible to the naked eye—and presumably to the Bifrost wildlife as well—that marked the trail without defacing the nearly pristine wilderness.

A ribbon of foamy lavender water etched its way through pock-marked stone. Some sort of indigenous algae gave the stream the peculiar tint that in itself served as a reminder not to drink the water without treating it first. In a narrow spot over the creek, three wobbly looking lichentree logs had been knocked over to form a corduroy bridge.

I gingerly started across, looking down into the angry cascade. Although none of the guidebooks had mentioned the presence of aquatic carnivores on Bifrost, the very idea made me scuttle quickly to the other side. Craig paused, bent over, and ceremoniously spat a glob of phlegm into the water. Although he's four years older than me, being out in the wilderness always seems to transform him into a little kid.

Once we were over the bridge, I let my eyes move back and forth, tracing the discouraging zigzag pattern of steep switchbacks up the other side of the canyon wall. When I groaned in dismay, Craig reminded me, "We do this for fun, remember? Asgaard awaits."

"Yeah, yeah, Asgaard awaits. It's sure better than sitting in my environmentally controlled cubicle."

I had long suspected that Craig envied my stable job with its regular salary, though he assured me he'd rather be footloose, traveling from system to system, than stuck at a desk. For most of the year I work sealed in a cubicle chamber surrounded by screens and interfaces, exploring all manner of networks, following faint data trails. I'm a specialist in tracking certain violations in the business world, a hunter hired by clients to scan the labyrinth of entertainment loops, advertising, and news stories for unauthorized use of someone else's intellectual property. In most cases the perpetrators are too naïve or stupid to be a real threat. Still, just because they're idiots doesn't mean they can't cause disasters. I'm paid to avert disaster. It's a subtle job, and I'm good at it.

Even so, I spend much of my time dreaming of Getting Away From It All, while looking at the images in my *Fifty Most Spectacular Sites* guidebook. Craig does the same on his long-distance hauls. And now that we were on Bifrost, we intended to make the most of our limited time here, and make a year's worth of memories along the way.

Soon after we began the climb, with my thighs hauling every gram of mass against Bifrost's gravity, I found myself regretting all of the supplies I had put into my pack. I reconsidered each item from a new angle: Why should I require a first-aid kit, if I was careful enough? Would I actually miss my sanitation amenities if I left them behind on the trail? And did I really need to eat *every* day? Besides, the ecosystem and indigenous species here were compatible with our biochemistry, so we could just live off the land, despite the potential fines. How would the rangers ever know?

Unfortunately for my weary legs, my ingrained commitment to averting disasters brought me to my senses, and we plodded onward and upward. After two switchbacks, we rested ten minutes, then staggered up two more. By early afternoon we climbed over the canyon rim and were greeted by the glorious sight of a thin, cool stream running across the mesa top. We bounded toward it and stopped on the bank to unlace boots, strip off self-cleaning socks, and dunk our feet into the frigid water.

Craig let out a long "Ahhhh!" He put his hands behind him, and stared up into the sky where vulture-sized butterflies drifted about on the breezes. There's nothing like the sheer delight of a simple pleasure when you're tired and dirty. "This is the sort of experience wives just don't understand," he said.

"Some wives do," I said.

"None of mine ever have," Craig said, and a shadow crossed his face. I thought he was about to say something more, but he yelped and yanked his feet out of the water. Several small scallop-mouthed bivalves clung to his bare toes and ankles, nipping at the flesh.

In the stream I saw a swarm of these small nibblers approaching my own exposed flesh and pulled my feet out of the water just in time. Inspecting his toes, Craig found only a pinch mark, no broken skin.

"We're making a memory," I reminded him—a phrase that had become a private joke between us when we ran into something unexpected.

He chuckled to himself as he pulled his socks back onto his moist feet and relaced his boots. I understood what he was thinking: After waiting so long and working so hard to get to Bifrost, we weren't about to let anything ruin our trip. "Rest stop's over."

On backpacking trips, I prefer to put on an extra kilometer or two the first day, when my energy is greatest. Craig has the opposite philosophy, not wanting to burn himself out too soon, so he likes to break off early. Therefore, we compromised and called a halt exactly where we had decided to stop during the months of planning for the trip.

In a pleasant clearing surrounded by huge blue ferns, we unshouldered our burdens, activated the self-erecting tent systems, strung up phosphors for light, and turned on the discourager beacons to drive away any nocturnal predators. Since regulations prohibit real campfires, we settled for a high-resolution hologram of crackling flames and rough logs. I'd considered bringing a can of aerosol woodsmoke, but discarded it when paring down the weight of my pack.

Craig selected a self-heating gloppy concoction of noodles and sauce while I, in a show of macho fortitude, intentionally chose a Spampak. He looked at me with a frown. "You're crazy. I'd rather eat indigenous invertebrates."

"On the trail is the only place this stuff tastes good." I proceeded to eat my meal with much lip-smacking.

We sat outside in the growing darkness under the

camp lights and talked. When you're hiking all day, you don't have much extra breath for conversation, so you can let your thoughts wander, clear your head, work out personal problems and questions or, better yet, just think about *nothing*. That's a luxury most people in the frenetic civilized world with families and careers and daily schedule grids don't have.

"I wish my life could be like this all the time," Craig said with a sigh.

"You'd miss the amenities of civilization. Eventually."

He gave an eloquent shrug. "But there are plenty of things I wouldn't miss at all." He leaned closer to the campfire image. "What a year! I don't know how I'm ever going to dig out from under the crap, Steve. Maybe it's impossible."

I waited. Craig didn't need me to ask questions. He'd tell me what he wanted to tell me.

"First, I lost a huge account. A shipment of extremely delicate—and extremely valuable—skreel embryos hatched prematurely while my ship was under heavy acceleration, killing every one of them. In the wake of that disaster, my transspace insurance carrier dropped me."

"Without insurance, how will you—"

"Then, before I could get even probationary coverage, I misaligned my ship in a spacedock on Klamath Station—and *that* caused damage totaling just about my entire net worth."

"Are you going to have to declare bankruptcy?"

From the dark forest came the sound of crashing trees, a loud roar, and a frightened-sounding trumpet as two large animals collided with each other. Craig listened for a minute, then with utter faith in our discourager field, continued, "The company's already planning to sever my contract, and if I declare bankruptcy, I'll lose my ship and any chance at a livelihood. At that point, my options narrow down to submitting myself for scientific research or volunteering for hard labor on a terraform colony."

"I hear terraformers get paid well. At least that's a possibility."

"And where could I spend the credits on a raw world?"

I groaned in commiseration. No wonder he needed to get away. "Trust me, someday when it's all over, this will seem funny."

"I don't think so, Steve. It's hard to imagine."

I might have tried to cheer him up, but then the large indigenous animals—any guidebook would have called them "monsters"—lumbered into view. One, an elephant-sized panther, ripped into a house-sized spiny ungulate that looked like a cross between a porcupine and a woolly mammoth. The ungulate tried to duck into a defensive posture, but the panther thing slipped under its guard.

They snorted and snarled. Spittle and blood flew. Lichentrees crashed into splinters. The porcupine creature raked a spine down the predator's flank, but the beast didn't seem to notice. The ungulate fled crashing away from our campsite. Without so much as a look at us, the panther sprang after it.

Resigned, Craig said, "Well, that gives me a whole new perspective on my trivial human problems."

"Amen," I said. "I'm turning in."

All the next day the trail led along a sinuous arid ridge dotted with surrealistic hoodoos, hardened clay that stuck out from the softer sandstone like a petrified alien army waiting to advance. I used my clicker to snap large files of images, though Craig just stared in peaceful satisfaction, drinking in the details, taking pictures with his mind. "I store the images in my brain," he'd once told me, "since I'm the only one who really cares about them anyway." I had to agree. There's nothing more boring than looking at pictures of someone else's vacation, no matter what planet it's on.

Late in the afternoon, the wind picked up and the sky congealed with ugly gray clouds, and I became uncomfortably aware of how exposed we were on this ridge. Rain and hail struck with the force of Thor's hammer, stinging my bare arms. I dropped my pack and ducked under one of the hoodoos for shelter. Overhead, sheets of static lightning and blue balls of Saint Elmo's Fire whipped about.

I scrambled to get out my electrostatic rain shield,

but my hands were already wet, and I fumbled it. An earsplitting clap of thunder was followed by a rumbling boom, and I dropped the shield projector. Naturally, it struck a rock, and the device sparked and fizzled out. "Great."

Craig crouched under the inadequate shelter with me, his head covered by his own electrostatic umbrella, a twinkling net that deflected the raindrops and the gravel-sized hail. He shifted it over so I could huddle under the meager protection that had never been designed to cover more than one person. "Here, I'll tough it out."

"You're getting drenched and bruised!" I said.

"I'm making a memory." Craig smiled, shrugging the droplets away. "Isn't that part of the charm of this back-to-nature stuff?"

"It's supposed to be a pleasant sort of misery," I said. "The kind that makes you appreciate your everyday life a bit more."

"Bifrost is going to need to toss some pretty big loads of 'pleasant misery' at me."

Watching the majestic storm and waiting for the hail to end, we each ate several handfuls of hyper-granola and chased it with some energized water. Then we passed the time chatting.

Craig was having problems with his current soon-to-be-ex wife Grace, who had filed divorce forms while he was on a long-distance run, making it impossible for him to finish the rebuttal phase in time unless he dropped his cargo and raced back home—which she knew, as did I, that Craig would never do.

"Grace figured out a new tactic for increasing alimony. She claims that since I'm flitting around between star systems all the time, the time-dilation effect, though small, is still significant. Therefore she has effectively put more time into this marriage than I have. She's trying to get 1.3 times the standard alimony calculation."

"Never heard that one before." It was just another nail in the coffin of his disastrous year.

As the storm rumbled and swirled around us, Craig continued to tell me about how all of his previous divorces had gone wrong. I'd lost track, unable to remember which of the women were legally bound wives and which were just long-term live-ins. He never learned to be more wary of the women he hooked up with.

But we were here on Bifrost, with only a few days to forget about the nonsense of our normal life. I tried to get Craig thinking about good times, positive things.

We both got a chuckle reminiscing about the previous year's trip, shooting the Hundred Mile Rapids on Beta Kowalski. No one could survive the legendary whitewater stretch in a traditional kayak or raft, so Craig and I rented armored ballistic projectiles. We both found them uncomfortably similar to coffins with picture windows built into every side. Unable to control our own paths, we simply laid back for the ride, in occasional radio contact, though the thundering rapids drowned out most transmissions as we went over cascades, plunged down giant drop-offs, then shot along the current to the next set of even worse rapids. It had been an adrenaline rush for five hours straight, and we were both so weak and shaky by the time we reached the pickup point that the expedition managers had carted us off for a routine medical check. The recovery facilities and the numerous saloons at the bottom of the cascades proved that we weren't alone in being stunned by the trip.

Afterward, Craig and I each had a different look in our eyes. "Most people don't do that, you know," I said.

He nodded. "Most people aren't crazy."

"Most people are boring."

When we showed my wife the pictures, she was predictably horrified and made me promise I would never try such an outrageous stunt again. It wasn't hard to agree, since I didn't need to shoot the Hundred Mile Rapids a second time. I had already checked that one off the list, and there were other things to see and do. I had them all in my guidebook, *The Fifty Most Spectacular Sites in Galactic Sector A.* Everybody needs goals.

The next morning we descended steeply into a swamp, with rivulets of water snaking around dubious-looking tufts of dryer ground. I found it ironic that our discourager fields were effective at keeping large predatory animals away, yet somehow they did nothing to block swarms of annoying skeeters. The small biting insects couldn't possibly have a natural appetite for Terran-based blood, but that didn't stop them from biting us.

The swamp foliage was so dense and the muddy ground so uncertain that we had to keep IR filters over our eyes just to spot the trail beacons, many of which were covered with moss or slimy fungus. I had to unroll the mapfilm and uplink to the surveillance satellites and zoom in on the detailed topography.

Splashing across the marsh, Craig misjudged a stepping stone and sank in up to his knee. He pulled out his foot, dripping with greenish-black muck so viscous as it crawled off his boot that it seemed alive. Maybe it was.

Halfway through a thicket, I saw some other hiker's carelessly discarded food foils, and my face pinched with annoyance. "Can you believe someone would go to all the trouble of coming to Bifrost, then be stupid enough to throw litter on the ground?" I worked my way off the marked trail to clean up after the slob. When I pulled at a polymer strap from a hiking pack, it came out of the muck connected to the gnawed remains of a human femur. Now it dawned on me that this wasn't merely careless litter.

"Yeah. I think we've found that one-out-of-twelve the ranger was talking about," Craig said, reading my sober expression. "He wasn't very successful at the Robinson Crusoe bit."

I know it sounds warped, but the only thing I could think of was, "I hope the poor guy got munched on the way *back* from his hike, so that at least he got to see the Asgaard Bridge." Sometimes my priorities sound screwy even to me.

I let the bone drop back into the swamp. "I'd better leave a radio flare so the rangers can come and gather the remains." I took one of the pulsers from my belt, activated it on nonemergency locator mode, and tossed it into the water. If I remembered right, the terms of our backcountry permits required the hiker or his surviving family members to pay all the costs of such a retrieval operation. Maintaining a wilderness planet is serious business. . . .

A large fern sprang back and slapped me in the face after Craig pushed into the dryer forest beyond the wet marsh. I wiped slime off my cheeks. We were both tired, but we had to do at least another kilometer. Otherwise, we wouldn't reach our destination tomorrow, and the whole schedule would fall apart.

We found an adequate campsite just after dusk. Too tired to talk much, we ate our meals. That night we went to sleep early after looking at our guidebooks again and drooling over the glorious pictures of the Asgaard Bridge—certainly one of the fifty most spectacular sights in Sector A, if not in the whole Galaxy. I couldn't wait to see it with my own eyes.

As luck would have it, thick fog had settled into the lowlands. The trail took us into a narrow gorge, where we couldn't see anything but a gauzy mist that hung like a suffocating pillow. We moved quickly: After days of hiking, our goal was near. We were about to join the very short list of privileged people who had actually been to the Asgaard Bridge. Mere pictures would never be the same as personally experiencing this wonder first-hand.

We began our long ascent, and once in a while we broke above the low-lying mists and saw outcroppings like islands in a gray-white sea. We climbed toward our destination—the grail. As if by some malicious joke, the clouds thickened even further, making it impossible to see more than a hundred meters in front of us, then fifty, and then twenty. In clear weather, the trail would have been plain, but we had to use the IR cairns just to find our way through the mist.

"Can't see a thing," Craig muttered. "This is *not* the memory I wanted to make."

"We're not there yet."

We kept hoping against hope that the fog would lift by the time we reached the Asgaard Bridge. It was mid-morning, and the sun ought to burn away the fog and leave us with clear skies and a beautiful view. It *had* to.

We reached the top of a mesa, then headed toward the edge of the gorge. Both the map and the IR indicators told us that we had reached our ultimate goal. And we could see nothing. Absolutely nothing. Days of hiking, months of preparations, countless permits, enormous expenses—all to get here.

To see thick fog.

The claustrophobic air intensified sounds, and we could hear the roar of the lavender river charging through the rocks and cascading into the distant gorge. I squinted, demanding optimism from myself, but I couldn't discern even a silhouette.

"The perfect ending to a perfect year." Craig shook his head. "It defies belief."

"You say that every time something like this happens." Resigned, I opened my pack, removing a snack and some juice. "Might as well have lunch."

Troubled and sulking, he tossed pebbles into the unseen chasm, while I opened the map and the guidebook, looked at the image of the Asgaard Bridge again, and tried to calculate just how long we could wait there. This weather couldn't last forever, but it could last longer than we had. We both remembered the ranger's admonition that he wouldn't wait for us—and I couldn't stop thinking of the skeleton in the swamp.

"Three hours is all I'm comfortable with. I sure don't want to miss the pickup shuttle. I've got a performance review and a raise justification when I get back to work."

"Yeah. And I've got my alimony hearing." Craig hurled another rock over the edge. "Sure wouldn't want to miss that."

I started figuring out how fast I could make my way back at top speed, how many extra kilometers I could put on my feet each day, but I doubted Craig could keep up.

On the other hand, I really wanted to see the Asgaard Bridge.

After three hours of growing frustration, the gray mist grew whiter and brighter, thinning. I finished packing up, reluctant to leave but watching my chronometer. We had never turned back before. Never. But our time was up.

Feeling as if a neutron star were weighing me down, I hefted my pack. "That's it." Many other choice words were running through my mind.

Craig didn't move to pick up his pack, just sat staring into the opaque fog. "You go ahead."

"You'll never catch up." My pace was always faster than his.

"I don't have to." He finally turned to me. I'd never seen such a bleak yet simultaneously peaceful expression on his face. "I'm not going. I'm staying here."

What could I say to that? "You're crazy! Come on."

"I mean it. What do I have to go back for? I'd rather go native here. I've got my equipment, supplies, guidebooks." The way he rattled off his justifications, I could tell Craig had been thinking about this for a long time—maybe even before the ranger had dropped us off. "The life forms are compatible, so I can hunt and forage. I can build myself a cabin. I'll be Robinson Crusoe, living off the land. Peace. Solitude. Adventure. *You* of all people should understand that, Steve."

"I understand it as a *game*, a break, a vacation. Not everyday life." Craig's expression wavered. I was articulating his own doubts. "Sure, we like doing this primitive thing every year, mainly because it makes our regular lives tolerable by comparison. The only reason we have fun getting miserable is because we know we're going back to reality when it's over. It gives us an appreciation for the simple pleasures."

"I don't have any simple pleasures left," he said. "I've got nothing. No job, no money, no ship, no wife. Tell the ranger that a monster ate me, or that I fell off a cliff. Make up a good story."

I could only stare at him. "You'll regret it in a week, Craig. A month at most. And nobody'll be there to throw you a lifeline."

"No other options that I can see. And I sure don't want to sign up for a bioresearch project. I like camping, roughing it, surviving by my own hands—" He stopped in midsentence and jumped to his feet, grinning. "You better take a look, Buddy! Get ready to hear a chorus of angels."

And he was right. The mist parted, and golden sunbeams stabbed down enough to impress even the most jaded photographer. Suddenly, there was the Asgaard Bridge, an impossibly delicate and poignant sliver of rock stretched across a gorge as deep and as sharp as if a cosmic scalpel had sliced the flesh of the sandstone all the way down to the bone. Directly beneath the arch flowed a foaming cascade of pink quicksilver, a perfect strand of water, pouring from between walls of natural diamondplate crystal. Showers of rainbows filled the air all around us. It was more stunning than anything I had ever seen, more breathtaking than any image in any guidebook. High spires of quartz-laced rock rose like crystalline spears on either side of the gorge, dazzling in the light.

Putting aside the crisis for a moment, Craig and I raised hands, and gave each other a high-five. This was exactly what we'd come out here for. "By far the best one on the whole list!" He said that every time.

I pounced. "And if you stay here, who am I going to see the rest of them with?" I pulled the guidebook from my pack. *The Fifty Most Spectacular Sights in Galactic Sector A.* "We've only done seventeen, Craig—that leaves thirty-three more to go!"

He wavered, looking at the Asgaard Bridge, then

back at the open book. Just to prod him, as the final part of the ritual, I found the Bifrost page and marked a big fat X on the checklist box. Another one down.

"I really wanted to see the singing cliffs of Golhem," he admitted. "And the refractory eclipses of Tarawna."

"Don't forget the fungus reefs and phosphor labyrinths on Kendrick Five-A. I was thinking of a way we could combine two separate checklist locations into a single vacation for next year. We *can* bag all fifty, Craig. But not if you're stuck here."

He looked as if his engines and life-support systems had all just shut down. I knew him well enough to read a flicker of doubt in his expression. Even he hadn't been so sure about his decision. "But what else can I do? This seemed like a decent way—make my own home, settle a plot of land. . . . I could pull it off. I know I could."

I had an idea. "If you're going to do that, then why not sign up for one of the terraform colonies instead? Same idea, but you'll get a huge financial incentive and gain title to half a continent. Pick yourself a hardworking colonist wife and form a dynasty."

He scratched his rumpled and sweaty hair. "Terraformers? I always heard that was miserable, no amenities, living with minimal resources . . . *no* amenities . . ." His words slowed.

"And exactly how is that different from turning Robinson Crusoe here?"

He remained silent. Then, like the mists evaporating to give us a view of the Asgaard Bridge, an uncertain smile broke through on his face. "The difference is, if I become a land baron, *I* can foot the bill for our next expedition."

Though I was anxious to start back, I handed Craig the guidebook and let him spend a few minutes mulling over the images. *The Fifty Most Spectacular Sights in Galactic Sector A*. I set the hook: "You know, there are books like that for Sectors B and C, too."

Craig shouldered his pack and looked at the Asgaard Bridge one last time before returning the guidebook. Shaken and still uncertain, he took the lead with a new spring in his step. "We'll have plenty to do for years to come, Steve—if you and I make the time to go to these planets."

"We will. As long as we get back to the shuttle in time."

DR. PROSPERO AND THE SNAKE LADY

by Brian Stableford

I'M NOT OFTEN AWAKE in the middle of the night in winter, especially when the skies are clear and the temperature drops to thirty below zero, but on the day Elise Gagne fell out of the sky I was unusually restless. There was a meteor shower due that night, so I decided to take a look. Caliban and Ariel don't care for things like that, so they were content to let me be whole, even though my being awake was depriving one or other of them a tiny fraction of existence.

Dr. Prospero didn't seem to care one way or another who I was. He'd become bored with me; the experiment's honeymoon was over and he was content to leave further formal monitoring entirely to

AIs. He, too, had been restless of late—awaiting new inspiration, I supposed.

The shower wasn't as spectacular as I'd hoped, but there was a fugitive aurora that made up for the thinness of the meteor trails. I'd read only a few days before that the aurora's lights are echoes of storms on the sun, and that made the flickering seem more romantic. There were a couple of airships above the island, running with minimal lights so that the sight-seers could watch the shower, but I didn't pay them much heed until one of them dropped a falling star of its own.

I guessed immediately that it was a parachute capsule, and that that it was aimed at the island. Dr. Prospero never invites visitors, but that doesn't prevent people from coming. For a while, when I was the apple of Dr. Prospero's eyes, there was at least one illicit visitor every week, and they all wanted pictures of me. Now I was nearly full-grown, though, it was as likely to be someone interested in the white mammoths, the tapirs or the giant rats—or even Python, who'd been old news for three centuries before I was even born.

It was a stupid time to come calling, I thought. There'd only be a few hours of meager daylight when dawn eventually came, and the night was so cold that even the mammoths were likely to stay in a huddle, deep in the pines. Python was safely curled up in the bowels of Dr. Prospero's ice palace, fast asleep and oblivious to the world of men.

I sometimes envied him that ability. Sleep, for me, is an eternal dream. Ariel and Caliban remember nothing of one another, but I remember every embarrassing moment of both their stupid lives.

There wasn't much wind, but the descending capsule drifted farther than I expected. It didn't carry as far as the ice-sheet, but it came down in the water a few hundred meters offshore. The parachute-rider's life raft inflated immediately.

I went down to the beach to meet the raft, in case its occupant needed help. She was so frightened by the sight of me that she raised her flare gun; I made frantic gestures to assure her that I meant her no harm.

Her suitskin's tegument was thickened against the cold, slightly inflated by an insulating layer of vacuum, so her face was slightly indistinct, but her features seemed bland enough. She was unfashionably tall, and her long limbs seemed to be unusually supple. There was no way to tell whether her eyes were wired up to record or transmit, but the way her gaze wandered suggested that she wasn't paying attention the way a newsvid reporter would.

I tried to sign to her—although I can write, I can't talk, because I don't have the necessary vocal apparatus—but she didn't understand. It obviously wasn't me that she had come to investigate.

"You shouldn't creep up on people like that," she said unfairly. "You're the smart orangutan that never sleeps, right? I saw you on the archive newstapes, but I didn't think you'd be allowed to run around at night. Can you see me safely up the mountain to your daddy's door?"

She seemed to think that I was some kind of pet. I was going back up the mountain anyway, but I had planned on going by way of the trees rather than the footpath. I didn't have Dr. Prospero's distaste for human company, though. I liked people. I could study them to my heart's content in v-space, and communicate with them, too, but there's no substitute for actual presence and authentic touch.

I offered her my hand, but she wouldn't take it.

"Just lead the way," she said. "Your name's Miranda, right?"

I nodded my head to indicate that I was indeed Miranda at present, not Ariel or Caliban, but I don't think her research in the newstape archives had been detailed enough to make her aware of my unique situation.

I meekly led her up the mountain. I even let her into the palace, although I wouldn't have been able to do that if Dr. Prospero had wanted her kept out. Even then, I assumed that he was just making the best of things, and that he'd get rid of her as soon as he could—but when he came to meet her, I realized that I'd been mistaken. He was expecting her.

He seemed less resentful of her presence than any other human I'd ever seen him look at.

"Miranda," he said, "this is Elise Gagne. She'll be staying for a few days. I've agreed to work on a project with her."

I was thunderstruck. Dr. Prospero working in collaboration! It was unthinkable. There were a thousand Creationists working on Pacific islets, of whom eight or nine hundred were probably obsessively reclusive—fully half of whom used silly pseudonyms in the great tradition of Oscar Wilde and Gustave Moreau—but Dr. Prospero was in a class of his own when it came to cultivated eccentricity. If Python and the white mammoths weren't evidence enough of his original turn of mind, and his determination to venture where other Creationists feared to tread, I was the final proof of it. Who could this person be that Dr. Prospero would deign to "work on a project" with her? I thought that I had made myself familiar with the names of the world's leading Creationists, but I had never heard of Elise Gagne.

I signed a question, curious to know what project Dr. Prospero was talking about—but he ignored me. The humiliation was bitter.

"You can go, Miranda," he said. "Elise and I have things to discuss."

It was not so much the fact of the dismissal as the tone that cut me. It was one thing no longer to be the focus of Dr. Prospero's minute attention or the object of his intensest study, and quite another to be waved away like some mere irrelevance. I had never felt so hurt. I had, of course, only been alive for fifteen years—a drop in the ocean by comparison with Dr. Prospero's 433 and Python's 399—but I had never expected that I might feel so wretched if I lived to be a thousand.

Elise did not wait for me to leave. She had already stepped into Dr. Prospero's private space, without causing any precipitate retreat. She actually reached out to touch his cheek.

"Thank you, Prospero," she said. "You don't know how much this means to me."

He didn't flinch. The omission of his title didn't disturb him any more than the pressure of her fingers.

I crept away, feeling like Caliban at her worst.

I had no difficulty at all finding out who Elise Gagne was. It was equally easy to discover what she wanted from Dr. Prospero. The woman was an open book: her life, her art and her ambition clamored for attention on the uniweb. She wasn't a Creationist at all. She was an exotic dancer.

She danced with snakes. What she wanted from Dr. Prospero was a perfect partner.

The one thing that wasn't a matter of public record was what she'd offered him in exchange for designing one, but that wasn't hard to figure out, although the answer was hard for me to swallow.

She had offered him fleshsex.

A year before, I would have thought the idea of any such exchange ridiculous, but not anymore. I had had a great deal more time to further my education since Dr. Prospero's observations had grown less intense—and so had Ariel and Caliban. Neither of them was fond of reading, and Caliban was no seeker after wisdom even in v-space, but there were kinds of experience for which each was avid, and I remembered every last detail of my dreams when I woke up. My partial selves had, inevitably, become the intensest objects of *my* study, as I struggled to understand the dream-stuff of which I was made.

Although I'm formed like an orangutan, that being the genome-plan and fundamental cytostructure with which Dr. Prospero worked when he shaped the egg from which I was born, the inspiration for my creation came from another mammal: the dolphin. Like orangutans, dolphins became extinct in the twenty-first century ecocatastrophe, but they were among the first of the recreated species. There are many things about them that are remarkable, but the one that seized Dr. Prospero's imagination was a consequence of the fact that a sea-dwelling mammal cannot go to sleep as a land-mammal can, else it will sink and drown.

Creatures with simpler brains than dolphins can solve this problem by restricting themselves to shallow sleep-states, but dolphins need to dream, and thus need deeper sleep. They solve this problem by letting the two hemispheres of their brain sleep in shifts, one at a time.

This is restrictive in a different way. It requires each hemisphere of a dolphin's brain to be able to perform all of the basic functions required to sustain it; there's still scope for some specialization, but not as much as a primate brain. That's one reason why dolphins aren't as smart as most dogs, let alone recreated orangutans, in spite of the potential offered by the size and complexity of their brains.

Dr. Prospero probably wasn't the only man ever to wonder whether such a situation could be produced in a brain whose functions were more elaborately divided—but it's his propensity for actualizing such wonderings that makes him the exceptional Creationist he is. He undertook to find out, and I'm the result of that inquiry. When both sides of my brain are awake, I'm Miranda. When the left hemisphere sleeps, I'm Caliban. When the right hemisphere sleeps, I'm Ariel. The specialization of my two hemispheres isn't as marked as that of a human brain, nor is it patterned in the same way, but the principle is similar. Ariel and Caliban are very different individuals, and I'm far greater than the sum of my parts.

At least, I like to think so.

Indeed, I feel obliged to hope so, now that Ariel and Caliban have become so obsessed with sex—in different ways, of course. It's easy to believe that Caliban would be male if he weren't stuck in my female body, and that Ariel would be some kind of polysexual sprite, but it was hard to think anything else after I'd read *The Tempest*, even though I knew that Dr. Prospero had just been carried away by the implications of his pseudonym when he named my constituent parts. I, by contrast, have only an intellectual interest in sex, perhaps because I routinely wake up in possession of a sated body.

A man of Dr. Prospero's age, intellect, and temperament should have transcended sexual urges long ago, in my view, or at least confined their expression to virtual experience—how, after all, could any mere partner of flesh compete with the exquisite subtleties of *his* artifice?—but I think I understand why it doesn't work that way.

Humankind took effective control of the species' evolution a thousand years ago, at the end of the twentieth century, but clung hard to as much of its inheritance as was not actually disastrous. By that time, ten thousand years of mental and social evolution had far outstripped the physiological evolution of a body whose emotional equipment had been shaped by the brutality of natural selection. Since then, physical evolution has outstripped the emotional evolution of a brain whose moral and emotional equipment was shaped by terror and lust. One day, no doubt, a reasonable balance will be struck, but today's emortals are no more than five generations removed from the rough-hewn products of natural selection, and the tools with which they reshaped themselves are still relatively crude. They retain the greater number of their follies.

Even Creationists, masters of evolution as they are, retain their follies: even Dr. Prospero, the greatest of the great eccentrics.

And that is why, no matter how absurd it seems, Dr. Prospero was willing to design a perfect dancing partner for Elise Gagne, in return for a fleshsex fling: a hectic *folie à deux*.

On the second day of Elise Gagne's visit I unearthed one of my old electronic voice-boxes so that I could communicate with her more easily. Dr. Prospero and I didn't need spoken words, because we had such expert fingers, but her fingers—long and supple as they were—were mute.

She appreciated the effort, I think, but she didn't really want to talk to me. She seemed uncomfortable in my presence, although I made every effort to be pleasant, and to take an interest in her art.

"Why did you come to Dr. Prospero?" I asked, one day when we were dining *à deux* because Dr. Prospero could not interrupt his work. "Couldn't any commercial engineer make you a dancing snake?"

The words were pronounced as I typed by a beautifully modulated voice that would have sounded perfectly human to a blind person, but they seemed alien to me. After all, I'm not human, let alone perfect.

"The kind of dancing I do is very complicated," she told me, seeming to look down at me from a great height even though we were sitting at a table. She used her lovely fingers to smooth her hair, which she was wearing Nordic blonde in honor of the latitude. If Dr. Prospero's island had been in the tropics, like the vast majority of Creationist havens, she'd probably have worn it obsidian black.

"Is it?" I said. Unfortunately, my artificial voice had politeness built in to its tone, and it wouldn't do contemptuous scepticism.

"I needed a snake with a brain larger than any ordinary recreated species," she went on. "Making a snake with a big brain is only part of the problem, though. Apparently, there has to be some specialization of function, which has to do with cytoplasmic determinants of formal and structural development . . . the jargon's beyond me. Anyway, everyone said that Prospero was the man, if I could get him to do it— they laughed when they said it, but I wasn't worried. You've already got a smart snake living in the cellar, I understand—old as the hills and nearly as big."

"That's Python," I said. "He was the best result of Dr. Prospero's first experiments with mammoth genes."

"I thought the white mammoths were recent—last century."

"Yes, they are. The mammoth genes Dr. Prospero works with aren't *the genes of mammoths*, except that he couldn't resist the temptation to make a few mammoths with them; they're called mammoth genes because they're so big. When geneticists began reverse engineering very large proteins, they ran into problems because of the size of the genes required to make them and the fact that their component strands have to be kept separate. Mammoth genes can have as many as twelve introns, and they're very prone to transposon migration. Natural ones are understandably rare. Heritable artificial ones tend to suffer fatal mutation within a couple of generations. They're used commercially in short-term somatic engineering, but Dr. Prospero is exploring other potentials, such as . . ."

"I just need a dancing partner," Elise put in. "I don't need to breed from it, but it has to be built to last."

She was rude to interrupt, because I hadn't finished. I had a lot more to say, even though my fingers were feeling the effort because I hadn't used the voice-box for so long.

"Dr. Prospero hasn't had any difficulty producing long-lived individuals with mammoth genes," I assured her, although it wasn't strictly true; mammoth genes often break down in routine mitotic cell reproduction, which can make longevity problematic. "Python's proof of that. Reptiles are easier to engineer for longevity than mammals. His giantism is a side effect, but it added further interest to the outcome of his brain differentiation. The other engineers probably advised you to come to Dr. Prospero because he's so good at organizing brain differentiation."

"Obviously," she put in. I assumed that she was thinking of me.

"It's not just genes, however mammoth or minuscule, that determine differentiation of function," I persisted. "The formal development of an embryo is dependent on an architectural blueprint carried in the cytoplasm of the egg cell. Dr. Prospero will be using one of Python's cells—carefully renucleated—as the parent of the snake he's making for you."

"Just as long as it doesn't grow to be half a kilometer long," the dancer said. "I wouldn't want it to be too smart either—I can do without it wanting to take the lead."

I could tell that she wasn't seriously interested in the science, so I stopped trying to explain. I didn't like her at all. Mercifully, Caliban and Ariel didn't like her any better, although that didn't stop Caliban wanting to have fleshsex with her. Caliban became quite jealous of Dr. Prospero, in fact, and I sometimes had to cope with the hormonal fallout of that when I woke up. I always preferred waking up after Ariel, who was just as silly in her own way, but didn't leave such discomfiting physiological aftereffects behind.

When I took the trouble to watch some recordings of Elise dancing, I realised that the contempt I'd tried to insert into my comment on its complexity was quite unjustified. I had recklessly supposed that no human dancer could perform as elegantly as a sim, but sims are, after all, *simulations*. Dancing may be mute, but that doesn't mean that it's not a form of communication, or that its communication is more easily reduced to bytes than any other form of human interaction.

I watched her dance from the viewpoint of an observer, and I danced with her by choosing the IDENTIFICATION option, although I always find it difficult to put myself in a human's place no matter what the human is doing, because my limbs are so different. It's easier to identify with fabers, even though it's hard to imagine what low-gee environments feel like.

Elise was a very good dancer. She was also a very sexy dancer. I hadn't expected the snakes to add anything to her routines but a certain vulgar symbolism, but I was wrong about that too. Her snakes were more than crude phallic symbols or emblems of Edenic temptation; their coils complemented the sinuosity of her own body—whose suppleness was not, I discovered, the result of genetic engineering or surgically-enhanced plasticity, but a matter of training and of art. I only had to watch half a dozen dances from a distance, and join in with half a dozen more, to appreciate how brilliant she was—and how much more brilliant she might be if she could get past the limitations imposed on her by stupid partners.

I understood why she needed a smart snake—and I do mean *needed*, because she was an artist, and I understand that artists have needs that we common mortals don't.

Dr. Prospero is an artist, too, as well as a scientist. Every true Creationist is an artist first and a scientist second.

I would have stopped watching after half a dozen dances, but Ariel and Caliban didn't. They don't remember one another's actions at all, or anything of my inner life, but they do remember actions that I perform repeatedly. I think it must be like remembering a repetitive dream, which overcomes the tendency to forget by sheer insistence. Caliban and Ariel both remembered Elise's dancing, and how to access the tapes. They both used that knowledge—which must, I suppose, have seemed to them a strange intuition.

They both liked Elise's dancing, although they liked complementary aspects of it. Ariel loved its lightness and its pace, and the ability to lose her physicality in the flow. Ariel was a music lover; for her, dance was a liquid expression of music, flesh made sound. Caliban liked its physical dimension, and the sensation of the snake's coils. Caliban was a sensualist; for her, dance was a celebration of brutality, flesh made self. They both thought that Elise Gagne's dancing was sexy, although they had different notions of sexiness.

I remembered everything. In theory, I should have been able to fit their different experiences together, just as a brain can combine the images transmitted by two eyes to make a more coherent, mentally three-dimensional whole. Perhaps I could have, if I'd really wanted to. But I didn't want to. It's all very well being more than the sum of your parts, but if you can't choose the parts you're more than the sum of, and actively dislike them, you can lose interest in deliberate addition.

Dr. Prospero spent more and more time in the lab, locked up with his blueprints and his embryos. Elise showed no inclination to join him, but she seemed to have even less desire to hang out with me. She never went out, even when the sun peeped over the horizon and the white mammoths started foraging. She didn't want to watch the mammoths on the move, or the tapirs following the ebb tide while the giant rats hunted them by stealth. She spent a lot of time in v-space, far beyond the walls of Dr. Prospero's ice palace.

I spent a lot of time in v-space, too, sometimes as

far afield as Titan and the patient ships journeying between the stars, but I did go out to ride the mammoth bull and dig for shellfish with the tapirs—with my fingers, not my snout. I played with the rats, who had become amusing companions since I'd persuaded them that I wasn't prey. And I visited Python, who is my favorite person of all, except for Dr. Prospero, in spite of the fact that he has no fingers and can't talk to me in signs.

Sometimes, I think it must be very frustrating to be Python, not just because he has a lot of cleverness in his brain and no easy way to communicate its findings, but because he can sleep for such long periods—not just months but years, spending most of that time in oblivion and the rest in dreams that he probably never remembers.

He was asleep when I went down into the mountain to see him, but he woke up when I stroked his head. He looked at me, first with one eye and then with the other, his patient brain waiting to collate the two images. Then he yawned—an impressive sight— and licked my face with his tongue.

The walls in Python's hideaway are just as thickly skinned as the walls insulating the rooms and corridors of Dr. Prospero's palace from the ices of its fundamental architecture, but they're neither translucent nor luminous. They could have been patterned even more extravagantly than the tapirs if Dr. Prospero had wished, but they were actually monochrome gray, so dull that the light-fittings seemed to blaze more harshly white. Compensation for that was supplied by Python's iridescent scales, which gleamed like nothing else on Earth or in v-space.

"Hello, Python," I signed, touching my fingers to his skin rather than displaying them to one or other of his eyes. "Are you hungry today?"

He didn't understand sign language, but he always seemed to pick up something of my meaning. He yawned again and smacked his lips, as if to say that he could fancy a tapir, but couldn't be bothered to chase a few snack-rats.

"No tapirs," I signed. "You'll have to stay in the tunnels for a few months yet—but there are rats a-plenty to keep you going. Did you know that you're going to be a clone-father? Well, not a clone-father, to be perfectly accurate, but a sort of clone-great-uncle. Anyway, there'll be something in you in Elise's new partner: a chip off the old genetic block; something to be proud of in your old age. You are old, you know, no matter how young you feel. You might live for another thousand years, I suppose, but you're still old. Older and wiser than me."

He licked my face again. He could have swallowed me whole, after squeezing me to death with the merest effort of his vast coils, but he knew that I wasn't prey. To the rats, I was an honorary rat; to Python, I was an honorary snake; to Dr. Prospero, if not to Elise Gagne, I was an honorary human being.

Or was I?

My fingers faltered as I stroked Python's mighty head. I'd been having a lot of anxious thoughts like that lately, although there was really no need. Dr. Prospero might be distracted now, but Elise would be gone soon enough, having completed her unsavory bargain. Afterward, Dr. Prospero would be his own man again, and the palace would be closed to everyone—including the island's uninvited visitors—for hundreds of years.

Elise had been in residence at the palace for nine days when Dr. Prospero called me into his study.

"How is the work going?" I asked him politely.

"Very well," he signed. "I've completed the DNA assembly and renucleated thirty cells stripped from Python's mouth. I anticipate a higher failure rate than usual because of the number of mammoth genes involved, but I should have several embryos ready for implanting in four days' time."

"Is Elise going to be here throughout the gestation?"

"No. She's leaving tomorrow, but she'll return when the snakes are about a meter long. The advanced training phase will be the most difficult of all; it will take her a week or two to figure out which one is the most promising. After that, it's up to her. I'll be involved, of course, but only virtually. Are you happy, Miranda?"

The abrupt change of subject startled me, all the more so because it wasn't the kind of question Dr. Prospero usually asked.

"Yes," I signed. It wasn't entirely true, but I expected to be a lot happier in two days' time.

"Elise says that you seem unhappy to her."

Elise says! I thought. The effrontery was appalling, and not just because she'd scarcely looked in my direction all week. Why was Dr. Prospero interested in her judgment, when he was in a far better position to form one of his own?

Dr. Prospero didn't wait long enough for me to frame a reply. "Elise thinks you might be lonely," he signed. "She thinks I ought to make you a mate."

That was beyond effrontery. It was something whose term I hadn't yet discovered in the dictionary: something esoteric, that even a garrulous human with a functional larynx might only have occasion to pronounce once or twice in a lifetime.

"No," I signed. "No. No. No." Unlike a voice-box, gestures aren't restrained by artificial politeness.

Dr. Prospero seemed quite amazed. "I thought you'd like the idea," he said, aloud.

"No," I signed. "No."

"What about Ariel?" he signed. "What about Caliban?"

I was immediately seized by the awful idea that he might actually put it to a vote—and that I might be overruled by the separate hemispheres of my own brain. But they were only half a person each, at best, and I was more than the sum of my parts. Surely my opinion ought to outweigh both of theirs.

"No," I signaled. "No. No." My hand seemed to have got stuck, possessed by a kind of nervous tic. It must have seemed like that to Dr. Prospero, too. I hoped that he wouldn't tell Elise, because I could guess the interpretation Elise would put on my confusion, even though such a thought would never enter Dr. Prospero's head.

It would never have entered mine, except that I had *bad dreams*: dreams of Ariel and dreams of Caliban; their urges, their whims and their poor excuses for thought.

"It wouldn't be a matter of breeding, Miranda," Dr. Prospero said, proving that his mind wasn't entirely isolated from the kinds of thought that Elise might put into it. "You have too many mammoth genes to be an effective mother. Like me, you'll never have offspring while you're alive—and in your case, it'll require a very clever Human Creationist to ensure that you have them thereafter. It's a matter of companionship—a matter of having someone to do things with, to talk to, to love."

Until Elise had come, it would never have crossed Dr. Prospero's mind to add that last word, whose sound was so much cruder than its sign. Why should it enter his head now, I thought, given that she'd be leaving in two days' time and would only return once more to collect her precious dancing partner?

"No need," I signed. "I have Python, the rats, the tapirs, you." I tried to make him into an afterthought, as if to sting him like a serpent's tooth—although, not having seen the blueprints, I didn't know whether Elise's new partner was destined to have teeth or not. Sometimes she danced with cobras, sometimes with anacondas—all recreates, of course; nothing of that sort had made it through the ecocatastrophe, in spite of the fact that there'd never been any shortage of rats and cockroaches to eat.

"They're not your own kind," he pointed out, reverting to silent discourse.

"Elise isn't your kind," I signed back. "Nobody is. Python's one of a kind, too. We all are."

I knew before his fingers moved what he was going to say. "What about Ariel?" he signed. "What about Caliban?"

They didn't matter. They were only fragments, figments cast out by the dreams that could only take possession of half of me at a time. They didn't really exist. They didn't have needs of their own, desires of their own, votes of their own.

Except that they did—have needs and desires, that is. Not votes, while I had any say in the matter.

"What about me?" I signed back to Dr. Prospero. "What about me?"

DR. PROSPERO AND THE SNAKE LADY

* * *

The tempo of life on most Creationist islands is rapid; the days and nights are more or less equal all year round, and the sun is always hot. The vegetation is avid, the animal life frenzied. Here in the cold north, where summer days and winter nights are all-but-endless, things move much more slowly. The evergreen forests have leaves like needles, which fix the sunlight with the utmost patience, and their undergrowth is grazed with equal patience. The mammoths are vast and majestic, like great drifts of dirty snow, far too self-possessed ever to turn avalanche. The omnivorous tapirs and rats are similarly unhurried, never condescending to anything as vulgar as pursuit.

I, too, am a creature of the island. By the time humans "discovered" them, orangutans were tropic-dwellers, like tigers and elephants, but they'd first been shaped—like tigers and elephants—by the rigors of oft-repeated ice ages, bulked up for insulation against the cold. Only the vagaries of chance and the competition provided by humankind's remoter ancestors drove them from the habitat to which they'd been adapted into warmer climes, where the ever-avid vegetation gave them greater scope for survival.

Even had I been a faithful copy of my clone-great-uncles, I wouldn't be out of place on Dr. Prospero's island. It isn't my mammoth genes that make me fit company for actual mammoths, nor my dolphinesque brain. I belong here—far more so than Dr. Prospero himself, who's a stranger, genetically speaking. His clone-great-uncles wiped out their Neanderthal cousins, who were better adapted to endure the continual advents of the ice, but they never learned to love the cold.

As for Ariel and Caliban—well, quite frankly, who cares? If I don't, who should? Can they really care about themselves, given that they only have half a brain apiece, and that each one only has that when the other is dreaming. No matter how intimately related we are, they're not my companions. I don't love them.

But I digress. The point is that the next two days dragged, even though they were only two days. They didn't pass as swiftly as I desired, or needed—and on the eve of her departure, Elise Gagne danced.

She danced with a cobra, but the idea of biting her probably never crossed its mind, any more than squeezing me to death and swallowing me with a single gulp would ever cross Python's.

I was allowed to watch, even though the occasion might have been thought preciously intimate by Dr. Prospero. Indeed, my presence was required, because Elise was a performer and needed all the audience she could muster—even recreated orangutans too stupid to know where their own best interests lay.

Perhaps she knew that I had been watching her

tapes, and taking her place in them as best I could.
Perhaps she didn't know that Ariel's and Caliban's
similar actions weren't mine in any true sense of the
word. At any rate, I was there for her performance.
I watched her dance, in the flesh. I might have fallen
asleep if I could, but I couldn't.

The cobra was less impressive than one of her anacondas, although it was a full two metres from nose
to tail and had a fine hood decorated with the eyes
of an owl. We have owls on the island occasionally:
summer strays from Greenland and Spitzbergen,
which fly over the pole.

Were I signing this instead of writing it, I could
probably give a more convincing account of Elise's
dancing, but even dexterous fingers could not give
more than the faintest impression of its charm. She
and the cobra were fused as closely as was possible
into a single soul, as carefree and innocently ec-
static as Ariel, but so much more indulgent of their
bliss; they flowed around one another with all the
grace of a DNA-helix, but with much more versatil-
ity, much more freedom of expression. They looked
at one another with such naked predatory lust,
such brazen physicality, that it was impossible to
judge which of them might be more likely to poison
and consume the other were they enemies instead
of lovers. They were as brutal as Caliban, and as
monstrous, but there was an art in their mutual
caresses that transfigured brutality into sublimity

and monstrousness into . . . well, something far more sinister than beauty, but far less sinister than love.

It was magnificent, in its way, but some way short of perfection. Elise knew that, even though she had reached the peak of her own achievement. When she finished, she looked directly to me, and held my gaze for longer than she had ever been able to before.

"It will be better when I have my asp," she told me. "You'll see, then, what dancing is."

Orangutans aren't built for dancing. Not, at any rate, the kinds of dancing humans can do. Our genes are very similar, but the instructions etched in my cytoplasm are more akin to fabers than walkers.

I nodded my head, as if to agree with her—but she refused to understand me, even in a gesture so simple. Her redirected attention was already fixed on Dr. Prospero. His had never wavered.

I left, and went to talk to Python.

"You're not built for dancing either," I told him. "I'm all arms, you're just a mammoth's thigh stretched to absurdity, too much mass to move with grace. But she's going home now, and Dr. Prospero will be all ours again. Yours and mine, I mean— because the mammoths and the tapirs, and Ariel and Caliban, too, are all too stupid to care. You and I are the only ones who really love him, because we're the only ones who can."

He licked my face when I finished, as if he wanted to comfort me but didn't quite know how.

I waited for life to return to normal. I waited for Dr. Prospero to return to himself. Initially, I put his increased distraction down to the stress of his continued labors in connection with the gestating asps. Then, after some thought and a certain amount of research, I figured that there must be some kind of hormonal echo afflicting him, the way Caliban's echoes occasionally afflict me. I thought that his body might be missing her, even though his mind must be eager to return to a more productively ataractic state.

I did what I could to help. I was attentive but discreet, always ready to talk and never to nag, always concerned but always careful.

It did no good. He remained moody. I'm sure that his work didn't suffer—his work on the asps, that is—but it had been dislodged from its proper context. It was almost as if he were leaving the island to do it, commuting to some private v-space a million miles away.

We had a hundred trivial conversations before he got around to it, but in the end the moment came.

"I've been thinking, Miranda," he signed to me, one evening after dinner when the stars shone brightly, darting their frail refractions through the infinite crystal corridors of the ice palace. "I think

I've done everything here that I need to do. I'm going to move south again, take an island nearer to the equator. The Continental Engineers have a couple of dozen virgins ready for allocation."

The word that hurt me most, oddly enough, was "again." Dr. Prospero hadn't worked anywhere else since Python was the size of his forearm. Given the limited carrying capacity of human memory, and the way in which human personalities reshape themselves over the centuries, he couldn't have any meaningful sense of ever having lived anywhere else. The Dr. Prospero I knew—the Dr. Prospero he knew—ought to have been as much a creature of the island as the alpha male of the mammal herd, or me.

"I don't want to leave," I signed, hastily adding: "Not yet. In a hundred years, maybe. Or two."

"You're only fifteen, Miranda," he signed back. "You have no idea what a hundred years means. In any case, you can stay here if you want to."

And there it was: *You can stay here if you want to.* As if I were capable of wanting to be here if he was somewhere else. As if I were just part of the artificial ecosphere he'd created here. As if I might welcome a new tenant to his ice palace, or become its chatelaine myself, or fade into the scenery.

As if, as if, as if. My fingers twitched as I repeated the phrase inside my head, itching with it even though it remained discreetly muffled.

"No," I signed eventually. "That's not what I want. I want things to be normal again."

"You're only fifteen," he signed, as if his fingers, too, were developing habits that were difficult to break. "You have no notion of normality. Fifteen years is a drop in the ocean. Things have been settled during that time because I've become stuck in my ways, but that's not normal. Moving on is normal. You have to keep changing when you're emortal, Miranda, or robotization might set in. It's time I moved on. Past time, I think."

"Is that what Elise told you?" I asked, recklessly.

"She mentioned it," he replied, "but she only started me thinking. I needed to start thinking along those lines. Once the asp is finished—finished here, I mean, not fully trained—it will be time for new surroundings, new stimuli. I need new ideas, Miranda. You have new ideas every day, simply because you're growing up, but I've been grown up for a long time, and I need to move on if I'm not to stagnate. I don't want you to stay here. I want you to come with me—but you're free to make your own choice."

What about Ariel? I thought. *What about Caliban?* Well, what about them. They wouldn't care, and they didn't have a vote. I was the whole person, the real me. I didn't want to go. But I didn't want Dr. Prospero to go without me either—even if tagging along with him, like an exhibit in his portable collection of samples, turned out to be anything but paradise, anything but comfortable and anything but endurable.

"There's no hurry," I signed. "We have all the time in the world."

"That's part of the problem," he signed back. "Time moves so slowly here, where the day seems almost as long as the year. It's worse than the moon. When Elise comes back . . ."

"It won't make any difference," I signed, suppressing a tremor in my fingers in order to make sure that my meaning was clear. "Once she has her asp, she'll have no further use for you. Your deal will be over."

He raised his eyebrows in sincere astonishment. "I know that," he signed. "It's fine by me. We both got what we wanted, and it'll be over soon enough for both of us. It'll be time for us both to move on—to seize new opportunities, to meet new challenges."

He couldn't see that the deal wasn't over, and never would be—because she'd changed him. She'd drifted into his life and drifted out again, but she wasn't gone. Even when she had her asp, she wouldn't be gone. Things had changed, forever. But what could I say? What could I say that couldn't be countered with that ridiculous, appalling, insulting rejoinder: You're only fifteen, Miranda. You don't understand.

Because I *am* only fifteen, and I don't.

When there was nothing further to say to Dr. Prospero, I went to see Python again, because he wasn't only fifteen, and he did understand.

"We're leaving, Python," I told him, my fingers dancing on his glittering scales as if on a dance floor that went on forever, glittering all the way. "We're leaving, and never coming back. Nothing will ever be the same. You're coming, too, of course. Just you and me and Dr. Prospero. And Ariel and Caliban, I suppose.

"Sometimes, I wish that I could go to sleep for a thousand years, and wake up when they've had a chance to grow up and become as wise as they ever can—but I can't, because regular wakefulness is just as essential as regular sleep to a highly-developed mind like mine. Even you're too smart to be able to sleep forever, Python. Truth be told, they can't grow up if I'm not around; they can't even live for long if I'm not around to draw them together and nourish their dreams.

"And while we're admitting the truth, it's possible that Dr. Prospero is right—that Elise is right, although it would choke me if I had to say it with my throat—and that he really does have to move on. He's only human, after all. Three's a crowd, you know, inside or outside your head, but everything on the surface of the Earth is one big crowd, even when you're on a tiny island surrounded by a little hole in an ice sheet that goes all the way to the pole on one side and calves bergs into the great gray sea on the other. I hate Elise Gagne, but she knows how to dance. She certainly knows how to dance."

Python yawned, and stirred. I knew that he was feeling hungry, that he wanted to be away. He'd probably been perfectly content before I arrived, but I'd sparked the restlessness in him and now he wanted to be off, hunting for rats in the tunnels, or tapirs on the slopes.

"It's still winter, old man," I said to him. "It's cold outside, even in the meager daylight. There's no hurry, is there? And there'll always be plenty of rats. Even in the depths of the ecocatastrophe, there were always plenty of rats."

I left him to it, and went through the tunnels myself, out on to the mountainside above the tree line. Far below, I could see the mammoths huddled in a clearing, like a great white tumor in the forest's dark flesh.

The stars were shining, but there were no stars falling, and no aurora to echo the storms on the sun.

If I were able to sleep for a thousand years, I thought, I might wake to a braver new world, when the legacy of billions of years of natural selection has at last been balanced by the legacy of two millennia of godlike power.

Or maybe not.

Anyway, I had no choice.

DR. PROSPERO AND THE SNAKE LADY

Wakefulness is as essential as sleep; ambition is as necessary as dreams. The only place on Earth that never changes is the utmost ocean floor, into which nothing falls but the corpses of sea-dwelling mammals that have finally been consumed by sleep, Ariel-twin and Caliban-twin alike.

But I cursed the homewrecking snake lady nevertheless, for not having the grace to wait just a little while longer.

BITTER QUEST

by Jim Fiscus

THE NOON SUN TURNED the great falls of the Columbia to burnished silver. Over a mile wide, the river frothed and tumbled five hundred feet over black volcanic rock into a dark, roiling pool. A bright rainbow crowned the mists at the foot of the falls. A mile downriver, the southwest bank had been excavated to form the Basin, which protected a handful of ships tied to docks and a dozen others waiting at anchor. Warehouses, shipping offices, bars, and brothels covered the steep hill between the docks and the black cliff holding back the river.

Rafael Baggett wiped sweat from his forehead and turned from the thundering falls. He inhaled deeply, smelling air tainted by the raw sewage and garbage that covered the backwaters of the anchorage, and coughed. He longed for the clean salt air of the ocean, some seventy miles away at the mouth of the Columbia.

"The falls are impressive, Hefmon Baggett, aren't they?" The ship's captain stood at his side.

Baggett nodded silently. At nearly six feet tall, he was a half a head taller than the captain, whose muscular build made him look squat next to the tall man. The high-crowned, wide-brimmed brown hat Baggett wore on his black hair made him seem even taller.

"Heavy cargo uses a cog railroad two miles west. You'll use the cable car. It rises from the terminal, that large white building against the cliff." The captain handed Baggett a telescope.

Jagged black rocks snapped into view through the long glass. Baggett moved the glass till he saw a small platform swinging precariously from a nearly vertical cable. "Almost looks like an elevator." Baggett handed the glass back. "Thanks for the look, Captain, and the smooth sail from Angeles. Would you please have my equipment taken to the terminal?"

"Already done, Hefmon. It'll be there before you are. Your local guide should meet you there." The man paused, clearly contemplating his next words. "My father died last year of fever, Hefmon Baggett. May your mission succeed."

"Thank you, Captain," Baggett said, remembering Miya's passage from burning fever to seizures and death. "My wife died three years ago from fever. She was pregnant. It always kills our children, our wives, our parents: then, we are alone." Unable to say more, Baggett turned from the ship's rail and shouldered a large backpack.

"Rafael Baggett." Baggett stooped to talk through the window grill.

A clerk pointed across the terminal's busy waiting room to a tall man leaning beside the back door. "That Souther in the red cloak asked for you."

Baggett wound his way between long wooden benches to the back of the room. "I'm Baggett."

"Kieren Vanslyke. How was your sail up coast, Hefmon?" The man rubbed his hand through his long, blond hair. His other hand rested on the hilt of a foot-long belt knife.

"Fast and smooth. Is the boat ready to go up lake?"

"Yes, Hefmon, and your trunks and other baggage are out back waiting for you."

"Good." Baggett studied the tall man. "You're far from home, I'd guess."

"Came north twenty years ago. Been trading on the lake since." The guide smiled. "Twenty years, and they still consider me an outsider."

"How long do we have to wait for a cable car?"

"One's just unloading from a downrun." The guide led Baggett outside to a concrete slab that filled the fifty feet between the terminal building and the cliff face. The cable car was a square platform, fifteen feet to a side, made of heavy timbers. Side rails enclosed the platform. A central stanchion rose to the overhead cable. Secondary stanchions attached fore and aft to keep the car from rotating. Handlers quickly loaded his baggage, lashing it against the central column.

Baggett slipped off his pack. He glanced up as a horn sounded. Seconds later, the car lurched into the air, swinging gently as it climbed. Looking around, Baggett realized that he and Vanslyke were the only people aboard. "Light load, isn't it?"

"Your trunks are heavy, so they decided to just send us with them."

Halfway up, the car jerked to a stop and Baggett staggered slightly. "Why are we stopping?"

"I told them you wanted a slow trip so you could see the sights." Vanslyke pulled a long cudgel from inside his cloak. "Sorry you're going to miss the view up top."

Baggett moved behind the luggage pile. Fear tightened his gut. He looked up, seeing only black rock and sky. No one—above or below—could see them clearly.

"You've no place to hide my body."

"Passengers panic and fall every so often." Vanslyke darted forward, snapped his cudgel toward Baggett.

Baggett sidestepped. He grabbed Vanslyke's wrist and smashed the man's forearm against the edge of a trunk. The snap of bones and Vanslyke's scream echoed against the cliff. Baggett grabbed the cudgel and cracked it against Vanslyke's knee, dropping the man to the platform.

Baggett pulled Vanslyke's knife from its sheaf. He grabbed an extra cargo rope and lashed his attacker to the stanchion. As the cable car rocked gently in the wind, Baggett grabbed Vanslyke's broken arm and twisted. As the thug's scream subsided, Baggett said softly, "Now, we only have a few minutes to talk."

The cable car bumped the edge of the cliff and slid to a stop on a wide concrete pad. Baggett stepped off the car, calling, "This man is injured."

The top cableman threw the cable lock. "What happened?"

"Lost his balance when the car stopped. Smashed his arm all to hell."

The cableman looked down at Vanslyke, grimacing at the white fragments of bone poking through the darkly tanned arm. The man leaned over Vanslyke, jerked up. "He's dead!"

"Pain must have been too much for him," Baggett said.

"Who is he?" the cableman asked, spreading his arms to hold back a small crowd of onlookers.

"My guide. Named Vanslyke."

Baggett glanced at the small crowd, "Anyone know him?"

A man about Baggett's 34 years, but at least five inches shorter, limped out of the crowd. His black hair was heavily streaked with gray. He had on well-worn leather pants and shirt. He walked over to the body, reached down and pulled the red cloak aside. "No idea," he said in a raspy voice.

Baggett nodded, said to the cableman, "Deal with the body as you choose," and to the crowd, "I need a wagon to take me to the anchorage. My name's Baggett."

The man with the limp tapped the wardrobe trunk. "Right over here, Hefmon Baggett."

"How much?"

"Two silver Columbians."

"Good enough."

The man gestured to two nearby men. Both looked about twenty, with the same green eyes and black hair as the limping man. They waited as the man with the limp crossed the dirt road to a wagon pulled by a swaybacked mule. He patted the mule on the muzzle and led him back across the road. Baggage loaded, the man with the limp climbed into the back of the wagon and perched on one sideboard. The younger men waited at the head of the mule, one holding a short lead rope. "I'd walk, but I twisted my knee last week. Please join me, Hefmon Baggett."

"How far to the anchorage?" Baggett sat across from the man.

"Two miles." He pulled a wrinkled envelope from his shirt pocket. "I didn't tell you my name."

"No, you didn't."

"I'm Kieren Vanslyke." He grinned. "The real one. The pair up front are my nephews, Styvie and Karim." Handing Baggett the envelope, he said, "Here's the letter Dr. Kreshfield sent asking me to guide you."

Baggett recognized Kreshfield's handwriting. "Who was the dead man?"

"No idea. I sent a message to your ship telling you to meet me at the upper terminal."

"I didn't get it."

"So I gather," Vanslyke said. "What happened on the cable car?"

"Answer a question for me first. When did you first meet Dr. Kreshfield?"

"I met Jaime fifteen years ago. We spent six months steaming up and down Lake Willmut. He stopped at every island and landing and spent days taking plant and insect samples and packing and preserving them. I thought he was crazy." Vanslyke chuckled. "But I liked talking to him about the days before the mountain blocked the river. We've written each other a couple times a year since . . . his handwriting in that letter looks shaky to me. Is he sick?"

"He came down with a new form of the fever two years ago. Nothing we have will cure it. He gets better for a while, then it comes back on him. It's doing the same for thousands of people. It kills the old and the children." Thinking of Miya, he added, "And pregnant women."

"A new fever?"

"It seems to be the same disease we've always fought, malaria by its old name. Records from before the great plagues say that they had a way to cure it and prevent reinfection. It's caused by a bug that swims in the blood and is spread by mosquitoes. But we can't recreate the old drugs. Our traditional treatment, quinine, does little."

"And the fever brings you here?"

"Jaime found records saying that before the collapse scientists up here created a plant that produced a kind of super quinine, and designed it to thrive in the climate they predicted for here. It's critical we find it."

"So you're looking for it?"

"Hefmon Vanslyke, plagues destroyed the old civilization after the warming. If I fail, the fever may break us, too. A year ago, northern traders started selling small amounts of a new type of quinine. It stops the fever, but we only have enough to keep a handful of people alive. Do you know anything about it?"

Vanslyke braced himself as the wagon hit a series of ruts, said, "No . . . no, I don't. Now, I ask again, what happened in the cable car?"

"He tried to kill me, and the shock killed him."

"The shock, eh?" Vanslyke smiled. "Did he say anything?"

"Nothing."

Baggett stood atop the ridge of lava that had blocked the Columbia River eight hundred years before his birth, flooding the land and eventually creating the falls. Two miles wide above the falls, the river ran south, gradually swelling into a small lake before narrowing to run east through its ancient gorge. To the southwest, Baggett saw the sharp peak of a tall mountain, looking as if it rose from the sheet of dark blue water. The top of the mountain had the jagged look of a broken tooth. Hood, the old maps called it, Baggett remembered.

Vanslyke's boat, the steam launch *Lake Queen*, was one of thirty boats in the small anchorage, ranging from skiffs to large sternwheelers that traded inland beyond the Gorge. The *Queen* looked rather like a floating tub to Baggett, about thirty feet long, with a wide beam and a shallow draft. A steam engine sunk into an open well took up the center third of the boat, with a long drive shaft running aft to the prop. Bright blue with red-and-yellow eyes on her squared bow, she looked freshly painted. Baggett's trunks and supplies were lashed on deck forward of the engine. Stacks of firewood filled the engine well and lined the sides of the ship. A faded tarp mounted on poles shielded the deck from the harsh sun.

One of Vanslyke's nephews fed wood into the fire box. He stopped and swigged from a water bottle.

"I'm afraid I don't remember which brother you are," Baggett said.

"Few can tell which is which. I'm the younger, Styvie. I'm a hair taller than Karim."

"Did your uncle say where I should set up my equipment?"

"Where your trunks are. You'll also sleep there. The forward cabin holds cargo. My uncle has the aft cabin. Karim and I sleep by the wheel."

Baggett swung open his wardrobe trunk. The right side held drawers that he inspected, ensuring that his chemicals and instruments had survived. The top of the left side dropped down to form a small table. The lower half held a kerosene burner and other equipment. He closed the trunk and looked ashore as the wagon rattled to a stop at the top of the dock.

Vanslyke climbed slowly from the wagon. Baggett helped unload the final supplies.

At dawn the next morning, Vanslyke stood at the boat's wheel, easing power to the prop. The brothers cast off stern and bow lines and *Lake Queen* eased away from the dock. The steamer nosed out of the anchorage, swung sharply when her bow hit the fast current, then steadied as Vanslyke increased power.

An hour upriver, the brothers lugged two wooden crates up from the forward hold, placing one on each side amidships. Vanslyke called to Baggett, "Time to unpack any weapons you brought with you. If you've nothing, I'll loan you a gun."

"I'm armed," Baggett said, watching the brothers unpack a crate. They pulled out a heavy stanchion that mounted to brackets on the bulwark. Next came the weapon itself. It consisted of seven breech-loading guns set side by side on a heavy frame, all fired by a single trigger. The barrels had a bore of about an inch and were set in a slight fan, widening their coverage. Heavy springs mounted to the frame would help absorb the recoil of the barrels. Baggett said, "Clever design."

"We make do," Vanslyke said, chuckling. "The guns take scatter shot. They'll clean out anything in front of them for fifty yards or more. We call them reapers."

"Why do we need that much power?"

"Trade has increased the past decade. So have the number of draggers who attack boats in the Narrows to Lake Willmut. Once we're south of the Narrows, we'll be safe. The folks living around the lake and on the islands are all good people. Some day, we're going to have to get together and clean the draggers out.

*   *   *

A long, low hill formed a barrier to the west. High-lands to the east at the head of the Columbia Gorge angled sharply to the southeast, forming a funnel into which they steamed. Ahead, several large islands offered two possible channels south. All of them were covered with a scattering of dry-looking brush and scrub trees.

"We stay west till we pass the next island, then cut to the eastern channel," Vanslyke called over the thud of the steam engine. He stared into the dark water. "Always feels eerie in the Narrows. Legends say there's a city down there that died when the waters backed up."

"There is," Baggett said. "The old maps call it Portland."

The brothers manned the side guns, regularly leaping into the engine well to toss wood into the firebox. Vanslyke stood at the wheel. He had two revolvers tucked into his belt and a rifle leaning against the wheel post. Baggett waited amidships, holding a short-barreled rifle. A slight breeze stirred the hot, muggy air. Baggett's shirt was dark with sweat.

The boat slowed as it nosed into the faster current. Closer to the islands, Baggett recognized manzanita and small oaks sheltering scrubby-looking rhododendrons. Grasses and scattered shrubs covered the rest of the ground. Willows held near the waterline, with reeds spreading into the shallows.

His rifle cradled in his left arm, Baggett drank deeply from a water bottle. A curtain of willows shielding the nearest island parted and half a dozen canoes knifed toward the *Queen*. Each held three or four men. Equally as many skiffs moved from around the island, each packed with men. Baggett yelled, "Ahead. Right," and raised his rifle.

"Got 'em," Karim said. He aimed a rifle at the oncoming boats.

Baggett glanced left, noted that Styvie knelt by his reaper, watching the islands on his side.

A crossbow bolt clanged off one of the poles supporting the canopy.

Baggett snapped his rifle up, aimed at the nearest canoe, fired, felt the stock slam back into his shoulder. He levered the breech open, ejected the spent shell, and loaded as white smoke cleared. He fired steadily, taking three men from his target canoe before the last man swung it out of the attack. Karim and Vanslyke were also firing steadily, ignoring the bolts and occasional bullets that slammed into the steamer. Baggett noticed a large boat, most of which was hidden in overhanging willow. Three men stood in the bow, firing at the *Queen*. "A hundred yards," he muttered. He adjusted to the roll of the *Queen*, and fired. A man jerked back, falling into the water. The other two scurried out of sight. "Bad shots and cowards both."

The attacking boats clumped closer together as

they closed on the *Queen*, each trying to be the first to reach their anticipated plunder. Several, nearly empty of men, drifted out of the fight. Baggett saw Karim drop his rifle, adjust his reaper, and fire.

A wall of metal shot swept men from the nearest boats. Other men screamed and fell from more distant boats. Karim snapped open the breaches of his reaper, slammed in shells. As heavy smoke from the reaper's fire cleared, Baggett saw that three boats still came on from the side. A man in the lead boat raised his crossbow at Vanslyke, who snapped a shot that missed. Baggett fired, taking the crossbow man in the chest.

Karim fired again, and the remaining boats were empty.

"Left!" Styvie called, followed by sharp clicks as he cocked the barrels of his reaper.

Baggett saw several canoes and skiffs among the fringe of reeds lining a tall headland, but no attack came.

"Nothing like slaughtering a few draggers to dissuade the others," Vanslyke said, laughing. He raised his hand to Baggett. "Thanks for taking him down."

Baggett nodded acknowledgment.

Vanslyke turned the *Queen* west into a wide channel between islands. "We should be clear. The folks on Chehal's Island and the mainland patrol this area. We'll be in Good-Bye Lake soon, and it's kept under tight control."

"Good-Bye Lake?" Baggett asked.

"It's a sidearm of the main lake: marked off by Chehal's Island and the Narrows." Vanslyke reduced power and angled toward open water.

That night, they anchored in a small inlet. Mosquitoes dove at them in clouds as they cleaned their weapons. The next morning, Baggett and Karim hiked inland, Baggett taking samples of every bush and tree he found.

For three weeks, Baggett, accompanied by one of the boys or Vanslyke, had hiked the lakeshore and islands of Good-Bye Lake. The only boats they saw were the skiffs of fishermen, with whom they traded. Vanslyke's knee healed quickly. Baggett collected bark from a dozen types of bushes and trees and spent the nights testing his finds. Nowhere did he find the dark, broad leaves of the tall tree that produced quinine in the mountains of Angeles. One plant, a low bush that looked like a dwarf rhododendron, contained traces of quinine. But there wasn't enough to test against his samples. Each day he failed to find the plant he sought it had became harder to force himself up and down the steep hills.

Vanslyke and his nephews were ashore chopping wood and smoking fish. Hunched over a beaker, Baggett pulled his coat tighter around his shoulders, chilled despite the 100-degree temperature. Shaking, he turned off his kerosene burner and collapsed into his bed roll. He found his last small bottle of the new, effective quinine, and downed a third of the bitter liquid. He lay, alternately chilled and burning with fever, till dawn.

Vanslyke's hand on his shoulder woke Baggett.

"Rafael, how long have you been this way?"

"Since last night," Baggett whispered. He sipped water from a flask held by Vanslyke. "Thank you." He raised onto one elbow. "I should be better in a day or two."

"We're pulling in to Academy. It's a town on the south shore of Chehal's Island."

"I need to keep looking."

"Sorry, but you need to rest."

Baggett started to argue, then nodded wearily. He swigged more of his quinine. "One week," he said, falling back onto his bedroll.

By the next day, Baggett was able to stand by the *Queen's* rail as the launch steamed up a shallow fjord, bordered by steep hills. Smoke rose from a village above the inlet. Most buildings were dried mud, baked hard under the harsh sun, and painted bright yellow or orange. The boys leaped onto the gray boards of a dock and tied the *Queen* fast.

Two large fish, which Baggett estimated must each weigh at least a hundred pounds, hung splayed open on drying racks. Several villagers carried another fish toward the racks, waving as they passed.

"Karim, Styvie, stay aboard." Vanslyke stepped to

the dock and offered a hand to Baggett, who shook off the aid and joined him.

"First thing is to report to the council leader."

Villagers were busy repairing fishing nets and tackle or working in garden plots. Several recognized Vanslyke and called greetings. Near the top of the winding main street, a man waited beside a white-brick building.

"Kieren Vanslyke," the man said, smiling, "You've not been here in a year."

Vanslyke bowed slightly, "Hefmon Smoth. How is the island?"

"We do all right." Smoth looked about fifty, and was inches shorter than Baggett with gray hair.

Vanslyke bowed again. "With me is Rafael Baggett. He traveled to us from the south."

"Come into the shade," Smoth said, leading them into the white building. The three men sat on cushions in the cool shade and several younger men brought them cups of bitter tea.

Baggett thought he detected quinine, but was not sure.

For an hour, Vanslyke and Smoth talked of the decline of fish in the lake and their smaller size, of the monotony of long, dry days, and of wives and friends. Baggett tried, without success, not to show his impatience and growing fatigue. Finally, he nudged Vanslyke.

Vanslyke glanced at him, and said, "Hefmon

Smoth, I'm sorry to be direct, but Hefmon Baggett is recovering from an attack of fever. To state it directly, he seeks a way to cure fever."

"We don't have a lot of trouble with fever," Smoth said, "but it still kills some." Looking hard at Baggett, he asked, "What help do you need?"

Baggett explained his search for the powerful quinine, and his failure.

"I don't recognize the tree you describe. When you feel better, we will help you search the island."

For two weeks, while Vanslyke traded with the islanders, Smoth or another villager took turns guiding Baggett on long hikes across Chehal's Island. Moving slowly for the first few days, Baggett recovered quickly. Again, he collected bark from every bush and tree he found. Again, he tested them. Again, he failed. The only encouragement he gained came from the beauty of the scrubby rhododendrons, which were now covered with brightly colored flowers. Each bush blazed with its own color. He took several dozen slip cuttings and wrapped them in damp cloth. That night, he tucked them into a side pocket of his backpack, determined to at least bring home a touch of beauty.

After another day of failure, he sat across a small fire from Vanslyke. "Every day I find nothing, hundreds more die," Baggett said, his forehead resting on his hand.

In the morning, they sailed south. Standing aft near

Vanslyke, Baggett saw a smudge of smoke in the distance. Neither of them could tell if the smoke came from another boat or a fire on land.

Baggett pulled the brim of his hat lower to shield his eyes from the afternoon sun. Standing on a mainland hill a week south of Chehal's Island, Lake Willmut spread in a dark sheet to the north and south. Baggett studied the dark line of shore thirty miles to the east. Looking north again, a smudge of gray smoke rose above a small island. *Nobody lived on that island when we passed it this morning,* Baggett thought. He hiked back toward the *Queen.*

Baggett jumped aboard the steamer and took a canteen offered by Vanslyke.

"What's the eastern shore like?"

"Much the same, perhaps a bit wetter," Vanslyke said. "We'll swing that way shortly. About fifty miles south of us the lake becomes a swamp."

Baggett took another drink. "I saw that smoke column again. It's as if they were laying back during the day and closing on us at night."

"Likely another trader."

Baggett turned to Vanslyke. "You've talked to a lot of folks as we moved south. Have you learned nothing to explain the shipments of quinine we've been getting?"

"Not a thing."

That night, Baggett lay staring at the dome of stars

over his head, their brilliance scarcely dimmed by the rising moon. "The old records say we once walked on the moon," he said softly. "Do you believe them?" he asked Karim, who was standing watch.

"No. They're just old tales. You?"

"I don't know. Our legends make the ancients as powerful as gods, and they weren't that. If they had been, they'd still be here," Baggett said. "But they did wonderful things. Take the plant I'm looking for. We can breed animals and plants and shape them to a degree, but the records we have speak of changes we can't begin to understand."

A week later, the surface of the lake vanished under a carpet of floating plants and the *Queen* sliced into the edges of a swamp. "It goes on for twenty miles or more," Vanslyke said. "We're as far south as we can go. Now we steam to the eastern shore of the lake."

Baggett glanced north as the steamer swung east. A trail of smoke rose from a distant dot on the lake. "Buggers are still there, and they look closer."

Vanslyke studied the lake. "They do, indeed."

"Draggers this far south?" Baggett asked.

"I don't know."

Another hour saw them back in open water, bow cutting east toward the distant shore. Working through the afternoon, Baggett tested the plants he'd recently collected, finding nothing. When he finally turned off his burner, the shore was less than a mile distant. Pointing to a hill, he asked Vanslyke, "Is that our landing?"

"Just beyond it, on the mainland. Town is called Pine Creek."

"Pine Creek?" Baggett asked. "Was it named after lovers who lost each other?"

"Nothing that romantic. There used to be a few scraggly pine trees, till they were cut down for firewood."

The *Queen* steamed around the corner of the island, and Baggett saw a wide inlet, its shore rising gently to high hills several miles inland. Tilled fields covered the nearly flat land north and south of the lakeshore. A large town perched at the apex of the inlet.

Villagers flocked to the dock, calling loud greetings to Vanslyke and his nephews. "They look more prosperous than the people we saw in most of the westside towns," Baggett said.

"Pine Creek has good farm land. It's also the start of the land route south. The villagers profit from what trade there is."

The Vanslyke boys tossed bow and stern ropes to men who tied the *Queen* fast to a wooden dock.

"Two more weeks. Same plants. I've tested them all. There are more of the small rhododendrons here, but that's the only difference," Baggett said. "Where else can I try?" Heavy clouds hid the sun for the first time since Baggett had been on the lake.

"What about higher elevation?" Vanslyke asked. "North a day, there's a deep inlet that will let us get closer to the mountains by three days' hike."

"Sure," Baggett said, depression hanging on his words. "Too many lives depend on me, and I've failed so far. When can we leave?" Rain started falling, gently at first, and then with growing force.

"We'll have steam in an hour." Vanslyke called his nephews over. "Load the reapers. We've not seen our shadow, but I suspect it's out there."

Baggett stood in the bow as they rounded the northern corner of the island guarding Pine Creek Inlet. A launch about the size of the *Queen* sliced out of the rain.

Baggett saw shadowy figures and the flash of rifle fire. He saw the fanned barrels of a reaper, a man kneeling beside it, hand jerking back. He bellowed, "Down!" as he dropped flat on the deck. Metal raked the *Queen*. A scream sounded behind him, then silence. Baggett rose, knelt, aimed through the smoke at the distant gunner, fired. The man jerked back. Slamming his breech open, Baggett dug a shell from his pocket. He loaded and shot another man who moved to reload the reaper. Guns fired behind Baggett, and more men fell.

The *Queen* swung sharply toward the other boat.

As they passed, the *Queen's* right side reaper fired. Vanslyke yelled from the wheel, "We board. Styvie, grapple forward. Rafael, get back here."

Baggett dashed along the left side of the deck, slipped, saw Karim, face blown away, and stumbled on.

"Hold the wheel." Vanslyke hurled the heavy stern anchor as the boats crashed together. It fell into the engine well of the enemy. He yanked the release valve, blasting steam into the air. "Don't want her to blow up on us. Come on!"

Vanslyke leaped across the narrow gap between the boats. Baggett followed, screaming his anger. He fired into the chest of a man at the wheel. A figure loomed before him, pistol firing. Baggett rammed his rifle's muzzle into the man's gut, then whipped the stock upward to meet the man's face. Forward, guns fired and men screamed. And it was over.

Energy suddenly gone, Baggett nearly collapsed onto a cargo chest. Vanslyke limped out of the rain, using a heavy pole as a crutch. "Damned nearly broke my knee this time. You hit?"

"No. Karim's dead," Baggett gasped.

"Had to be," Vanslyke said in a near whisper. "He was hit by most of the reaper's load." He called forward. "Styvie!"

"All clear. Six dead."

"Three here."

Hearing a moan, Baggett turned. A man by the

wheel tried to pull himself up, slipped, and fell back to the deck, wet with rain and his own blood. "Vanslyke, you fooker. You killed us all."

Vanslyke knelt, pulled off the man's hat. "Yamota? What in hell were you doing?"

"You know."

"No, I don't." Vanslyke's belt knife slashed across the man's throat. "For Karim."

Baggett wished for a moment that he'd wielded the knife, then doubled over with nausea. He staggered to the rail, vomiting into the lake. "Shouldn't react this way," he mumbled, "I've seen a lot of bodies." He slipped to his knees, shaking with cold.

Later, through the haze of fever, Baggett recognized the *Queen's* deck. Dimly, he saw Vanslyke taking a handful of leaves from a chest, grinding them, adding them to water. Still later, he gagged down hot tea. Shaking with cold, he tasted bitter quinine, and slept.

Morning light filtered through the awning covering the *Queen*. Baggett lay on his bedroll and felt a slight chill. Not again, he thought, then realized his chill came from a cool dawn breeze and not the fever. He heard boots on the deck and looked up at Vanslyke, who sat down on one of Baggett's trunks. "I didn't expect to live through that attack," Baggett said.

"You scarcely did. The new fever is hard. Even here."

"How long have you known about the special quinine?"

"All my life," Vanslyke said, "though I didn't realize it was different from what you folks have down south till a couple of years ago."

"How did I miss it? I tested every plant up here."

"You tested their bark." Vanslyke pulled a branch of dwarf rhododendron from his jacket. "It's in the leaves."

Baggett stared, feeling overpowered by his own foolishness. "It's always in the bark. Sure it is." He shook his head, smiled, added, "I underestimated them. They'd helped create plagues that destroyed their civilization. At the core, they had to be fools. I was the fool for not thinking more broadly. I have to test those leaves." He stood slowly, still feeling weak. He pushed open his portable lab and turned on his burner.

Vanslyke handed him the branch. "You might as well."

"Why the deception? Why not show me the leaves?" Baggett asked, as he worked. He pulled off several leaves.

"We ship it to you in small loads. One trip gives the trader enough money for a year. That would stop if you get the plant."

"And that's why," he hesitated till the name came to him, "Yamota attacked us? Why you've lied?"

"Greed and fear. This is not a rich land. We survive. We do not thrive. I argued in council to set up a factory to process our quinine so we could ship you more, even if we had to ask your help. I was voted down. I agreed to not interfere with their attack on you, but when the assassin failed, they attacked us both at the Narrows. They became my enemies, while you saved my life. Yamota's faction will be waiting at the narrows and at Basin. I'm sending you home through the southern pass. Styvie will guide you. You'll leave in a week."

"Will they come for you?"

"Not here. I live near Pine Creek."

"Please, can I take my samples?"

"You can't harvest seeds or cuttings," Vanslyke said. "We can't afford to lose the trade. We can harvest the leaves and process the drug here. We'll work with your people to send as much quinine as we can produce. We live. You live."

"And the Yamota gang?"

Anger flashed across Vanslyke's face. "We'll deal with them. Soon."

Standing and pulling his heavy coat more tightly around himself, Baggett looked at his wardrobe trunk and bundles of samples. "I'm leaving all my work, everything I found."

"I'm sorry," Vanslyke said.

"At least I return home with hope," Baggett said. He thought of the small bundle of slip cuttings in his pack, and regretted his betrayal of Vanslyke. Then he remembered Miya's death, and the cost of failure.

NOSTALGIA 101

by Dean Wesley Smith

WE LEFT THE DOMED city of Portland through the western gate, moving along the old Columbia River bed. Centuries ago, ice had jammed up the Columbia Gorge to the east of Portland, forming an ice field that stretched for a thousand kilometers. Nothing existed in, on, or under that ice field. It moved and shifted too much to be safe.

The wind bit at my shield-protected face, cutting through even my special thermal suit. An unprotected human body in this cold would die in less than a minute. A bad suit tear could kill if not fixed quickly enough.

The danger of being out of the dome always excited me, got my heart racing, made all the research and work leading up to this trip worth it. I loved going out of the domes, had since I was a kid a few hundred years before. Just as everyone did when leaving a dome directly into the snow, we got the standard lecture of too much time in the cold can kill, too much time free breathing can kill, and on and on. Exciting stuff the first time, the two hundredth time, it was real boring.

"Ree, can you hear me, son?" the Professor asked through the com-link in my ear. "Stay to the right and in the river basin."

I was leading, Lara followed me, then Torman, then Jeanette, then the Professor. Five sleds, five self-contained living units if they had to be. We didn't plan on being out long enough to use those features.

"Will do, sir," I said.

I always addressed Professor Barren Stanton as sir. I never called him by name. I didn't feel I had the right to call a man almost a thousand years old by his name. Besides, he insisted he be called Professor or sir, and who was I to argue?

As I accelerated away from the base of the dome, the wind force field on the front of the hoversled rose into place, blocking any blowing snow and ice from hitting my environmental suit. I eased the sled up to one hundred and twenty and settled there, the agreed-upon speed.

The snow-covered terrain sped past in a blur. There was really nothing to see, since the ice and snow had killed everything hundreds of years ago. I clicked on the hoversled autopilot controls and sat back, adjusting the controls only when I thought the computer needed the help to make a bend in the riverbed.

Thankfully, mankind had discovered the cooling of the sun hundreds of years before it happened and had prepared, after a period of panic and religious insanity. As the sun's cooling phase started, some people had left the planet, moving into self-sustaining stations closer to the sun. Some day I hoped to visit one of those stations on vacation from my job managing a restaurant. I just hadn't had the chance yet.

Other groups had built large spaceships, Generation Ships as they were called, and simply headed off slowly toward other stars in search of a new home, one that wasn't about to be covered in ice. Nothing had been heard from those ships in hundreds of years. Nothing was expected for hundreds more.

Most of the population of Earth had decided to stay and wait out the sun's cooling phase. With the help of nanites back in the early twenty-first century, humans now lived thousands of years, maybe longer. No one was sure, since only a thousand years had passed. With nanites, humans had time to wait for the melt. Scientists predicted the sun would start into a heat-up cycle in less than five hundred years. I wouldn't even be as old as the professor by then.

It took just over an hour for us to reach the frozen Pacific. Millions and millions of humans lived under the frozen oceans of the planet, in the depths near thermal trenches, in domes that hugged the ocean floors like ancient coral. I had been into an ocean dome twice and both times didn't like the damp feel and the darkness that seemed to creep in from all sides.

I liked surface domes, with the intense white of the snow and the constant of the deep blue sky in the day and starfields at night. Surface domes were kept clear, ocean domes opaque. I loved the openness, the whiteness of everything. I had been born in the Reno dome three years short of two hundred years ago. I sure didn't feel that old, especially around the Professor. Nevertheless, on my two hundredth birthday, I planned on closing the restaurant and throwing a private birthday party for myself. I always figured that starting a person's third century of living should be celebrated and I planned on doing just that.

How could anyone get anything done in a short seventy to one hundred years of living? I worked full time, sure, had had a couple of marriage contracts with women, but basically, I was still in school, and would be off and on for another thirty years. Only after finishing all my classes would I feel really ready to contribute to society.

This class had become a prerequisite to any professional jobs above waiting tables. Nostalgia Factor 101. The problem with living a long time had not been boredom, as many had predicted, but nostalgia.

Dreams and thoughts of a time that seemed better, seemed more comfortable, seemed easier, often pulled a normally productive human down to a complete standstill. Or worse, it made them collectors of things from the long dead past. Collectors wasted dome space, inflated prices of worthless things, and basically contributed nothing to the forward progress of society.

Five hundred years ago, nostalgia had become such a debilitating factor in society that suicide became the main cause of death above accidents. Classes were mandated to cure the problem. Hospitals were set up to treat the worst inflicted. Living basically forever was a wonderful thing, as long as you remained looking into the promise of the future.

For me, the dreaded nostalgia so far hadn't become a factor. I liked new everything, didn't collect anything, and didn't even much like old movies. I was happy with my life now, but even still, I had to take the class, prepare myself for the time when nostalgia might take me over.

I turned south along the old Pacific shoreline and kicked the speed up to two hundred kilometers per hour, skimming over the frozen ocean surface. The others followed at safe distances.

I couldn't imagine being born into a predome life,

back before nanites. But as the professor said, this expedition was going to help me with that lack of understanding. We were in search of a home he had known existed when he was born. A cave home that had survived the big Pacific fault quake of 2067. He claimed that after the quake, the house had been closed down and sealed by its owners. It might be possible that artifacts from over a thousand years ago were still in that home.

The problem was, of course, finding it under the hundreds of feet of snow and ice, using only records from three coastline shifts before the freeze. The five of us had signed up for this class with the professor four years ago. We had traveled the world searching through ancient stored information and books, arguing, learning, pinpointing what we thought might be the exact location of the home.

One of the main things I had learned in the process was that looking into the past was a very time-consuming and expensive thing to do. Why anyone would do it as a hobby was beyond me. It had to be a sickness, of that I was sure.

Now, we were approaching the agreed-upon site, the one place all our research led us to believe we might find the old building and thus discover something about ourselves, human history, and more importantly, nostalgia.

My screens showed I had almost reached our destination. I slowed and turned the sled toward the slopes and ice cliffs that indicated the old coastline. Hundreds of thousands of people had lived along this ocean's shores before the freeze. I had seem images of these places, old movies of walking on sandy beaches. I just couldn't imagine it. My entire life had been in the comforts of the domes and the white nothingness of the snow.

I eased my sled up onto a slight incline and then stopped when my computer told me I had arrived at the right coordinates. I did a quick sounding of the slopes and cliffs above me, checking for any chances of ice slides, then signaled the "all clear."

"Well done, son," Professor Stanton said to me as he pulled up his sled beside the rest of ours. I nodded and stayed on my sled. I could monitor all the progress of the search from there on the sled's screens.

Torman and Lara already had out their equipment and were scanning the ice field below us. They looked almost identical in their environmental suits and masks. We all looked the same, even the Professor.

"There's something down there," Lara said, her voice level.

I could feel the excitement of a possible find surge through me. Could we get lucky enough to actually find the old cave house so quickly?

I watched the information come over my screens.

The details were correct, the shape of the opening that we had trained to look for, the age of the blockage in the cave mouth. All fit. Thirty-six meters down.

But something about the ice and snow around it didn't seem right. I couldn't put my finger on exactly what it was.

"We have found it," Professor Stanton said, his voice flat as always. "Jeanette, are you ready?"

"I am, Professor," she said.

I could hear the excitement in her voice. She was the youngest of the four of us at just under one hundred and fifty. Like me, her job in the Portland dome was to manage a restaurant. I would have been interested in a contracted relationship with her if she hadn't already been in contract with another woman. And she seemed neutral to me, so I never pushed anything.

"Then open us a path to the cave home."

Jeanette moved her sled back away from the hill, then watching her screens instead of the white in front of her, she turned on her heat drill attached to the front of her sled.

I watched as the drill melted the ice, fusing it into a ten-meter-diameter tunnel down toward the cliff house. The tunnel formed very quickly, almost too quickly.

I ran a few nonconnected scans of the snow and

area we were in. I could see traces of the remains of other closed-up tunnels. Many others. Maybe thousands.

Jeanette drilled down right along the path of a former tunnel, which caused her much easier digging.

I said nothing about my findings, but I instantly lost the excitement I had been feeling about the find. Excitement that Professor Stanton had warned me to contain.

He had said, "From this excitement comes nostalgia, and from nostalgia comes death. As a society, we must never look back. We must always look to the future. It is in the future that the true excitement lies."

Realizing that this wasn't an original find, that we were only going over the same stuff a hundred or thousand classes before us had gone over, made the professor's point very clearly.

Finally, Jeanette reached the mouth of the cave and shut off the tunneling device.

Professor Stanton climbed off his sled for the first time and using hover pads on his feet, moved to the mouth of the tunnel. "Shall we take a look at the past?" he said.

I wondered if he said the exact same thing to every class he taught. More than likely, he did. I didn't know if I should be angry at the years we had spent researching to find this place. I wasn't sure of the point of that part of the lesson.

I sat there as the others went to join the Professor.

"Are you coming, son?" he asked after a moment.

"Wouldn't it just be easier to look at the images recorded by earlier classes?"

The others spun to look at me through their environmental visors, but the Professor just nodded. "Yes, it would be, Rees. But that's not the point of this class, is it?"

"I'd be very interested in what *exactly* the point might be," I said.

"To give each and every one of you an understanding of nostalgia. That was in the course description. I'm sure you read it."

"By going to an old site where hundreds, maybe thousands have been before?"

"Of course," the Professor said. "History is where people have been before. Did you expect anything different?"

I started to say something, then realized he was right.

He went on. "Nostalgia is the disease that makes us continually want to be where others have been before, where we have been before."

"And what's the point of wanting that?" Jeanette asked.

"There is no point," the Professor said. "True excitement is always the unknown ahead. Torman, Lara, you saw in your scans that there had been many tunnels here before us."

"We did," Lara said.

Torman nodded.

"How did you feel?" the Professor asked.

"Disappointed," Lara said.

"Tricked," Torman said.

"And you, Jeanette, you saw it as well. How did you feel?"

"The same," she said, nodding.

"Yet, for the last few years, our mission in this class was to find this cave house in which people had lived, where people had been before. What is the difference that others had visited this site in the last hundred years, or a thousand years ago when it was built?"

I was starting to see his point. "The search for anything in the past is always the search for where someone else has been."

"Exactly, son," Professor Stanton said.

"But no one has been to tomorrow yet," Jeanette.

Professor Stanton nodded. "Now are you starting to understand why nostalgia is so dangerous? You just spent almost four years of your time to discover a place that others had been to, that others had lived in. Couldn't your time and money have been spent so much more constructively?"

I nodded, as did the others. Point made.

"So," Professor Stanton said, indicating the tunnel "anyone want to take a look at the past?"

"Why bother those who are dead and buried?" Jeanette said.

We all agreed with her and she closed up the shaft so that the next class might have its object lesson.

"Come in for one final discussion next week," Professor Stanton said. "I can safely say, you all passed with top marks."

After a few minutes, I turned my sled back north up the coastline, setting the speed at two hundred kilometers per hour. I had to admit, I was glad we hadn't wasted any more time going down that hole. It would be nice to get back in the dome, maybe check in with the restaurant and see how the dinner rush was doing.

And it felt very good passing this class. Now, I could sign up for my next class. "The Proper Use of Nanites in a Sexual Act."

That promised to be very informative.

GO TELL THE SPARTANS

by Sarah A. Hoyt

THERE WAS NO BAND playing as I stepped off the ship in Terra Nova. No crowds of anxious miners fighting for their first glimpse of a Show Girl.

Instead, the spaceport looked deserted. Dust blew over it from the barren plain stretching west. To the east all was verdant, silent fields. Ships took off and landed all around the circular landing strip, close enough that I could feel the singeing heat of their exhausts.

Robots loaded and unloaded cargo from the yawning bays of landed ships.

It took me a moment to locate my reception committee of one, a blond man who stood well away from the robotic bustle and looked at me with impassive, almost vitreous blue eyes.

I smiled at him. "Lil of the Spaceways," I said, and held my arms at my side, hoping that my girdle held and that I didn't show my growing middle section. "Just as advertised."

If only the girdle held for this one show. With the small fortune they'd promised to pay if they were happy, I could afford to have my middle and tits redone as soon as I got back to Terra Madre. And that would add fifty years to my career and allow me to retire later in comfort, instead of now, in penury and squalor.

He raised his eyebrows and said, "The show is tonight." Then turned his back and started walking away.

He made me think of the marble statues I'd seen once, on a school trip in Terra Madre. Tall, blond, beautiful and remote, in his shimmery white tunic and pants. His perfect features didn't reflect the rough eagerness I'd met with in miners' worlds, or even the carefully disguised interest of scientists and literati in other, more civilized worlds. I could not fathom what made his perfect, sculpted lips tighten in a firm line.

I cleared my throat. He didn't turn. I huffed and picked up my suitcase.

I'd been a Show Girl for twenty-two years, and I'd never had to carry my own bags. Even the roughest miners knew that a lady didn't carry.

Not this gentleman, though. He walked ahead of

me, oblivious, head held high, without a look back to see if I was following.

Gods, my tits must be sagging more than I thought.

We walked out, between two spaceships, onto what looked like a parking lot beyond—a parking lot filled with egg-shaped vehicles in all colors of the rainbow.

He approached a purple one, opened a door on its side, and turned and waited for me.

I followed, huffing and puffing, the strap of my bag cutting into my palm, my resentment at him growing with every step. When a girl aged, she needed more makeup and props than ever. When a girl aged, she needed more than ever to have her bag carried.

"My name is Kaltar," he said, as I got close to his ship. "Kaltar Nedan. I am the promoter that contacted your agent."

Oh. Maybe that explained it. Maybe the booking was all business and no pleasure. I mean, I didn't kid myself. I had known for many years what happened in those far-off worlds, when a Show Girl didn't happen to be visiting. No more than you'd expect, men being men, and most women Earthbound for century upon century upon century. What was weird was that some of them felt better that way, and didn't appreciate Lil when she came to town.

He stood aside, to let me step up into his vehicle and stepped in, all cool formality.

And that was just all right with me, thére being a majority of men who liked me just fine, thank you—and never mind that I didn't look as pretty as I once had. They didn't care either. Most of them had never seen a woman in their conscious lives and had nothing to compare me to.

The inside of Kaltar's car looked like any Terra Madre Flycar. Correction, any family flycar. It had ample seating, for five or six passengers, and the smell about it was fruity and sweet, like kids' drinks. It reminded me far too much of home and my mom's car.

It didn't help things that I found a doll—a male-looking doll, not anatomically correct, with long, blond hair—wedged between the seat and the arm of the blue, scuffed passenger seat in which I sat. Mom's flycar all over, with all of us packed in, screaming and shoving and babbling, strewing toys and candy all around.

I was the eldest of eight sisters, and just remembering home gave me a headache all over again.

Kaltar put out his long, impeccably clean hand for the toy, and smiled, for the first time as he tucked it into a storage pocket beneath the dashboard. He mumbled something that sounded like, "Sorry. The children," as he turned around to program a course into the onboard computer.

As we took off and flew over a long barren plain dotted with verdant oasis, I watched his long, limber fingers dance over the keyboard. He wore two rings on the middle finger of his right hand, both silver.

Halfway through the trip, I broke silence. "This world—" I struggled for the name, retrieved it, "Terra Nova, your world—what do you specialize in?"

He turned to look at me, surprised, as if he'd forgotten my presence. "Bio-gen," he said. "We are the foremost experts in the modification of the human genome." He smiled, a tight smile. "The fauna and flora of this world are genetically very similar to humans, though in many ways very different, and they lend themselves to being used to modify the human genome, where needed. We have hospitals, where we can do most of the operations spacers require. We cure most illnesses of spacers and colonists. Even those considered incurable in other worlds. We even tried—" He stopped suddenly. "Forgive me, you probably didn't want a dissertation on my people's accomplishment, and all this must be boring to you."

To me? Oh, of course, being a Show Girl I was supposed to think with my gonads. "Actually, it's fascinating," I said, in my best ladylike voice. "Pray continue. I was very interested in bio-gen, myself, and in biology in general, and thinking of being an obstetrician or a pediatrician when I was tested and recruited by the Show Girls."

"Recruited?" he raised his eyebrows again, in that gesture of incomprehension.

I looked away from him and out the window. The ground over which we were flying had changed from featureless plains to tight-knit woodland, broken here and there by clusters of inconspicuous, squat buildings. "Yeah," I said. "Recruited. I could have stayed on Earth and worked and been a mother, or I could come to space and earn more in a year than any of those women earn in twenty years and ten babies. I thought I'd come out for a year and then go back and maybe become an obstetrician or pediatrician after all."

"You didn't," he said.

Actually, I had. But I hadn't realized what going back after being to space meant. I couldn't have children. Not one. In a world filled with pregnant women, women having babies, women walking around in clouds of daughters and talking about the gaggles of their boys that they'd sent out to space, I'd felt ugly, unwanted, lacking.

I'd been back in space within months, touring Canopus and shaking my ass in the Centauri system. I'd been back in space, flaunting my lucky pink feather boa, enjoying the rough attentions of miners; getting well paid for allowing the gentlemen to experience that marvelous half of humanity that had to stay back on Earth while men went to space.

I wanted nothing to do with Terra Madre. Never

again. Not until I was so old that no one expected me to have babies anymore. And even then, I'd feel left out. Most old women lived with one of their daughters. I'd better go to Luna and settle in the home for retired Show Girls. "Yeah," I said. "I didn't."

He didn't—fortunately—start talking about the price at which Earth sold male babies to spacers anxious to play daddy. Or the even more outrageous price it charged for producing a male baby from the spacer's own genes.

The flycar descended, slowly and gracefully, and stopped, with barely a jar, besides a small, orange building that looked like an egg cut in half and set on the ground, flat sides down.

Kaltar slid the door open, but got out ahead of me. I followed him.

Outside, a brood waited. I upgraded my opinion of Kaltar's wealth by a good ten times. No less than ten children surrounded him. He held a toddler in his arms, and two other toddlers, about the same age, held each of his legs. The other kids ranged anywhere between three and ten years of age, and most of them bore some resemblance to Kaltar's lean, perfect profile, though their hair colors ranged anywhere from dark brown to as blond as Kaltar.

'Course they would. They would all have different mothers, back on Earth. At least if Kaltar hadn't specified a preference, and he obviously hadn't. It was impressive enough that he'd used his own genes. Those kids amounted to a walking, talking fortune of ten thousand hydras, at least.

Kaltar was talking to them, in a rapid-fire lingo that had no more than a passing resemblance to the Glaish of Terra Madre.

His face had relaxed into almost friendliness, by the time he deigned to notice me. "Pardon me, Lil. My family."

I nodded a general acknowledgment and walked past him, toward the building, hoping he'd get the hint and not try to introduce the litter to me. I had no interest in children. Children other women had. Children I'd never have. Bad enough that all my sisters insisted on sending me holos of all their skinny, buck-teethed daughters. Not one among them with the looks to become a Show Girl, even if they should prove barren. Not without some major cosmetic surgery.

Kaltar got the hint. I heard him chatter at the kids, and then heard their steps go another way and his quick steps following me, catching up with me.

"The theater?" I asked, pointing at the building nearest us.

Walking beside me, he raised his eyebrows, again, in that puzzled look, then smiled. "No, no. My home. I thought you'd want to change. Maybe eat something. Before— Well."

Uhm. Normally I changed in the theater proper. In

most of the ice-miner worlds, it wouldn't be safe to change in my host's house. But then—I looked at Kaltar out of the corner of my eye—this one's interest lay elsewhere and I'd be perfectly safe.

As if to confirm my thoughts, the door was opened, before we reached it, by a tall, dark man. As inhumanly beautiful as Kaltar—but then, if they specialized in bio-gen, their whole world would be beautiful—he wore dark red, velvety pants and tunic. His curly black hair tumbled over his shoulder and to his waist.

He leaned to kiss Kaltar, casually, then stepped back from me as though I carried a dangerous infection and watched me, wide-eyed as I walked into the narrow, cool corridor.

I put an extra swing to my hips, aware of his eyes on me. Gods, how long had it been since these people had seen a Show Girl? My agent had said this was a great opportunity, right at the edge of the galaxy. Not that distance made much difference to the quantum-drive equipped ships. Every trip took about twenty minutes. But a place this far away from Terra Madre took more energy to reach, and therefore more money to buy that energy.

Kaltar followed me, and his lover followed him, speaking to him in the same quick, light lingo that the children had used. Kaltar responded with monosyllabic words.

The hallway ended in a large, round open space

furnished with what could be either very low sofas with neither arms nor backs, or very tall and wide cushions. Another man lounged there, on one of the cushions. As blond as Kaltar, and again as beautiful, but smaller, though miniaturaly as well proportioned, he rose on an elbow to look at me, his pale gray eyes growing as wide as the darker man's.

I stopped.

Kaltar came to the rescue. "This is Len," he said, gesturing toward the reclining man. "And this," he gestured toward the darker one who stood, two steps behind Kaltar, scowling intently at me, "is Lar. They're my—family."

He didn't need to be embarrassed. I'd run into it in every other world, and I suppose the same—in another flavor—would happen on Earth if we didn't keep just barely enough males to go around.

Lar, the dark one, let loose a long string of incomprehensible language and Kaltar blushed darker and answered something terse, and shrugged, as though to indicate it wasn't his fault. He touched me, lightly, on the shoulder and withdrew his hand as though burned. "Come with me. I'll show you to a room, to change. For the show."

The show. My agent, Maya, had told me it would only be one show. One show for five thousand five hundred and fifty hydras. It had been such good money that I couldn't figure out why none of the higher-paid agents, none of the younger, more shapely Show Girls had taken it. It must have been the location, out here in the middle of nowhere, away form civilization.

Or perhaps it was that they knew more than I did about these strange, aloof people.

I'd found precious little in the encyclopedia, except that Terra Nova was one of the oldest colonies, started over eight hundred years ago, at the beginning of colonial efforts and that the world had been selected for its capacity to provide pharmaceutical compounds.

Kaltar showed me into a cool, small room, furnished with a bed, a bureau, and a fresher at the far end. "You take a bath," he said. "And change and do your show, and then you can catch the evening shuttle back to Thule and from there you should be able to get back to Luna easily enough."

I nodded. They wanted me out that quickly. I'd assumed the good price was for private entertainment after the show.

I watched Kaltar, as he walked out and closed the door.

Was it the promoter's particular bias? Was he afraid that a woman here would remind the locals that there was such a thing as women?

Was he afraid all of them would be buying tickets to Terra Madre, on the next shuttle?

I chuckled to myself, as I opened the door to the silver cylinder of the fresher. It looked like a normal, compact style fresher, with a toilet in a corner and a shower-massager-vibrating exfoliator in the center.

I availed myself of both facilities. I never used the bathroom in the ships, if I could at all help it. To go in a spaceship, meant to live with the stench of it the rest of the time. And a Show Girl should never stink.

Out here in space—as they told us in training—we were the representation and embodiment of hallowed femininity, the perfect, helpless and yet unattainable, delicate and yet desirable half of humanity that had kept men fighting and dying for them over the centuries and that still made men pine for them, all the way from the immense colonized space.

Since most women couldn't go to space—where their eggs became tainted and where they, themselves, tended to succumb quickly to breast cancer and other feminine illnesses—it was left to us, the few, the proud, the barren and cancer resistant minority to show the men who were sent out as children or sold out as infants, what women were all about.

We were supposed—they had told us—to keep the two halves of humanity together.

They hadn't told us most of that keeping together would be done by wiggling our behinds at the crowds and by offering private "show sessions" after the show proper.

They also hadn't told us that the shows proper would become grueling as we became older. That, when we were aware of what sagged and what wrinkled and what draped strangely, we would no longer take an interest in showing it off to men.

I put on my net stockings, my lace panties and bra, my see-through, pink negligee garment, and wished this room had a mirror, in which I could watch myself and make sure I didn't look too gross.

They also hadn't told us that after the first twenty or so shows, every world ran into each other, and men—all men—became somewhat sickening in their lust, their pawing, their hunger for our bodies.

Yet, lust was better than the bewilderingly cool reception I'd got here. What if they claimed I'd disappointed them and didn't pay my fee? I applied my make up by touch, putting on the lip enhancer and the tint improver with the practice of years.

I'd make them yell and scream, and surge on toward the stage like those miners from Arcturus, who'd almost brought the house down.

My cool promoter would be forced to acknowledge my talent, and book a few more shows, and pay me the same royal rate. I tucked my brown curls up on my shoulders, picked up the pink feather boa and stepped into my pink high heels—hell for the joints, but they sure made your legs look good—and opened the door.

Kaltar and Lar stood outside the door.

Lar made a choking sound.

Kaltar looked apologetic. "Are you ready?"

"As ready as I'm going to be, honey," I answered.

He turned and walked away. Lar covered his face with his hands, as I passed him. Already, I was getting a reaction.

And if Kaltar didn't like it, that was his problem. Catching up with him, in a flurry of clicking heels, I tickled his face with my boa.

Kaltar looked surprised, and took a step away from me.

This close up, I noticed he didn't have beard growth at all. That, of course, didn't mean anything. A lot of the little boys mutated, after you sent them out to space as infants. Not as drastically as women did, and rarely with fatal results, but men changed in space, too. Different radiation. And different plants and different animals. Different everything.

We walked down the narrow corridor and out of his house, and across what looked like a little wilderness area, then into another building, larger than his house.

It was definitely a theater, laid out as all of them had been laid, ever since ancient Greece in Terra Madre. I was led into a private area, behind a holo-curtain that looked like impenetrable fog.

From outside, I could hear the subdued noises of a crowd trying to behave.

A very large crowd.

This was going to be my greatest show ever. They would too like it. I'd give them their money's worth.

Feeling warm and happy, I essayed a few steps on the stage. The board felt like real wood boards, and creaked beneath my heels. Soon, soon.

Kaltar left.

I'd knock them dead. I'd have everything tucked and pinned and maybe a rejuv treatment, and I'd be good for another fifty years without having to face dreary Earth or even drearier retirement in Luna.

The curtain started dissolving, slowly.

The room beyond was in utter darkness. A strong light shone down on me.

I started walking across the stage, swaying my hips.

The bright light became blinding. I couldn't see at all beyond it, to the audience. Well, an audience was an audience. I didn't need to see them to know what they wanted. But their strange quietness made me uneasy.

While we were at it, I would have preferred music, but I hadn't had time to request it. I pulled off my negligee, moving to an unheard beat.

Gracefully, I pulled down my panties, removed my bra.

The silence of the audience was absolute now. I held them spellbound.

The quality of the light around me changed. It somehow jelled into a shape-form. Until I felt it restrain my arms, I didn't realize it was a tractor ray. And then it was too late to protest.

Completely immobilized, naked before the audience, I stood there, while a voice droned on, in the language I couldn't understand. But I understood enough. Enough words to realize that this was a didactic presentation on the subject of the human female.

Of all the dirty tricks. I was no classroom exhibit. I didn't feel like a museum piece.

Immobilized, I felt my annoyance grow by degrees, until the light on me went down, and the lights in the house went up, showing face upon face, row upon row of infants, children, toddlers, teenagers, all looking at me, like a child in a museum, viewing an artifact from an ancient civilization.

And then shock stopped my anger.

"Of all the awful, rotten tricks," I told Kaltar's impassive face on the way to the spaceport. It had taken me that long to recover power of speech, to comprehend the enormity of what they'd done. "You should have told me you wanted me for an anatomy lesson." A whole world of men indifferent to women? Or Kaltar's own bizarre scheme?

He blushed.

Maybe the latter. "I'm sorry," he said. "I *should* have told you. Lar told me I should. He said it was . . . despicable. But so many of the others refused the offer when they found out . . ."

Of course they did. To have all the feminine allure

they'd taught us reduced to a classroom model was the ultimate humiliation.

"We're paying really well," he said.

"That doesn't matter," I said. "I'll talk. This will get about. When your boys are teenagers, they won't thank you that they can't get a Show Girl to come to their world."

He opened his mouth, closed it, took a deep breath. "There are no boys in this world," he said. "And they'll never think of Show Girls in the sense you mean. Earth's monopoly on reproduction is over, her crushing yoke on the colonies is lifted."

He smiled. "Pardon me. I should have told you that, too, but I thought you might know. The news has been spreading throughout the galaxy. More and more colonists are coming here—we can change the human genome, make boys into hermaphrodites. Humanity can reproduce and go to space without having to be born on Earth. The umbilical cord has been cut."

"But . . . the radiation," I said. "Hermaphrodites' eggs would be affected, just like women's eggs."

He shook his head. "No. Our . . . our ovaries, or what works like ovaries, function differently and eggs, like sperm are formed every few days, not carried around lifelong, to accumulate mutations. And besides, men have always suffered less from radiation than women have." He pronounced *women* like an alien word. A blind man describing an elephant.

"I realize I used subterfuge," he said. "Lar said it wasn't right. But women are so anatomically different that . . . Well, I wanted our children to have a chance to see a representative of the species we've superseded. Only once, at least." He was quiet a long time, and then jutted his chin aggressively forward, as though marshaling an irrefutable argument. "We've had a lot of other endangered Earth species up here," he said. "Species that don't travel well out of Earth. We had them sent up for one appearance. For the children. And we're recording it all on holo. In case . . . So if Terra Madre doesn't survive the economic collapse, after spacers stop buying babies for good—or if we go so far we forget about Earth, there will be an accurate accounting of our origins."

I looked at him, openmouthed, speechless, something churning in my mind that could find no words to express itself.

My gaze seemed to undo his calm. He looked away from me. "I'm sorry," he said. "We can't alter women. It's . . . chromosomal. The alien species we use need the Y to bond to. You're just— We just can't."

It wasn't until I was on the shuttle, headed for Luna, that the shock wore off enough that I could feel what hid beneath it: a kind of longing sadness.

Humanity would go out to space, unfettered. At long last, humans would be born in other worlds.

Eventually, they'd forget the Earth—Terra Madre—forget there had ever been such a thing as women.

This lesson, in which I'd served as a model, was probably one of the last few.

Women and Earth were part of humanity's past. For centuries we'd survived selling babies and making those babies, later, pay for their replacements.

There would be no more selling babies, no more producing babies for the colonists.

Earth economy would wither and die.

I had enough money in my account now, to repair my breasts and my middle.

But it didn't matter, anymore.

The future had left me behind.

A BETTER PLACE

by Kristine Kathryn Rusch

"**N**OW WHAT DO WE do with him?" I asked.

Angus pushed Sven with his foot. Sven's prone body covered most of the plank floor, his arms outstretched, his legs bent at the knees and curved to one side, and his eyes wide open.

That was the strangest part: the eyes. I'd never seen anything like that. Wide, unblinking, and . . . empty.

"How'm I supposed to know?" Angus snapped.

I shook my head, feeling too influenced by all the studying I'd done. Everything said that unblinking eyes were empty. I crouched beside him and poked my pinkie into his right pupil.

He still didn't blink, and the soft squishiness of the eye itself made my stomach turn.

There were still a few things about this Experiment in Living that got to me, and one of them was the way the body, moving forward in time, had visceral reactions to external stimuli.

Who would expect that poking my little finger in my best friend's eye would cause my stomach to do that nauseous folding that the ancients called "turning?"

So many things to note in my livejournal, so many more to attempt to explain in the flashnotes I sent every evening, although I wasn't sure if they got read. After all, the scholars who studied them, the people we still called "normals," were—as it was explained to me (or attempted anyway)—unstuck in time.

That did not mean that they time-traveled in the ancient sense. It meant that they perceived time differently, as a constant, like air, something that surrounded and enveloped you, not something that moved in a particular direction, like wind, and eventually faded out or disappeared altogether.

I wasn't sure I understood that—I am a construct, albeit a human one, grown from the genetic material of the ancients and placed in this Life Experiment so that I would understand time as the human race once did.

But unlike them, I hadn't grown from an infant. I

arrived here fully formed, a replica of an ancient at twenty or so, skin young and toned, body at the perfect weight, hormones in place.

I did go insane around females, just like the learning said I would. I would find myself following them, literally fantasizing about them, and my appendages, particularly the penis, did seem to act of their own accord.

After a few months of that, I could understand why humans decided to step outside of time. What I couldn't understand—and would not be told (because, as the elders in this make-shift village tell me, it would ruin the experiment)—was why they want to know what human lives lived in chronological time were really like.

I had no idea how the humans would understand this stuff we send them if they couldn't understand the ancients' documents, videos, and digital records, but who was I to ask? I wouldn't be around if it weren't for the Life Experiment.

At least that was the conclusion I had come to when Angus and Sven and I tried to parse this thing. They had become my best friends in the short time we'd been here. We all lived in different cabins, in different families—each constructed human age-appropriate for their role. For example, I actually had a mother, even though she didn't birth me or raise me (although she did shepherd me through from that lump of code into the creature I am now, and she injected me with the Understandings at the correct point in my development).

She's about forty or so, in ancient human terms, and as such, her skin isn't as firm, and her hair has started to change color.

My perceptions overlay each other: I am always astonished by the changes made visible by chronological time (those are the Understandings provided by the Experimenters), and yet part of me accepts these changes as natural (those are the Understandings threaded through ancient philosophy).

I am, in other words, the perfect tool for attempting to understand the Chronological Lifestyle.

Except for this.

This, as I mentioned before, was Sven lying prone on the cabin's plank floor. This cabin belonged to Sven's parents, his true biological relatives (the Experimenters tried to reinstate "real" families wherever possible—apparently it hadn't been possible in my case), and he just lived there, with the understanding that he would "move out" as soon as it became possible.

Possible, in the ancient term, was as soon as he had enough money or wherewithal or gumption to leave his parents' home. In our term (what the elders were beginning to call the Cottage Terms), it meant as soon as this little patch of chronological time grew. The patch, which existed in an actual bubble on a section of the home planet (we were trained to call it "Earth"; whether it was or not was irrelevant: as Angus said, we lack the Understanding for that), did extend as far as the eye could see—at least, as far as my eye could see, since I was beginning to believe the ancients were right:

Sven's eyes saw nothing.

As Angus and I examined Sven's prone body, I noted that my feet were beginning to feel warm and wet. I looked down, and gasped in surprise: Blood, which we had only previously seen in pricked fingers and accidentally slit skin, oozed out as if it was water leaking out of a cracked glass.

The smell was odd, too: rusty, almost metallic, with some other, more familiar stenches.

Angus examined Sven's lower body, noting with a grimace that Sven had soiled himself like the village infants do. We were stunned by this and his leaking blood and his unblinking eyes.

Yet we did not find the condition horrible, as the ancients implied, or even maddening enough to rend our garments, bare our breasts, and weep copiously.

We were mostly perplexed.

After all, this had been Sven's idea, and he was not here to tell us what to do next.

Of course, we would have to do tests for that. It was an assumption that he was not here, as opposed to trapped within his prone body which would, if the ancients were to be believed, now decay. Even if he wanted to return to it, he could not, an argument both Angus and I made when Sven first came up with this plan.

He always had a morbid bent, and a tendency to focus on the unanswerable. At our lunch breaks from work, he would ask a thousand questions, all of them perplexing and seemingly irresolvable, like:

If all humans (except us) experience time as a constant— each moment lived at the same time as other moments—do these humans have the lifespan of a gnat or do they have no life "span" at all? Are they effectively immortal?

We, of course, had no answer for that, and any elder listening in would have quashed the discussion immediately. Our lot is to focus on the minutia of our lives, and then to use the Understandings as a basis for explaining those lives to the Experimenters.

Sven, of course, wanted to know why the Experimenters needed such explanations, and those questions he would ask an elder directly.

The elder would always tell him, *Ours is not to ask why. Ours is simply to exist.*

Sven did not like that either.

But he knew his not-so-idle questions would someday become an issue within the community: he too had been programmed with the Understandings and knew he was distracting all of us from focusing on important things.

So he went from the irresolvable and unknowable

(at least for us) to the Great Mystery of Life, something the ancients never ever understood: Death.

He pored through his Understandings and forced Angus and I to do so as well. He even gave us assignments: he would handle the philosophical, I would get the spiritual, and Angus had the practical.

And then, without consulting us, Sven took it one step farther.

I repeated my question. "What *are* we supposed to do with him?"

Angus glared at me. He was the largest of the three of us, square shoulders, square jaw, square forehead. A throwback, one of the elders had called him, which was funny since we were all technically throwbacks.

"And I'll repeat my answer," he snapped. "How'm I supposed to know?"

"You were assigned the practical parts of this. You're supposed to know what to do next."

His eyes moved, something I'd missed in Sven's eyes. Angus's eyes had actually widened. But the difference was more than lack of movement or "emptiness." It was also a matter of brightness and moistness. Sven's eyes were drying out. They lacked that shine that Angus's eyes had, even in their anger.

"I suggest we wait for Sven to return." Angus crouched beside our friend, poked him in the shoulder, and added, "Enough of this, Sven. We'll report what we learn, but we don't have the time to waste."

Then he leaned forward, as if Sven could hear him, and whispered, "Besides, you've created quite a mess, and I'm not in the mood to clean up after you. We have work in the morning, not to mention the fuss your parents are going to make."

They would make a fuss, too. Sven's parents believed in excessive cleanliness. The cabin even lacked clutter—to the point that most of the five rooms had only the important items: the couch in the living area, the table in the dining area, the beds in the bedrooms.

His parents would be quite distressed over the filthy floor, the soiled garments, and the rising smell.

"You tell him to return," Angus said to me.

I brushed a hand against Sven's forehead. It felt wrong. Skin, I had learned, should have a firm texture and a certain warmth. Sometimes it had too much warmth, which indicated illness, but usually the temperature was consistent.

I had heard that dead skin was cold, but Sven's wasn't. It was just not warm. And it certainly wasn't hot.

And skin should never feel spongy (the word I'd seen was "rubbery" but I did not have a context for it; "spongy" was also incorrect, but closer than "pliable" as all skin was pliable, even when it felt like it always did).

Only his hair felt like hair, and somehow that wasn't as reassuring as it should have been.

"I can tell him to return," I said, "but I don't know if he would hear me. I'm not sure his ears are working."

Angus cursed. "He's the one who studied the philosophy of this phenomenon. You're the one who focuses on its spirituality. Stop sounding like a philosopher."

"Sometimes there wasn't much difference," I said.

"Well, I'm the practical one, and I'm telling you to make him return."

I frowned and rocked back on my heels. My shoes squooshed against the plank floor, and my stomach did that odd little turn again as I realized the squoosh was the soles of my shoes interacting with the blood and the wood.

"In all of your studies," I said, "have you found any evidence of commandments to someone in this condition working?"

"Of course." He crossed his arms. "The religious leader Jesus often did this sort of thing commanded other people to rise from death, and even managed it on his own."

I had studied that case and knew it was a faulty example. "From the spiritual perspective, he had the help of a higher power."

"The Experimenters?" Angus asked.

I shook my head. "A god—you have reference to those in your Understandings, surely."

"An idol," he quoted. "Or, any of the various beings conceived of as supernatural or immortal. A person conceived of as such. Or in monotheistic religions, the supreme being, leader and creator of all."

He frowned and there was a long pause as he considered what the Understandings had brought him.

"In other words," he said at the end of that pause, "the Experimenters."

"No," I said.

"No?"

"I was the one to examine spirituality in depth, particularly spirituality as connected to death, which is where it all seems to find its center by the way, and here is what I've gleaned. A god is an other, not human. Something other than human, something greater than human. The Experimenters, according to the Understandings I've received, are human, only they perceive time differently than we do. If they were gods, they would have no need of the Life Experiment because they would have created Life and therefore, they would understand it."

"But they did create Life," Angus said. "They created us."

"Using scientific techniques. If you make that argument, the elders Margitay and Lars are gods because they created Life the old-fashioned way, and then Margitay ejected it through her body, and now we all watch it grow."

Angus sighed. "This is more complicated than I thought."

"Me, too." I caught my breath. My argument, while on the spiritual side, sounded a lot more like philosophy than Sven would normally have liked. I was a bit surprised that he hadn't bounded up, yelling at us for ruining his thought experiment or for poaching on his own thought-territory.

"I'm still confused." So far, Angus had not touched Sven. In fact, Angus had his arms crossed and his fists buried under his armpits. "The ancients called Chinese often consulted the wisdom of their ancestors. The ancients called Western had digital recordings of humans contacting those who have died—and those who died would often answer. There were boards and cards and other devices that guaranteed contact with those who have died, which tells me that somehow, we can get Sven to answer us, if we're only diligent enough."

"That was your area," I muttered. "The practical side."

"We don't have the tools," Angus said. "I have never seen most of the devices, and the Understandings say the way of them are lost to human knowledge. Except the ancestors part. That had something to do with shrines and incense."

I shook my head. "I don't recall encountering that. I think some of these things you refer to are philosophies."

165

"All right." Angus stood. He walked to the far end of the room, peered out the window, and then pulled the shutter.

I had no idea why he did that, but the action made me feel better.

"Here's part of the practical learning I have done. In death, the body—" He waved his hand at the growing smell that Sven was becoming, "—separates from the spirit which some term another name for consciousness. Since you are in charge of the spiritual, you must figure out where Sven's consciousness is."

I sighed. That seemed impossible. I had only just begun to touch the ancients' knowledge in this area, but a quick review of the Understandings had shown me that there was much debate and little consensus. In fact, Angus had just spoken to the consensus: a separation of body and consciousness.

"I don't know," I said. "Some of the ancients believed that the spirit ascended to another realm—"

"Such as where the Experimenters live?"

"No. Such as the clouds above us."

"Quite silly. No humans live on clouds," Angus said.

"Not humans. Consciousness," I said.

He shook his head. His skepticism surprised me.

"Others believe that they become recycled into new bodies when children are born."

"No child had been born since Sven took this action," Angus said. "Obviously that does not apply to us."

"And others believe that in death, the spirit ceases to exist." I was leaning toward that one, but again, this felt more like philosophy than spiritualism.

Angus frowned at me as if I had made all this up.

"Occasionally," I said, "a spirit will become trapped between the higher plane and this one, which makes it a ghost."

"Which is what?"

"A disembodied spirit of a dead person, one that everyone can see." I had no real idea. I was parroting my Understandings, not the learning I had done from the various built-in texts.

"I don't see anything," Angus said. "How do we trap him?"

"I think it's too late," I said. "But I'm not sure. Once again, this sounds like a practical consideration to me."

Angus cursed a second time. Obviously, we were going to have to do this without Sven's assistance. I wondered if he had thought of that.

Was this some kind of test for our sincerity? We'd always followed Sven faithfully. We'd argued with him, of course, but in the end, we had always done what he wanted.

If he had wanted the physical side, why hadn't he assigned it to himself? Or had he believed that his actions led to a better understanding of the philosophical side? Still, he had had to take physical actions to reach the philosophical one, and now, judging from my cursory review of the Understandings, he wouldn't be able to report to us any findings if, indeed, he was still conscious enough to have them.

"Physical, that's the practical stuff, right?" Angus asked me.

I nodded, even though I didn't know. I felt adrift without our leader. Had he done this so that we would move forward, taking control of our own lives?

I doubted even Sven thought that far ahead. I rocked back on my heels (trying to ignore that awful squishing) and studied the room.

He had stood near the far wall. Blood spattered some of the furniture as if it had flown in a great wind. Then, judging by the position of the body, he had fallen backward, landing with the thud that one of the neighbors had reported as we walked to the house.

(Are you going to see your friend Sven? she'd asked. We'd nodded. Good, she'd said. I heard the most awful thud fifteen minutes ago and I've been afraid to go in there.

(We, of course, were not afraid. Until we saw Sven lying prone on the planks. Angus had closed the door, and we had crouched, wondering how he could sleep with his eyes open, even though I knew—deep down—that he was not asleep at all. In my short time in the bubble, I had never seen anyone sleep like that.)

"What're you doing?" Angus asked me.

I shrugged. "I was just trying to figure out if he had found a way to trap the spirit."

But the room looked no different—except for the blood stains, Sven's damaged body, and the seeping puddle.

"If the physical is the practical stuff," Angus said, "we've got to get him out of here, and clean the place up. Then we have to decide what tradition we're following."

"Tradition?" I asked.

"If we follow something called Ancient Egyptian, we must go through an extensive ritual that cleanses and prepares the body for its future in the underworld—whatever that is. We must remove parts, add stuff, and then wrap it all in a linen bandage and put it in a carefully prepared home called a tomb. I'm not sure what that is, but some say the ancient pyramids are home to these long-dead humans."

"Pyramids? The geometric form?" I asked.

Angus nodded.

"We haven't prepared anything like that," I said. "How long will it take?"

He blinked, clearly checking the Understandings. "Some say forty years. Some say a hundred years. Some simply say a generation."

"I haven't even been here two years. I think that won't work."

"Good." His shoulders drooped in relief. "Because if we did all that, we would be considered unclean and have to live in another part of the village."

"Unclean?" I wrinkled my nose. "Sven's clearly unclean, but I think we can wash him up."

Although I didn't relish it. Touching his skin had been bad enough. Touching his eye was somehow worse. I didn't want to think about touching his entire body.

That just seemed—wrong—somehow.

I shuddered.

"That's another choice." Angus's arms seemed to tighten even more around his own body. "We could remove the blood, add another fluid to preserve him—"

"So that the spirit could return?"

"I don't know. This stuff isn't kept in any logical order. I'm getting all kinds of things." He was beginning to sound angry. He had no reason to get angry with me. I had nothing to do with Sven lying on the floor.

At least, I had no more to do with it than Angus did.

"If we do give him that fluid, then we put him in an expensive satin-lined box, and bury it in the ground."

That last threw me. "We what? We preserve him and then we trap him underground? No. What if he does come back? It took your friend Jesus three days to return."

"See?" Angus said. "You think he'll be back."

"I don't. There are millions—I mean millions—of examples of people who never returned or went onto another realm or disappeared or passed on or whatever you want to call it, and only a handful of people who didn't. So I think the percentage chance of Sven waking up in three days is miniscule. But someone did it, so there is a percentage chance, and if that's the case, I'm not trapping him in a satin-lined box under mountains of dirt."

"I didn't say mountains!" Angus backed toward the door. He left footprints on the only planks that hadn't been covered in blood. "We could burn him."

"Burn him?" I blinked. That shocked me more than the burial thing did.

"We have to do something," Angus said. "I know that much. All of the practical stuff starts with what happens when bodies are left untended."

"What happens? Besides rotting." I knew that much.

"Horrible diseases. Tainted water supplies. Flies."

"Flies?"

"Some kind of insect that lays eggs in the dead person, and then hatches—"

I waved a hand to silence him. That funny flip-flopping stomach thing happened again. "Okay. We do something with the body. What do we tell his parents?"

"Technically, they make the decisions," Angus said. "Most human models from chronological times have the families make all the decisions. If there is no family, then someone else does."

I stood, wiped my hands on my pants, and frowned at Sven. He didn't seem to notice. In fact, just in the amount of time that we had been here, debating over him, he looked even less like Sven than he had when we arrived.

The percentage chance of him returning seemed smaller than miniscule. It seemed impossible.

"But we can still have a physical job to do," Angus said. "We can discover how he died. It is an elaborate process that involves searching for clues, looking for answers in tiny drops of blood, and then, if we are successful, making entertainments from our findings."

"Entertainments?"

"In my searches through the Understandings, much of the materials I found were entertainments. As humans became separated from death—" He was quoting again. "—they needed something to remind themselves of its existence. Humans love a mystery, or so the Understandings teach. Perhaps we can solve this one."

I sighed. "We know the solution."

I pointed to the knife near Sven's right hand. Its serrated blade had hunks of skin and other stuff as well as clotted blood.

"He did this to himself as part of his thought-experiment," I said.

Angus looked away. "It seems painful."

I crouched again, this time looking at Sven's throat. He had punctured a carotid artery, then moved the cut toward the other side of the throat. However, he had not followed through, the way that I understood he should have. He should have slit the entire throat, not punctured one part of it.

My eyes ached, and my nose felt full. He had started, then changed his mind. I was convinced of it, based on what I saw.

But I decided not to tell Angus, for the news was too difficult. My mind wanted to shudder away from it—and Sven had always told me not to shudder away from anything.

"What?" Angus asked.

"You're right," I said. "This is for the elders, and Sven's family. They've been in the Life Experiment longer than we have. Perhaps they'll know what to do."

I felt bad that we could not continue, but we could not. We were in over our heads as the saying went, and we needed help extricating ourselves.

Since Sven usually provided the help, and Sven was not available, we had to go to the elders.

It was the only logical thing that we could do.

The elders had theories and assignments about death, practical considerations already taken care of. In the same way that the Experimenters provided a definitive means for growing and creating food, building and surviving in homes, and for structuring a community, they had also given guidance for the end of life.

The elders were surprised, just as we were. Only their surprise had a different element to it. They had thought that all of us chronological humans would reach the end of the designated lifespan, and then we would have to deal with the remaining bodies.

There were actually plans on how to deal with the elders who had arrived chronologically aged—we had two elders who began their lives here at the chronological age of 95. They were always thought to be the first to go.

But Sven was the first, finally showing us by example—or so the elders said—what the ancients meant by the recklessnees of youth.

Sven's parents decided to burn his body, despite Angus' argument that an infinitesimal chance of returning was better than none, and we should prepare, just in case. The burning had to be done at a specific temperature for a specific time, and although I wanted to attend, I did not.

My rebellious stomach kept me away. It folded whenever I thought of witnessing the event.

I have tried to spend my time doing other things. Useful things.

I have made several studies of the spirituality, and I have come to the conclusion that Sven did try to trap his spirit. It would return in the place where it had died, violently, and perhaps be seen as a wisp or a patch of light or perhaps even as a Sven-like shape.

But his parents want nothing to do with me or Angus or our theories, so we cannot visit the floor where he died. I am given to understand there is a bloodstain there that cannot be removed. I am also told that nothing has been seen there, no wisp, no light, no spirit.

I believe that, although I do not say so to Angus.

I do not say much to Angus any more. The loss of Sven took much of the joy from my life and my emotions, never the most stable part of my body, have become as unpredictable as my penis. I am difficult to speak to, difficult to be around. My eyes leak tears at the most inconvenient occasions, sparked by the oddest things.

Sometimes even the mention of the word "theory" is enough to provoke the leaking.

I tried to discuss all of this with Angus, but he quite angrily told me that I was speaking of philosophy, and we had to wait to discuss that part of the experiment until the day Sven's spirit returned.

So far, the spirit has not returned.

Angus believes I have done nothing to coax it. I think the responsibility lies with him, for it takes physical action to attract the spiritual being.

At least, that's what I say to him. A great part of me has come to understand that there is a reason the ancients had not resolved this Great Mystery in any meaningful way.

It seems impossible that a man who was here one moment could leave the next—without moving his body, without leaving a room, without announcing a plan for return. And yet it has happened.

And not only has it happened, but it has happened to someone I know.

The Understandings provide no answers, and one of the elders told me that he believes the Experimenters have set up this Life Experiment not to understand life (which he believes they comprehend quite well, or they would not be able to tamper with it so) but to understand this thing the ancients called death.

I don't know the answer. What I do know is the person I would discuss this with, the person who would actually have an opinion about it right or wrong, can no longer talk to me. Even if he wants to return, he cannot.

They have burned his body.

He is gone.

I prefer to believe that he now lives in a better place.

TO THE UNIVERSE STATION

by George Zebrowski

> I backward cast my e'e
> On prospects drear!
> An' forward, tho' I canna see,
> I guess an' fear!
> —Robert Burns

THERE WAS NO FANFARE for a new beginning. The sleeper opened his eyes and felt the same dismay about his own kind which had impelled him to close his eyes. It weighed on him again, with all the great datamass of history, and he recalled with a twinge of pain how he had forced himself to keep on caring about what was going to happen next. Hope was an engine that ran out of fuel too soon, in a vehicle too small for its ambitions. That was when he had decided to run up ahead and see, for as far as he could go.

The sleeper from the second millennium asked the flickering male face leaning over him, "You do know now, don't you?"

"Know what?"

"What this universe of ours is all about." He had always felt that all the questions of life, however local, would reveal themselves to be matters of cosmology; if you could see the large picture, you'd know what all the figures in the foreground were doing.

The face smiled, looking at him with unblinking kindness. "We have brought you back to health."

"This is three thousand and something, isn't it?"

The face still smiled, then nodded but gave no verbal answer to his first or second question.

"But it's a big thing, what the universe is all about. You'd think we'd know by now." About the cosmology, he thought, if not the date, he thought confusedly. With cosmology you have to find the beginning. You'd think . . .

"No," said the hazy figure.

"How about the last thousand years?"

"You have recovered well. What did you do . . . back then?"

"I wrote science fiction stories."

"Whatever for?"

"Don't you read?"

"Read?"

"Words on a page, a screen, whatever."

"We do it differently."

"How?"

"Fast-in."

"How's that work."

"Just what it sounds like."

"But how do you . . . pay attention?"

"You remember it," said the man, and was suddenly gone.

Ben Paine lay back, noting that he felt well, if a bit tired. He closed his eyes and withdrew into himself, wondering what kind of world he had been born into this time. He was living a science fiction writer's thought experiment, as he had lived the nightmare of the first decades of the twenty-first century. *Gotta get a historian,* he told himself, *preferably one on the outs with the current regimes, who knows something more than organized rumors about the past.*

He opened his eyes and looked around the room. It was not where he had started. Bare white walls, no windows, no doors. He wondered if he was being observed, then asked himself whether someone from his time would be of any interest to anyone in this world. What kind of world lay outside this room?

The doctorlike figure was suddenly at his side,

looking at him with the same unwavering kindness. "There's really nothing wrong with you," he said, smiling, "but you have to rest a while yet."

Ben Paine fell back into his own thoughts about futurity. Always a new idea. There was nothing else like it, always waiting up ahead as it did, so that everything didn't just pile up in the present. Most imagineers had never seen very clearly into the unfolding nature of futurity. Near projections had been nearly useless, the far ones unseeable.

He was the past—now separated from it by ten centuries—and he wondered if he would understand anything.

Then he noticed that the doctor figure was still standing there just staring at him—and suddenly winked out.

Hologram or teleportation?

"Hello? Anybody there? I'd like to know what happened to the rest of the twenty-first century for starters."

The room said, "Select period."

"The twenty-first century," he said.

Another figure appeared in the center of the room, a tall thin man with sandy brown hair, aged anywhere from fifty to a hundred. He wore what seemed to be the green coveralls of a house painter.

"I'm Dr. Warren," he said. "You may ask . . ."

"Just an overview of the twenty-first century—most important developments, please."

Ben waited outside a thousand years of human history, ten centuries of inhumanity, if the previous millennium of hellish horrors was any guide.

Dr. Warren winked out suddenly, then reappeared, dressed this time in blue coveralls. "Sorry to break in on my standard self," he said, "but I suddenly realized . . ."

"Yes, I'm the damned sleeper from the past," said Ben, hoping that he was finally talking to a living person.

"Oh, it's not that. It's just . . ."

"You mean I'm not the only one?"

"It's happened quite often," Dr. Warren said. "You asked about the twenty-first century."

"I was on my way out of that time."

"It's not recorded when you started your bio-stasis, but I'll take your word for it."

Ben Paine felt that he was becoming more wakeful, and exclaimed, "That was my world!" as implications began to circle in his mind.

"Now the factual presentation," said Dr. Warren and winked out, and Ben suspected that he had been talking to a person who had wanted to conceal the fact.

Then he realized that no one had asked him his name—the name on all his books, if they still even existed in any form.

And suddenly he didn't know his name.

Sweating, he closed his eyes and floated in darkness, imagining that the room was filling with water, and that he would either drown or learn to breathe it. . . .

He opened his eyes and asked, "What is my name?"

After a silence he shouted, "What is my name!"

"Your name is Ben Paine," a voice said within him. Of course. How could he have forgotten?

A voice replied within him, "Errors creep into brain memory, but there are enough echoes with which to rebuild."

"What about the history?" Ben asked.

"Already fast-inned."

"I didn't feel anything," Ben said, wondering if somehow the history of ten centuries had pushed aside his name.

"Relax and sleep. You'll true-dream everything you're curious about, all we have on record, while we finish out your bodily repairs."

"Nanoguys at work?" Ben mumbled, remembering his old unfinished story about tiny intelligences.

"We have another term."

His eyes were closing, and he thought it odd that he should be so tired after sleeping so long. Of course, it had not been the usual sleep. . . .

Now he dreamed a thousand years, in neatly arranged swirls of ten centuries, and smiled at the reality of the fast-in retrieval, admiring what would have once been for him a convenient literary device, but was now as intimate as circulating blood—

—and he was there, everywhere! In crowds and courtrooms, peering down and sideways through walls and skylights, doors and spyholes, in a wind of whispering voices . . . and heard his own words sorting through the drowned past, reminding him that genius had come to him too late, unexpectedly, out of practiced skill, just in time for him to know that he would not serve it long before the blackness took him. . . .

But returning strength unfroze the pity in his heart, firing up his brain, recalling him to life. . . .

A time of truth and reconciliation, though some called the twenty-first century one of revenge and justice, equally mixed.

By 2040, from Afghanistan to the Mediterranean Sea, the oil pipelines were empty and cracked, homes and highways for scorpions. The refineries stood like skeletal saurians on the brown and blackened land, their steel and iron bones resisting the earth.

The Fossil Fuel Families of oil, gas, and coal stood before the World Court, summoned to answer for delaying the world's transition to clean fuel and quickening the global greenhouse effect toward runaway change. Half the world's people were starving and diseased, beaten down by drought, floods, hurricanes, earthquakes, and ever more bitter winters.

A large share of the Fossil Families' fortunes had gone into private redoubts, retrofitting small cities for indoorsmanship, and, secretly, for the building of mobile habitats in sun orbits. The excuse, and it had some merit, as to why these habitats were justifiable as more than the ultimate in "gated" communities, was that the Earth had to be shielded from the inevitable, world-ending asteroid impact.

But even as the World Court unveiled crime after crime, the mobile habitats waited as an extradition-proof refuge for the criminals.

"We did not know," said the Fossil Families, even as documents revealed the pathology of regime overthrows that had begun with Iran in the 1950s and set back democracy for another half century, not only in the Middle East but also throughout Central and South America, even as the words claimed that democracy was being sown. The Middle Easterners had resisted by retreating into the ancient default settings of nationalism and religious fundamentalisms, destroying all enlightened gains, even as the oil ran out.

"We did not know!" pleaded the Fossil Families.

"You knew," said Lou DeGrinzo, the chief prosecutor, "that your pricing of resources was being swept away. Your sway over governments was threatened, so you delayed clean energy benefits because that would end your self-serving economies of greedy thievery, end the myth of profit, which is only an accountant's trick of excluding everything that would reveal the impossibility of profit, which occurs in the books only by disallowing costs that should be charged against it. Count every effort in play and there can be no profit."

"We did not know," cried the Fossil Families, "that the end would come so fast! Someone had to build the human surplus that would help us escape the past!"

The legal struggle went on for a quarter of a century, as the planet swung on a pendulum of changes. The sons and daughters, grandsons and granddaughters of the Fossil Families sat and watched their parents and long-lived grandparents tried, and felt shame to have come from such a tribe, which controlled them from birth, left them to futile rebellion in their teen years, and in adulthood forced them back into the financial and political bosoms of their families. They were shunned by their outclassed friends. Lovers turned away. Terrorists came to kill them.

The most fearful evidence revealed that a meeting of Fossil Fuel Families had concluded that the environment and its peoples was beyond salvation, unless the Families used up most of their wealth to save it. The meeting concluded that a small number of humankind would be permitted to survive as the majority died off. The Fossil Families intended to make the transition to becoming the only humanity. To do true justice to the world, to deal with all the root causes of strife, would require a loss of wealth and power that would never be regained. A saved world would no longer be their world. . . .

"And you lost us the time we might have had to work miracles," said the prosecutors. "Whatever happens to us, your fantasy of wealth and power and the projection of your progeny into the endless future is over."

As the trials spiraled toward their endless end, the hapless world burned its last drops of oil, caught the last fish in the seas, killed the last big mammals, and cleared the skies of feathers.

But new powers were moving upon the Earth, as Brazil, Russia, India, and China formed BRIC to restrain first American, then worldwide Fossil Family policies. For a time, Washington's masters toyed with the idea of a limited nuclear or biological holocaust, perhaps as a regional "example," unable to accept that their host nation would be reduced to the position of Britain, or the European north countries of huddling, overly suicidal populations . . .

The Fossil Families shifted their wealth and fled across borders, abandoning America and Canada to populist regimes, which now decided that they should export science and culture rather than economic brass knuckles and military threats.

But BRIC was doing as much, leaving the North Americans in also-ran positions. The new sharks circled, eyeing each other and sniffing Old North America for what might still be taken from it.

"Do you have anything to say," intoned the panel of World Court judges in unison, "before we pass judgment?" Even in his retrieval-dream, Ben Paine doubted the "in unison" stage direction of the record but smiled at the incoming justice, now nine hundred sleep years past.

"Your judgment will be dishonest," said the chief defender, his own head on the block with the hundred thousand outgoing masters of the Earth. "You would not have done better than we did. You are not better than us!"

"You were cruel," said DeGrinzo, "to the future which you now complain judges you. You brought into being those of us who now judge you, and future survivors will condemn you even more harshly." He looked around the great hall, and Ben Paine looked with him. "I know from the records that many of you here are more than a century and a half old—life bought by your greed, by the artifact of the monetary accounting system which you call profit, harvested from the peoples' lives and skills, for your benefit."

"We curse you!" cried the Fossil Families in the great hall. "We regret the life and warmth we brought to so many."

"That was never your purpose," said DeGrinzo,

then added, "Oh, there were those of you who became conscience stricken with age and did some good, but you cast them out."

"But we saved the world from the asteroids!" shouted the chief defender. "When nothing could be done about hurricanes, tsunamis, tornadoes, and earthquakes, we did what counted most, to save the history of the world!"

"You saved yourselves," said DeGrinzo. "Now you have gated communities in Earth's sky, above the teeming planet that you have ruined."

"Yes, but the Earth is saved."

"Not by design, and perhaps not for long."

"Some of us thought to do so. We, too, are human."

"Yes, of course," said DeGrinzo. "Some of you are."

"Can we back up a bit?" Ben Paine asked in his dream state. "I don't quite understand how . . ."

A voice quickly said, "Basic changes in outlook did occur in the twenty-first century, forced by larger events, of course. The keynote was sounded by the long suppressed, posthumous *Confessions* of Henry Kissinger, released in 2042, in which he repudiated American policies begun in Iran in the 1950s and continued in Chile, East Timor, Iraq, and Central America, of overthrowing regimes feared to be unfriendly to American economic growth. But it was the world's declining fortunes on a number of fronts that made possible the admission of widespread culpabilities. Although the Fossil Families denied the genuineness of Dr. Kissinger's confessions, the visual record of his admissions to his agent dispelled most doubts. It was an admirable legacy in a long life of rationalizations and lies, the equal of repudiations left by Albert Speer and Robert McNamara, putting to shame the plea bargainings of Bush II and his banana republic gang."

Ben Paine laughed and nearly wept, wondering if there was such a thing as dream tears. . . .

In 2048, President Edward Chavez proclaimed in his inauguration speech: "Our American Empire must admit the crimes that have been the source of its wealth and power. If we do not do so, we will suffer continuing crimes against us, and dissipate all the good that we have done and still hope to do. Our crimes were never unique, of course, only the most efficient and successful. Now, if we can summon the courage and it isn't too late, we may be the first great power to achieve lasting self-correction and reconciliation not only with the world's less effective thieves but with their powerless peoples. We are all part of a flawed, greedy species, unfinished in the creative possibilities that war with our natural inheritance of survivalist violence. We will not soon become angels, but we surely have enough mirrors to look into, for those who will look."

The words of this martyred president made his

death the servant of his life, and moved us all, for a time, into the waters of hope, where we navigated uncertainly, defying the cruelties of the past. The difference was described as a form of societal feedback producing remedial actions that could not be suppressed by private wealth and its usual artifact, power. The frauds of the past would be admitted and set aside, and we would live through our shame, quarreling, yes, but never again warring, viewing the remedies of the past, revolutionary, insurgent and counter-insurgent, or blackmailing deterrence, as crimes in themselves.

So the Fossil Families were put on trial, so that wealth would never again do as it pleased, permitting its owners to live as wolves among us. And it was asked how they had failed to see themselves for what they were, even though they constantly revealed themselves by conflating their interests with those of their own people, whom they sent out to die in wars. . . .

The century also accumulated smaller examples of unconscious, revealing confession. One was the prudish shrouding of the naked statue of justice in Washington from television cameras; another the cloaking of Picasso's *Guernica* tapestry at the United Nations to silence the ironies ringing out from a century of American bombings . . . these resource wars of the 1990s and early 2000s also tested new war technologies, and were meant to instill fear, as did the German Reich's bombing of Guernica in Spain just prior to the great central war of the twentieth century. . . .

The great show trials of the Fossil Families revealed their true nature to themselves much too late, but well in time for their children and grandchildren. We must recall that the Fossil Families were *us*, part of us raised up and made monstrous by the magnifying power of wealth and its first social disease, unregulated power, communicable across generations.

"We didn't want to be monsters!" they cried, unseeing that all violence, however justifiable by the argument of self-defense, only precipitated vendettas and horrors greater than any that had been remedied. . . .

Ben Paine smiled at the words put into the mouths of the dead, recalling how the ancient historian Livy had convicted Hannibal with convenient but fictitious dialogue. . . .

The dream of a past thousand years flowed on. Fully awake inside it, he reminded himself that there was something waiting up ahead, here in the present in which he now rested, which viewed the past out of which he had come in the way he was dreaming it, using it for its own needs, which he had yet to discover. Beware, beware, he told himself; history was often a recorded rant, quarreling with itself, events might have happened otherwise. Even the truth can be told with a lie in one's heart, as Hermann Goering and Karl Rove had so effectively proved.

. . . it was a failure to see that all of space and time were not ours, that we did know how *not* to produce criminals and murderers in our midst, when we burned whatever burned to make heat and power, when our accumulations of wealth flowed from the laboring many to the very few, and there was no decent economic bottom. Whenever decent middles arose, we eyed them with suspicion, and stole back what they had gained. Rome would not permit the other Rome glimpsed in the mirror of Carthage; and the American Empire, having escaped Europe's power, would not permit another in the East.

It was well known, even in the twentieth century, what was right—and not to be permitted by the world's wealthy. National regions should have been left to grow out of their own pasts and to awaken to their own futures, however painful the changes might seem to other regions. Few had even entered their own presents by the time the imperials came, setting back cultural clocks with violence, awakening national feeling and its sibling, religious tradition, to further violence, rather than letting culture and lawful ethics grow through long, peaceful persuasions of the survivalist organism. . . .

When nations would not get out of one another's way, the losses of empires increased, and the world hit a bottom of means; burn the plantation, and for a while you have nothing left; and then the world climbs to repeat itself, or else finds a new way. . . .

Ben paused the fast-in, thinking that all of history was a series of stepbacks. Stepback, look, stepback again, and maybe see better. Even the ways of stepback and lookback needed stepback and lookback. . . .

He asked, "May I have a recitation of facts and less moral rant? How about I ask questions and get back only what I ask about? Give me the ten centuries quick and simple."

—and the fast-in came through him with a kinetic rush:

—2000–2100 took the first major shock of diminishing oil reserves and increasing energy prices, followed quickly by shrinking gas supplies. Worldwide recession brought BRIC and the USA into conflict over oil, less over gas since BRIC relied more lightly on gas. China's use of massive, dirty coal reserves escalated to a military standoff, but all sides left it there, since China was only doing what the world had already done. Taiwan slipped back into the PRC without anyone's protesting. . . .

—2100-2200 saw an undeniable saturation of all environmental sinks. Greenhouse gases in the air and heavy metals in soil and water brought climate changes that limited food production. Scarcity of oil was offset by reliance on coal and nuclear power as renewable energy was brought into play. This did not prevent widespread famine and an ever-growing gap between rich and poor countries. The 2140s saw the final social-legal condemnation of the descendants of the Fossil Families, and the beginnings of several large projects to prevent runaway climate change. . . .

—2200–2300 erased the line between the rich and poor regions of the world. Anyone linked with the companies or political entities that had depleted the planet became a wanted criminal. Gaia-centric religions vied with each other for control of traditional faiths, and the world drifted into a dark age. . . .

—2400–2600. Many records of this period were lost, hidden, or confused, including databases from the prior two centuries, which showed how heroic technologies had helped stop runaway greenhouse climate change. Religious groups preserved much, but could not access the data, much of which was forever lost or had to wait for later times to be read. Paper records in landfills were highly prized by various groups, which devoted themselves to retrieval. Sleepers from the twenty-first century were cared for, but many of these perished. . . .

Who or what was caring for him now, Ben Paine wondered.

—2600–2700 saw new alliances develop. Political boundaries were redrawn dozens of times. A new human expansion rediscovered technologies and moral lessons from the past. . . .

—The 2800s saw the rise of a highly decentralized world that rejected the old de facto monolith and marveled that it ever worked at all. Fusion power and renewables ran a reduced economy of some two billion people. Then, from 2800–2900, as political and military power was concentrated again into fewer hands, a struggle began between a new breed of empire builders and those who had come to love the decentralized model. . . .

—The world that emerged by 3000 is a mixed model. What was once called Asia is now only a few large countries, though they do not use that term. The rest of the world is even more decentralized, into what is known as New China and South America, North America and Europa. Africa and Australia are vast wastes, only slowly being repopulated. The Gaia-centric religions have fallen back into calling themselves by traditional names that were familiar in 2005, but retain the worship of environment and are in many ways very different from the various Christianities, Judaism, Islam, Buddhism, Hinduism, Neo-Paganism, and the Unitarians of a millennium ago. . . .

The fast-in paused, and Ben Paine noticed what was missing from the account. There had been no miracle scientific breakthroughs. No alien contact, helpful or hurtful. A life-ending asteroid had not struck, despite the odds. And there had been no happy cultural changes of heart except those forced by bad experiences, which might in time be forgotten and all the good undone. Do and undo was a human pattern. Nations, corporations, and individuals all suffered memory loss; old victories had to be won again. The Earth was a generational starship parked around a star, each generation born amnesiac, scratching for a new start.

"Tell me," Ben Paine said, "how was the struggle of 2800–2900 resolved so . . . acceptably? Was there a world war?"

His body shuddered as the fast-in resumed:

—The world explained itself to alien visitors, telling them that we are not perfect. There was still a top and bottom, and a lot of middle for the top to recruit from; but the bottom, for those who must fail, was decent and provoked few complaints. And we knew now that how power is used is more important than who wields it, teaching its dangers from childhood, installing our consciences as eagerly as we try to love one another. . . .

—We told them that we now seek new knowledge and longlife, both too long delayed. We assume that you have imaged the horrors we have shouted to the stars, but they are old horrors, not as we are today. . . .

"What!" Ben Paine cried out, pausing the fast-in.

"You *explained* yourself to aliens? What did they say?"

—They replied: "It is early days for you. You have progressed, and we understand because we have climbed as you have. Far in your past, we diverted asteroids that would have destroyed your world, even as we saw that your own destructive behavior might race to preempt natural disasters. You looked at your battered moon and could not see your future fate. You neglected to become a spacefaring world, even though that would have ended your resource and energy problems; but it would also have swept away all the old power structures of your history, so you moved only slowly toward sanity.

"Why do we care?" the visitors asked. "Because intelligent life, although not rare, fails, too often, before it has a chance to contact other forms. Even successes are unlikely to meet during their matching times, given the vastness of the sevagram, and are thus unable to learn from one another's accumulations of knowledge and history. We have chanced upon you, and will not risk leaving you to your fate, on the eve of your latest struggle. We must at least deal a set-back to your violence, to give you another chance.

"Disarm now. Our incinerators are being placed at convenient sites. Deposit your weapons and prepare for inspection.

"Pax!"

"Stop!" Ben cried out. "Why are you lying to me? That's an old story of mine from 1998! And *sevagram* is a mysterious term from an old A. E. van Vogt novel!"

—A synonym for universe . . .

There was a sudden break in the fast-in, and it occurred to Ben that he had probably been cared for by automatics that had little or no contact with the real world of today—except perhaps for that Dr. Warren, who had not returned. The year might be much later than what he had been told, the truth lost in a stew of old records, swirling and distorted across a thousand years, with his old story fragment mixed in. The old AI that ran the fast-in and this sleep facility did not know fact from fiction.

As he lay in the darkness and fought panic, Ben Paine realized that he would have to get up and out into whatever world waited for him. Would anyone, or anything, be able ever to tell him what had happened, even what year it was?

He sat up, realizing that he had silenced the fast-in with a question it could not answer. "Why are you lying to me?" he asked again, and once again it failed, because the answer required data it did not have.

"So the aliens stopped our war and left," he said, giving the ending to his own story. He sat up on the edge of his bed, expecting dizziness.

Ben sighed. It had been a pretty story—but what had truly happened to his world?

White light slowly filled the room, and he realized that he felt just fine, which meant that this world had some advanced medical knowledge, or maybe that the facility into which he had been transferred had . . . simply lasted. Would anyone come to help him? The fast-in had been in English and visuals, but it was an old program. He would not be able to talk to today's people.

Were there any? Maybe this facility was all there was, a relic like himself. An ambitious story would leave him in a cul-de-sac, an easy one would bring help to him. Was ambitious the same as realistic? What about a story being honest before the constraints of a lawful universe? Fiction was too often a gauze-wrapped wish, reality a medusa into whose face few dared to gaze. Yet we had always sought, he reminded himself, to move creative, rehearsing fictions out of the merely possible into reality, to make dreams real, even to make possible the impossible, or what was life for? To follow an enigma-bestowed reality into death? Worship of the impossible, the miraculous, seemed to be an old program in human nature. A complexing psychology of brain and nervous system had grown rich enough to pull far horizons to itself and peer over not only into mere improbability but into the impossible. His kind had grown tired and unhappy with a chance-given universe, which clearly was a first or second effort and needed more than just editing; it needed a complete rewrite, when its awakening intelligent life had learned enough to do so . . .

He stood up and turned to look at the bed. No sheets, no pillow, and yet it had felt as if these things had been there for him. He turned again and approached the white wall. There were no doors in any of the walls, but when he touched the wall it slid back to reveal another room, identical to his own. That bed was empty. He stepped back and the wall closed.

He tried the two other walls and saw identical chambers. Then he tried the third wall, and saw a white corridor leading to what seemed to be a panel of light. He hurried toward it and saw that the panel was the same kind of wall material. He touched it and was startled when the wall slid back to reveal a misty view of the outdoors.

He stepped outside and peered into the mist, suddenly fearful that he had awakened to an Earth suffering from the runaway greenhouse effect.

He stood there, finally noting that the air was too cool for a greenhouse planet. And as he waited, the sun rose, burning through the mists, unveiling gently rolling countryside, trees, a distant stream, a blue sky that was nearly cloudless.

He breathed air that seemed full of life. As his eyes adjusted to the bright rising sun, he scanned the hilly green horizon, overcome by the beauty of the scene. Hope invaded his heart—that he had somehow awakened from the nightmare of human history, that it had all been a mistake, corrected now forever.

After a few moments he became aware that someone had come out behind him and was standing behind his left shoulder. He turned and saw a young, dark-haired man smiling at him.

"My name is Jean Lukacs," he said with what sounded like a French accent. "I've been waiting for you to awaken for some time." He held out his hand.

"Ben Paine." He shook the man's hand, then asked, "But you're such a young man . . ."

"I'm from 2098 Canada. There wasn't much to look forward to by then."

"Aliens?" Ben Paine asked.

Jean Lukacs smiled. "Oh, you heard that foolishness."

"I think it was an old story of mine."

"There's a lot of fiction in that jumbled database. Let's walk a ways. The exercise will do you good after a millennium, despite the reconditioning."

"When did you awake?" Paine asked.

"Some years ago."

"How many were in there with us?"

"Oh, maybe a dozen. All the chambers are now

empty. The others got up well before us, and probably wandered off, years, decades ago. I've not met a one of them."

"Is this year accurate? And do you know where we are?"

"Perhaps not. I think we're somewhere in the northern hemisphere. The facility doesn't answer that question, and we don't have any way of taking a navigational reading."

They walked out toward a group of trees. Paine asked, "So what happened in 2098?"

Lukacs shrugged. "Famine, war, die off, the rich abandoning their hell for heaven in their sun orbit."

"And you?"

"I was only rich enough to abandon my time."

Paine looked up at the sky. "Are they still out there?"

"Who knows? But you can see the habitats at night."

"And here? What can you tell me?"

"I think I have guessed a few things about this Earth. Few people, but those nearby seemed to have protected and passed along our sleep facility. They bring food and leave it regularly."

"Have you talked to them?"

"They stand and watch me when I come out, then leave when I go inside."

"So you live here?"

"It's a convenient hotel. I go out and try to talk to

our caretakers, and they do seem to be picking up some of my words, better than I learn theirs."

Jean Lukacs led him into a group of trees. Paine sat down against one. Lukacs sat cross-legged in front of him. Paine looked into his face, but could read little beyond open-faced youth, perhaps a bit afraid, more resigned, glad of company.

"May I ask," Lukacs said, "what you had in mind when you went ahead?"

"I thought that the future, as a place of possibility, was always a new idea. I was a writer. I wanted to see more."

"But surely you knew enough human history to know that it was a repetitive mill."

"I'll be honest with you," Paine said. "Human futures always interested me less than the future of intelligent life—and cosmology."

"Ah, yes," Lukacs said, "the words of great Clarke, that the proper study of man is not mankind but intelligence."

"Yes, the contemporary writers always mocked science fiction for not dealing with human character, which was deemed changeless, refracted through endless dramatic variations of story, but never becoming more. Wearing the blinders of your own time was everything, and history, well, the details of past blinders made little difference. If one read and studied much, one arrived at the feeling that here was where I came in."

"And cosmology?"

"What it's all about."

Lukacs smiled, "You and I will never find *that* out."

"I will ask our caretaker's fast-in . . . maybe something was discovered."

"You can ask . . ."

"Have you?"

"Of course not," Lukacs replied. "How can we even conceive of a cosmology that lets us imagine our universe from the outside, especially if that is an infinity that insults our minds. Oh, it may be that our local region might be some kind of single . . . thing, but that only opens up the larger enigma— either it's a standing infinity or a series of endless stepbacks, or it turns back on itself. Even an all-powerful deity would be an enigma to itself as much as to us. Yet a standing infinity is just as inconceivable as an always existent deity. Perhaps we finite beings will just have to get used to an infinity, because that's the way things are however we approach the problem. There is no deeper insight that would reveal to us what it *all* is, as if we were looking up an answer at the back of a book. The virtue of an eternal-infinity is that it ties off the questioning. The buck stops, as you Americans once said." Lukacs smiled. "And God stops the buck also, if we don't question further."

Paine said, "But still, it seems to me that to grasp

even the idea of our universe as a whole, as something to be questioned, seems right. I don't accept that there are questions or conceptions that can be ruled out of order, as not being real directions of investigation at all. If we can say it, there must be something to it."

Lukacs laughed. "Yes, you *can* speak nonsense! You are an American—always so . . . generous in your thoughts, about what could be known."

"What do you mean?"

"Their ambitions lacked all constraint. They believed Virgil's words about the Romans—'To these I set no bounds in space or time; They shall rule forever.'"

"Yes, the Rolfe Humphries translation," Paine said. "But why not try?" he added. "What is there to lose?"

"We are here, my friend, because all *was* lost."

Paine looked at the young man, and was seized with a sudden suspicion. "You know more than you're telling me, don't you? You've been awake longer. Yes, you *do* know more!"

Lukacs gave him a look of boyish shame, then nodded and said, "My friend, the only friend from my times, roughly speaking, I will tell you more, and only hope that you can accept it. . . ."

"I haven't come a thousand years without hope. What could be so terrible? The best of us were always time travelers, looking ahead while others looked back. We had to be ready for the worst, as we wrote and argued over possible futures."

"But few ever believed in the worst possibilities," Lukacs said. "They were always just so stories of possible worlds, held at arm's length, written to profit a publisher and feed an author. Provocation was the sensationalist's method."

"So tell me more of what you know," Paine said.

"I'll tell you. The people here think they *know* what the universe is all about. I mean the cosmos."

"They do?" Paine asked. "I mean not just thinking they do."

"Yes. I'll take you there and show you."

"Where?"

"Outside."

"Where is that?"

"I'll take you to their Universe Station. That is how I think of it."

"You're kidding me," Paine said.

"Consider," Lukacs said, "the malaise that ignorance brings, the yearning for revelation, the impatience of unknowing, the horrid demand that has always lived in all of us, expressing itself in countless ways—the so-called awful rowing toward God. I'll tell you how all this happened—"

"What are you saying?" Paine demanded. "Do they know or don't they?"

"Patience, my friend. Let me tell you in a way that will help you, as I have tried to understand."

"Go on," Ben said, wondering if the youth was painfully mad.

"The centuries known to you and me gave us no answers, either through the mere insistence of faith or from the descriptions of science. At the beginning of the last millennium we tried to punish and repudiate our human crimes, find better ways of living, but still were left with living in an inconceivable mystery, and thus found our human progress, hard won through bad experiences of one another, still unsatisfying. We wanted for something to rip open the sky and show us *what* and where we were, and what it was all for."

"A wrong demand," Paine said, "it has been claimed."

"Patience, let me summarize. The great question became, what is it? *What* do we live in? All the old answers had fallen away when we came out of the dark age of the mid-millennium. And all the reasons why the question was invalid continued to be unsatisfying. We, and certainly intelligent life everywhere, live *within* something, and no accumulation of self-defined descriptions will ever be enough. Some kind of transcendent explanation is needed. But we fear that. The diehard holdouts came back and cried that it was never a real question. If we could do such a thing as rip back the veil and see outside, we would only push the problem away to another level of questioning, and ask about *that*, whatever it is, as if we had made no progress! The illusion, some said, lay in the very idea of believing, or suspecting that if we could answer the cosmological questions, know who and what we are, then we would solve all our problems. There was a kingdom within us to know and conquer, then inhabit and be saved."

"So where are we?" Paine asked. "With an eternal God or an infinite background of superspace that needs no beginning but is inexplicable, or with a God who can't explain Itself or an Infinity that just *is*, assembling and reassembling itself forever, with no explanation needed? I know, I know, we want a God who speaks, even if we have to talk to ourselves and call it God."

"Close enough?" Lukacs asked.

"How about accepting things as they are, and reclaiming our freedom?" They sat still for a moment, and Paine felt a slight breeze. "Is this all you have to tell me?" he asked.

"You must see the Universe Station," Lukacs said.

"So you've been there. They've shown it to you. What did they tell you about it?"

"As I told you, they have some of my English, but I have still not picked up enough of their language . . . mixture."

"What kind of people are they?" Paine asked.

"They farm, use what technologies they can handle without much understanding. I don't think there are more than a hundred million people on the planet."

"So what is it, a shrine of some kind?"

"I'm never sure, when I visit. What I have picked

208

up from their words and behavior is very suggestive and disturbing."

"You've become superstitious," Paine said, wondering again about what Lukacs knew and wasn't telling, or whether the young man was simply afraid, or just reluctant to show that he was afraid.

"But wouldn't it be grand if it were true?" Lukacs asked.

"What would be true?"

"The story they tell of local universes in an infinite superspace, each region eventually revealed to itself from the vantage of a . . . universe station. I don't know what else to call it."

So they had told him a story. Paine imagined an endlessly expanding space-time, and outside of it an endless open-curved space. And it was inconceivable, a black mirror for superstitious fools in which they could see their reflections.

"And then?" Paine asked. "You go see it, and then what? You're sobered by the sight and leave?"

"I would say inspired," Lukacs said. "We'll go, you and I, and you'll see for yourself, think for yourself, and we'll compare our impressions. I need someone to do that for me."

"You've been there?"

"Yes."

"And you've haven't made up your mind yet?"

"I can't say. Perhaps I've been alone too long."

"When do we go?"

"This evening," Lukacs said.

They sat in silence for a while. Paine felt the warm breeze quicken. What had he done to himself by severing his mind from its own time, first in his writings, then through the persistence of his body into futurity? Was it best to live and die among familiarities, or forever flee, like the distant hurrying galaxies, into the night. . . .

Dismay, not quite despair, had loosened him from his time. But a man's mind was not a stone set in place, he had told himself. A man tires and dies away, but sings a poem as he goes, sending it against his own running time, in a present that is also fleeing with him, into futures that are also fleeting presents, in a rush that seems to stand still as he departs. Change desires a standing infinity in which to shape its malleables. A man tires and smiles, and wonders if it all might have been something else entirely. . . .

The breeze chilled him. What have I done? he asked himself. Lukacs had stood up, and was offering him his hand.

They came among smiling people who were dressed in what looked like hand-woven clothing, mostly trousers, loose shirts, and skirts. Their faces seemed to be of all ages, but not aged. A crowd of about a hundred was marching across a meadow to some kind of building.

Paine and Lukacs followed. Close up, Paine noted

that the rectangular structure seemed to be made of ceramic or plastic. The building reminded him of an insect trap with its row of doorless entrances black in the sunlight. People were approaching the outer walls from all four sides, so there had to be entrances there also. Paine began to feel that he was going to church, or to some kind of rite.

"Did you meet any scientists among these people?" Paine whispered to Lukacs.

Lukacs shook his head in denial as they came to one of the openings and waited for the couple ahead of them to enter. Lukacs went in and Paine followed.

His eyes adjusted and he saw the Canadian's dark shoulder ahead of him, moving toward a distant blue lit dawn. The light brightened as Paine caught up, and they emerged into a large oval area, with what seemed a curved gray lens-like wall ahead.

Paine came up beside Lukacs and looked around at the other dark human figures in the chamber.

"Is this the place," Paine whispered, ". . . outside our universe?"

"Yes," Lukacs whispered.

"This can't be serious," Paine said, but suddenly wondered whether it might be that these people had somehow wandered into a revelation and did not know what to do except visit it.

"I don't know where it is, but we reach it in a roundabout way."

"How's that?"

"Let's say that down the corridor we came is a kind of topological walk. Didn't you feel the odd inertial stresses?"

"I felt nothing," Paine said, "except strangeness."

Lukacs was silent.

"So this is it?" Paine asked.

"Yes," Lukacs said.

Paine saw an arm rise up against the gray lens and point to a faint blue blotch, and Paine heard a soft sigh from the people around him. A thrill went through him as he imagined that after a thousand years humankind had found a terrace from which to see the universe. Would it be like this if it were true—a mere blotch in a gray superspace?

A fraud was alive around him, standing in for and concealing an unattainable reality. This structure, he realized, had to be some kind of astronomical showplace, a teaching aid, like a planetarium—a relic out of time, embraced by the needful as a reality.

As he gazed at the gray lens, he began to see other blotches, smaller, meant to appear more distant, and he imagined the builders saying, "We want answers, so we must build a station outside our universe. It's important to have an answer in place of none. No one will ever really get out because there is no outside. But we're still *inside* something, without a doubt, unless there is no inside either, and it's just a way of talking. We can guess where we can't ever know, and so unmask the teasing truth even if no one ever gets out."

No one ever gets out alive, Paine thought, *but show me*, he said silently to the gray wall. Show me something to make me . . . accept this as real. Belief had always fled from him. It had always insulted him, so he had insulted it back. No wonder it had fled from him, said the nightmare of his unreason. He had as much of it as anyone.

Yet he still felt, inescapably, that he was inside, that all of human history was inside, and needed desperately to break out. He imagined that every blotch in the gray infinity would grow its own universe station, and that one day they would talk to each other, bridge the universes into one station . . . and then look outward to an even greater . . . space? Endless breakouts of scale would be launched, but there would be no end of breakouts . . . and for an instant he knew that would be best, with no final answers needed, thank you.

The human shapes around him were kneeling. Jean Lukacs kneeled, and Paine felt suddenly sorry for his capitulation. What were they worshipping? Nothing that seemed likely to speak to them, yet they seemed comforted, and Paine felt a momentary panic about being left out, of leaving himself out when he might easily let himself succumb. *Let himself*, he thought, knowing that he would never be overwhelmed.

Lukacs, for all his show of Pascalian intellect, was weeping on the floor beside him, and Paine wondered if the error-laden sleep facility would take them back. Maybe one day, humanity would know more. Knowing more had always seemed like a good battle cry, and so did the lure of futurities. *What else did we ever have*, he asked, to *match the glimpsed freedom of possibilities, to struggle against constraint, and even logic itself?*

Crossing a thousand years had brought him to this gray wall of blue patches that purported to show all and hid everything. Was the entire history of science, he thought with a shudder, merely a display of self-referencing language, leading, it had to be admitted, to a greater control of nature, but failing to answer any basic question of the kind that might be asked by a naive child? Yet predictive ability and control meant that there had to be *some* truth in the formulations, unsayable in any other way. Physicist Feynman had once said that science could say something, but should not be expected to say everything. Yet so many had hoped for much more—something that would say, "Reality is such and such, and that's it." And the response would be, "Is that what it is? Is that what it was all along?" And how could any answer imaginable ever satisfy? Most likely it would be denied or even start a revolt against the heavens that had made the answer so unbearably plain.

Paine reached down, grasped Lukacs by the shoulders, and helped him to his feet.

"Come on," he whispered. "We've got to get out of this place."

The blue patches seemed to be flickering as he steadied Lukacs. Bright stars appeared in their haze, as if struggling against his unbelief as he turned and led the young man away.

They came out into a bright late afternoon, and Paine knew that the dark age was not over; it had not been over in 2000, or in 2026, when he had begun his attempt to sleep off human history; it might be necessary to do more than that—to sleep off humanity itself, its needful, adaptive nature too long preserved by Darwin's survivalist natural selection. How could it have selected anything else, given the tyranny of environment? Something else would have to do the selecting . . . self-selecting?

As he watched Lukacs stumble ahead of him across the bright green grass, Paine wondered what might be made of such a revision. New laws for a new universe? A new kind of game to play? Was the universe into which he had been born a failed attempt, forged in a lost imaginary time and forgotten when its cruelties became unbearable? Made by whom?

Lukacs regained control of himself as they neared the sleep facility. He turned to Paine at the entrance and asked, "So what is to be done now? Do we go on ahead to some other time?"

"What else?" Paine mumbled unthinkingly.

They went inside—and heard distant voices.

Paine stood still and listened. The voices grew quieter. Lukacs went ahead toward the sleep chambers. Paine followed, realizing that these voices were not those of the nearby villagers.

Lukacs whispered excitedly, "Some of our fellow travellers have returned."

Suddenly, a tall heavyset man dressed in a long coat appeared in the corridor. He stopped and looked at them, then nodded.

"English?" he demanded.

"Yes!" Paine cried out.

"Jove Regis," the man said loudly. "From 2102," he added. "That's when this place was built and we transferred sleepers from older places. I helped build it. Took you two in, I think." He drew a deep breath. "But it's no good now."

"What are you saying?" Lukacs demanded.

"We can't sleep ahead anymore," he said. "The facility is empty of biotiming drugs. All gone, even the spooks who talk to you when you wake up."

The man came forward and stood with them.

"It can't be resupplied?" Paine asked, feeling a strange sense of relief.

"Maybe," the tall man said. "But we'd have to do a lot of searching across this . . . world. There's five of us just wandered back here. Found a lot of empty places, small groups of people living with what they could use of the past, getting by. God help them if their numbers increase, and there's not enough to go around. We thought to go ahead again, to a better time, but the facility just announced that it was failing. None of us know enough to even know where to look for refills. It's a bunch of tanks, I think. Maybe stored nearby, but it would be hard to know how to hook things up."

The big man stopped and sighed, and looked as if he was about to collapse on the floor.

They sat on the grass in the fading afternoon. Lukacs and Paine made the acquaintance of sandy-haired Ernest Jones, bald-headed Ray Winks, a wounded looking Milo Engal, and long-haired Jove Regis. The only woman in the group was Hanna Oslo, which was obviously not her name. Ben found her to be a tall, handsome, gray-haired woman, with piercing blue eyes and pale complexion. They were all later than Ben and Jean, from early 2100s Europe and Australia, and seemed reluctant to speak of their motives for timing out of their lives, except for Hanna Oslo, who said, "I had to get away from too much crazy family, which could only treat me as . . . well, old. They were all about seventy, of course. Besides, dying isn't very original."

"So what do we do?" Jones asked in a raspy voice.

"Can't fix it," Engal muttered.

Ray Winks laughed and rubbed his shiny head.

Jove Regis stared at Paine.

Lukacs smiled and said, "I guess we'll just have to stay awake."

"But we can still use this facility as a base," Paine said.

"If the locals continue to bring us provisions," Lukacs added.

"I wonder why they bother?" Jove Regis asked.

Unable to sleep, imagining skeletons voyaging forever into deep time in a now useless sleep vessel, Ben Paine got up from his sheetless, blanketless, pillowless desert of a bed and went outside, where he looked up at the night sky, saw the bright pearls scattered across the ecliptic, and knew that these had to be the proliferating habitats in their sun orbit, where the rest of humankind now lived. A great change had divided humankind, liberating it from its planet; yet the ring of skylife hung close to home.

With so many habitats visible, he now realized that they could not be failures. Earth was getting a rest from the mistakes of its childhood cultures. Out there, an ongoing humanity would tell him the true history of the last ten centuries. After a moment it occurred to him that the local peoples here had seemed too well organized, almost if they were being guided and cared for in their choice to stay with the planet. The two humanities had a continuing, subtle connection with each other, and he realized that Dr. Warren had perhaps been evidence of that link. . . .

He breathed the night air, feeling fit, wondering how much work the sleep facility had done on his body before failing, then looked up again and felt his face relax with happiness, because he knew that what he saw among the stars was the best dream ever created by the visionaries to whom he had always belonged, a dream now written across the sky, waiting for him to join it, to become whatever he might still become. The old dream had grown old enough to become real.

What are the moments of happiness? he asked himself. When one is poised between extremes but able to go on, full of sweet possibilities better savored than realized? The lesson of the stars, he thought, was that they had cooked up our necessary conditions, but the sufficient ones became increasingly our own to seek and to find. . . .

"Paine! Paine!" a young voice from his own time cried out.

Lukacs was suddenly beside him. "The facility—it's up and running again. It was only dormant for self-repair. We can go ahead again."

But Paine realized that he would not close his eyes again, even though once more the choice to cross time was being offered to him. . . .

"No," he said to Lukacs, pointing up at the night sky, "here I begin again," then added, "there we can begin again."

Lukacs looked up and Paine waited for the vision of humanity's skylife to work its wonder on his fellow voyager.

"I see," Lukacs said slowly, then added, "I shall be going with you, if they'll have us."

"We did the right thing," Paine said, "to get here. No more sleep. We've awakened in the right place."

"Who was that president," Lukacs began, "at the hopeless turn of the twenty-first century, who said that he didn't care about the judgment of history because by then we'd all be dead?"

"Oh, yes, what's-his-name," Paine said.

Lukacs laughed. "He was right."

"Took a while," Paine said. "He's dead and his world with him."

"Think they'll have us out there?" Lukacs asked.

"They'll have us down here," Paine said, "—at least."

"But out there . . ."

"It won't be perfect, but I think so," Paine said, wondering how the current populations regarded the criminals who had founded the sun habitats. Were there any "Memoirs of a Millennium" in which all was admitted, if not forgiven? He glanced up at the glittering castles in the sky and wondered if this new starry humankind had made sure to leave out the dungeons. . . .

"Will they come to get us?" Lukacs asked.

"I hope so," Paine answered.

"We'd better go in," Lukacs said, "and tell the others."

IN HIS OWN IMAGE

by Mickey Zucker Reichert

> *And God said, "Let us make man in our image, after our likeness; and let him have dominion over the fish of the sea, and over the fowl of the air, and over the cattle, and over all the earth, and over every creeping thing that creepeth upon the earth."*
>
> *So God created man in His own image, in the image of God created he Him . . .*
>
> —Genesis 1:26,27

BRUCE FABER SQUATTED in a trench and fired his M-37 assault rifle blindly into clouds of swirling, ebony sand that reeked of tar, smoke, and animal musk. He ducked between the ridges of sand and replaced his projectile cassette and propellant charge.

The rhythmical pops of his platoon members' fire played a sharp counter to the growing roar of approaching wind. Faber stood, steadied the green dot of his laser sight a meter above ground level, and pulled the trigger. The M-37 bucked repeatedly against his shoulder.

A darker shadow moved within the shifting curtain of sand. Faber swung his rifle toward it. *Steady. Steady.* Anticipation thrilled through him, warring with fear; and he wrestled down the instinct to open fire again in wild, erratic bursts. The green sightpoint slowed as Faber drew it across his target. *Now!* He pressed the trigger. The shadow split in two, then dropped gracelessly to the ground. *Got him.* Faber gritted his teeth in a rictus grin. *First kill.*

Bruce Faber had often wondered how taking a life might affect him, braced for everything from mind-numbing grief to desperate, life-staggering shame and remorse. To his surprise, he suffered nothing worse than a warm flush of satisfaction and a deep-seated relief that the enemy had fallen instead of one of his own.

The reloading indicator blinked an insistent red. Dipping below the edge of the ditch, Faber replaced the propellant, his back pressed against the cold trench wall. Enemy fire splattered sand from the ridge above him. Instinctively, he hunched, drawing into himself to make a smaller target. His chest rose and fell in swift, shallow breaths. *Calm, calm. They're coming.*

Faber's heart hammered, and he fought to control a swell of excitement. Barely nineteen, he had been sent to a planet thirty-five light-years from Earth's sun, fighting an enemy that looked like werewolves from an ancient movie, an enemy they derisively referred to as "Rover." Now, his first day in combat, he felt like a kid playing army. *Less intelligent, armed with inferior weapons, and too damned ugly to inspire guilt. It's like slaughtering plague rats. Or robots on a vid-game screen. Whatever these monsters have done, the universe is better off without them.* Faber released a dragged-out parody of their enemies' howl and stood, firing into the billowing sand.

Down the line, Faber's brother, Harold, the platoon's heavy gunner, yelled. "Kid brother's got first blood!" The pounding of the launcher, mixed with the soldiers' mocking wolf howls, masked the raging bellow of the wind. Silhouettes darted through the sand. Multicolored spots from laser sights played through the chaos. Individual shadows among the enemy split and toppled, but, en masse, they pressed continually closer.

Faber ducked, recharged, and fired again, repeating the sequence until the process became mechanical. Sweat drew lines in the fine, black sand covering his face. His exhilaration gradually died, long before the struggle ended. Apparently undaunted by casualties, the enemy surged relentlessly onward in a silence that made an eerie contrast to the soldiers' animal howls. *Like rats*, Faber reminded himself. *Like unfeeling, uncaring, inhuman robots*.

Far to Faber's right, the commander yelled, "Body count!"

Faber wondered why it mattered or how anyone could see well enough to give an accurate answer.

Nevertheless, a man's voice returned, "I count eighty-nine."

Suddenly, the enemy disappeared, baying like injured hounds. Surprised and uncertain, the soldiers stopped howling, and even the brutish noises of Rover gradually sank into a strange quiet filled with coiled menace.

Faber's brother shouted, "Sirocco!"

Understanding dawned. Rover could not attack during a sirocco. The fine sand, driven by 400 kilometer per hour winds, would strip exposed flesh to bone in seconds. Breath quickening to an unsteady pant, Faber dug into his pack and retrieved his microatomic armorcloth bivy. The material could withstand the storm and provide air for 48 hours. He unrolled the stiff bundle, crawled inside, cinched the opening closed, and activated the compressed air cylinder.

Pressure lifted the hard, yellow fabric, forming a turgid cylinder isolating Faber from the approaching sand. Lying on his back, he tacked the bivy's sphincter cover in place. He waited, reviewing the survival manuals in his mind: "A severe drop in pressure immediately precedes the onset of a sirocco. The first thirty seconds are critical to the survival of a bivy and its occupant. Full pressure must be reached and maintained during the course of the storm. If the sphincter cover is removed, or pressure is reduced for any reason, the probability of survival is severely compromised." He remembered his training, bashed into his brain until it became unthinking impulse. *Let nothing, NOTHING interfere with the installation of your bivy. The slightest mistake, the smallest hesitation, may cost you your life.*

The roof of the bivy sagged to Faber's chest. He squeezed his lids tightly closed and prayed the bag would hold.

The next moment passed like ten. Then, compression returned in a rush. The roof stretched taut. The initial wave of sand struck Bruce Faber's bivy with a deafening hiss, drowning all sounds except for his own pounding heartbeat and the fast, superficial gasps of his breathing.

The sphincter cover snapped loudly against the bivy's mouth. Hard grains of sand drove into Faber's scalp. Fine dust filled his mouth and nose. *Breach.* Icy terror washed through him, threatening panic. He choked, squinting toward the opening. Sand stung his eyes. He coughed and struggled to breathe. His throat pinched closed, making inhalation impossible. Wildly, he groped for, then gripped, the edge of fabric, forcing the cover back over the sphincter. At the opening, he felt a hand clawing through the fold. He tried to scream but only exhaled his last lungful of air. *No!*

Faber struck the hand.

It recoiled, then lunged forward, reaching for the cord holding the sphincter closed. Faber swung at it again, more feebly, losing strength to pressure, to the battering sand. *I don't want to die.* Frantic, he drew his knife from its thigh sheath and drove the blade into the hand.

The knife snapped from Faber's grasp. The blade and handle wedged across the gap of the sphincter. The hand twitched and jerked violently, held by a ring caught on the blade. Then, the finger severed, and the hand ripped free. Finger and knife fell to the floor of the bivy.

Faber lunged for his sphincter cover, his only thought for his survival. A weight collapsed across the bivy, pinning his arms above his head. He reached to press the cover in place. One edge flapped maddeningly. His consciousness swam from lack of air. He squirmed and stretched, but the edge remained just beyond his fingertips. *Can't . . . die . . . here. So close . . .* Faber dug his heels into the floor and made a last, desperate lurch for the opening in the sphincter cover. As he hit it, consciousness escaped him, and the world went dark.

As Faber's awareness returned, he knew only a dull itch over his entire body and a droning hiss. He rubbed at his closed eyes. Sharp grains dug into his lids. He shook, dislodging the fine covering of sand that had settled after he secured the flap, and opened his eyes.

Light shined through the yellow fabric hovering over Faber, and black sand coated the floor, his limbs, and his uniform. He remembered the fight with the hand and the struggle to reseal his sphincter cover. *A human hand.* Realization struck Faber like madness. *One of my platoon members must have gotten separated from his own bag. By refusing him entry, I killed him.*

Tears filled Faber's eyes, making a paste of the grit and burning like acid. Guilt swirled through his mind like the sand storm raging beyond the bivy's protective wall. *I murdered him.* All the grief and remorse that had eluded his first kill rose now, worse than any agony he had anticipated. His entire body felt battered, broken. His mind refused to function, stuck on that single, self-accusatory thought. The shield protecting his body isolated him from the companions who could offer solace and forgiveness. The tears finally beaded and fell from the corners of his eyes. He gasped for air and gagged, coughing up mucous black with sand. *I hate this frigging war. I hate what I've become.* He sobbed hoarsely, the will to live that had driven him this far utterly lost. *I wish I were home.*

Home. The word instantly conjured memories to

the fore of Bruce Faber's mind. His one-dimensional recollections returned verbatim, as they always did: *The smell of home-baked bread wafting through their tenement on Sunday mornings. Standing knee-deep in a stream of ice-cold water waiting for the klaxon proclaiming seven o'clock and the opening of larnfish season. Hugging Harold at his parents' funeral after the rocket crash, then huddling beneath a blanket, sipping hot chocolate with his big brother, the brother who echoed the same memories in the same words.*

Faber felt an overwhelming need to speak with Harold. The similarity and strangeness of their remembrances had forged a strong bond between them. Harold had a knack for putting everything in perspective. As soon as they could talk, Faber knew his brother would assuage his terrible guilt. But, until then, he could only wait alone and cry.

The continual hiss of the storm lessened. Faber reached above his head to check the seal on the cover. The edges held tight. He noticed a glint near the opening, covered partially by his knife. He pushed away the blade, and a disembodied, bloodless finger rolled free, still wearing his brother's class ring. Faber stared, stunned.

And screamed.

"Harold!" Faber ripped at the cover. "Harold!" *I have to save my brother!* Sand poured through the opening, a grainy avalanche lacking its previous wind-driven ferocity. *God, Harold. Don't die!* The bivy drooped. Faber grabbed his knife and cut the cord tying the sphincter closed. "Harold, please don't leave me." He gasped, a lump growing like an instant cancer, his throat nearly too tight to breathe. "Don't leave me. Don't leave me . . ." The roof collapsed. ". . . alone." Sobbing, Faber wriggled from the opening and stood. Sand stung his face and hands, lacking the force to cut through skin. "Harold!"

Faber turned. A body sprawled across his deflated bivy, twitching and clutching an M-37. Sand obscured the features, but the patches of an allied, heavy gunner's uniform showed through. *No God, not Harold. Not Harold. No. No. No!*

Tears smeared through the grime on Faber's face and pattered like raindrops, leaving darker spots in the endless ebony wasteland dotted with bivies and mounds of sand. He felt nothing but a fierce hole in his chest, an emptiness that seemed so vast and unfillable that he would never feel emotion again. Unable to recognize reality, Faber squatted next to Harold's head with some stupid, heroic notion of rescuing his brother. Gently, he brushed the sand from the still face, revealing a fine wire mesh covering thin wafers of microcircuitry.

Shock jolted Faber to his feet, and he stumbled blindly from the corpse. His foot mired in the collapsed bivy, and he managed to stagger half a circle before tumbling onto his brother's body. Faber gasped, shoving to his knees, and one of his fingers snagged on the pocket of the tattered uniform. Its label read "H. Faber" in clean, bold script.

Bruce Faber's mouth gaped. His jaw trembled. No rational explanation fit the sight of his brother lying dead and faceless except for wire mesh and circuitry. Faber clenched his teeth, fighting the hysteria threatening to overwhelm him. Then, a movement caught the corner of his vision.

Again, Faber noticed the hundreds of small heaps that littered the sand plain beyond the trench. A large, shaggy beast rose from one of them and shook sand from its fur. Slaver dripped from its fangs. Its glowing red eyes locked on Faber. It stooped slowly and lifted a rifle from the sand. Its lips curled, and its ears flattened against its skull. It shouldered the gun.

Panic seized Faber. His eyes darted between the wire mesh of Harold's face and the Rover. *I don't want to die.* Diving, Faber snatched the assault rifle from his brother's body and swung its blue dot to the monster's chest. His finger spasmed on the trigger.

A burst of fire pierced the monster's abdomen. It howled in pain. Bright, living blood sprayed the ground. The creature toppled, tearing frantically at its belly.

Sand ground into the M-37's bolt, jamming the mechanism, and it stopped firing. Faber dropped the rifle.

Hundreds of the enemy appeared from beneath piles, clutching rifles.

Faber ducked into the trench and screamed, "Rovers! We're under attack!" *Plague rats*, he reminded himself. *Robots*. The repetitive notion, once a mantra, now chilled him. Images of his brother's faceless form overtook all reality. He amended his thought; he had to: *Filthy, snarling dogs.*

Bullets strafed sand from the ridge above Faber. A chorus of howls echoed, genuine ones, not the sardonic rejoinders of his companions. The enemy swarmed into the trenches.

Faber watched, pinned by enemy fire, as his platoon members were dragged from their protective bivies. The wolf/men wrestled the soldiers to the ground, slashing at their throats with curved, razor-sharp claws. Skin tore with the high shriek of wire stretching. Finding no blood, the Rovers clubbed or shot the remaining androids as they emerged.

Alone in his trench, Faber huddled, trembling. Tears still streamed from his eyes. *I'm real. Human. They're all different. I'm a man.* He screamed, "I'm a man!"

The fire spraying the ridge above Faber ceased. His companions lay in the trench, nonfunctional. Faber examined his memories again. Their shallowness and distinct resemblance to his brother's, his not having a clear memory of his parents, all made him an ideal soldier. With nothing on Earth to make him want to return, he was willing to die to protect his home planet. He screamed again, "I'm a man!"

Suddenly, proof of Faber's own mortality seemed more important than survival. The will to live was replaced by the desire to die. Life creates, gives and receives love, and survives; a machine only responds to its environment. Death proved life. Being turned off or malfunctioning meant Bruce Faber never existed. He prayed, "God, let me die that I might have lived!"

A Rover approached carrying a captured M-37. Its necklace marked it as an officer.

Faber looked into its blood-red eyes and read an emotional mixture of fear and triumph. Its lips drew back to reveal sharp, yellowed teeth.

Tears ran along Faber's cheeks. "I'm a man," he whispered. "You can see, I'm a man."

The beast's muscles tensed. The butt of the assault rifle rose and slammed into Faber's head. Darkness surrounded him. He fell to his side. Meaningless images played repeatedly across his vision: a jagged chaos of stripes, patches of light and darkness, strings of 1s and 0s.

Then, Bruce Faber knew nothing more.

TAKE ME BACK TO OLD TENNESSEE

by Allen M. Steele

ONCE UPON A TIME, in a small valley cupped between two mountains, in a place once known as Tennessee but which now had no name, there lived a young man named Jed. Tall and strong, with skin the color of a burnt olive, he lived alone in a grass hut within the village he'd known as home since the day he was born.

Indeed, Jed was aware of little else except for the valley. When he was very young, shortly after the seventh anniversary of the day his mother had drawn her last breath giving birth to him, he'd slipped away from the other children while they were toiling in the fields and, after crawling through the corn, commenced to climb the forested slopes of the mountain that lay to the east. At first he'd followed the game trails frequented by the tribal hunters, but after a while he'd left even those behind and struck out through the dense woods until he finally made his way to the top of the mountain. When he reached the summit, where the pines grew thin and the air was cool, he stopped to behold the world, and discovered nothing more than he'd left behind. Mountain upon mountain, valley upon valley, all shrouded by the thin bluish haze that had given this range its long-forgotten name. He remained only long enough to look around, then he went back down to the village, where he received ten lashes from a hickory switch wielded by an angry elder and was sent to bed without supper.

From that day on, he remained incurious about what lay beyond the fields of home. True, he'd heard the legends, told in song and dance around the campfires, of great villages beyond the mountains, long-lost paradises where people flew through the air and lived in towers higher than the clouds, never having to work yet nonetheless fat and sleek from a never-ending supply of food. Since he'd seen none of these things when he'd climbed the eastern mountains, though, Jed believed them to be nothing more than fables. Far more believable were the stories of the great walls of ice that had come down from the north, driving his ancestors before them until they'd found refuge in this warm and isolated place. Ancient pictographs, etched in charcoal upon strips of birch and carefully preserved by toothless crones, were the sole remaining record of this exodus; he'd seen them once, yet they'd provoked little wonder in him. So far as Jed was concerned, history was inconsequential, time itself without meaning.

He lived a simple life, uncomplicated by anything except the basic necessities. He awoke early, usually an hour or so after dawn, and began his day by wandering over to a hole he'd dug in the ground near his hut and squatting over it to relieve himself. If he was hungry, he'd eat whatever food he'd stored in the basket by his bed. Then he'd go into the village, where he would join the others at work in the fields: ploughing, planting, spreading manure, weeding, harvesting, whatever needed to be done to tend to the crops that kept them all alive. In Jed's village, one received in equal measure for what one gave; there was no money and no one kept score, except perhaps when it was noticed by all that someone wasn't doing their share of the labor. This rarely happened, though, because work meant food, and no one was willing to risk starvation by shirking their chores. Anyone who lived more than forty winters was considered old, and the sick either got better or they died, and when that happened everyone ate a little better that night.

There were other jobs that needed to be done. Wind and rain took their toll on the huts, so they were in constant need of repair. Hunting parties would journey into the mountains, returning days later with animals that had to be skinned, butchered, and smoked; nothing was ever wasted, not even their bones. Waste pits needed to filled and dug, away from the stream that supplied water to the village, and the stone dam that kept the stream from rising above its banks during rainstorms had to be kept watertight. There was never any shortage of tasks, and all able-bodied men, women, and children in the village were expected to pitch in.

Yet Jed's life wasn't without distraction. There were games, such as the one where young men would divide themselves into two groups and take opposite ends of a field, upon which they'd try to kick a ball made of a deer skull wrapped in hide away from one another. And from the moment he entered puberty, he enjoyed the pleasures of sex, with any girl who would have him. Women often didn't survive childbirth, and usually there was no telling who the father was—in Jed's case, it could have been any one of a half dozen men who'd regularly copulated with his mother—so offspring were raised by the community as a whole. As a result, Jed himself had sired several children before he was twenty years of age, but called none of them his children.

In the evening, after the chores were done and the sun had set behind the western mountain, Jed often lay on his back outside his hut, watching the stars as they glimmered into sight within the darkening sky. Sometimes he'd have a girl with him, and he'd gently stroke her hair before he mounted her, but more often than not he was alone, which suited him just as well; the night sky fascinated him as nothing else did. He had no idea what those lights in the sky were—some said that they were the souls of those who'd perished during the coming of the ice—but he studied their patterns, noting how some appeared during one season but would be absent in the next, while others remained constant. The Moon was a mystery; on certain nights, during its dark phases. he could see tiny lights upon its face, yet although legend had it that men lived there, he doubted this was true.

And then there were the stars that raced across the heavens, shining more brightly than the rest, appearing shortly after sunrise and again after midnight. They always followed the same course, season after season, rising from the west and disappearing to the east. If he stared at them long enough, he was almost certain that they had distinct shapes: tiny cruciforms, or miniature rings. These were the most tantalizing of all, and Jed never grew tired of watching them . . . although, again, he seldom wondered what they were. Jed's life was uncomplicated by such deep thoughts, and imagination wasn't one of his gifts.

So his days were spent in sort of a timeless pastorale, one whose rhythms were orchestrated by the passage of the seasons. Seeds were sown and harvested, huts were built and repaired, children were born and old people died; he played kick-ball and humped girls, and ate well when there was plenty of food and tried to ignore the ache in his belly in times of scarcity. When the weather was warm, he walked naked beneath the sun, and when it became cold, he wrapped himself in skins and joined the others as they huddled around the fire. And on occasion someone else would climb the mountains to see what lay beyond the valley. Usually they would return, reporting only what Jed himself had seen long ago; sometimes they wouldn't, and their absence would be felt for a short time, but not very long.

Then, one summer night, as Jed lay outside, he spotted a star more brilliant than any he'd ever seen before, one which left behind a thin trail as it streaked across the moonless heavens. Startled, he sat up in time to hear a thunderclap just before it vanished behind the western mountain. Yet there were no clouds in the sky, so he knew that it couldn't have been caused by an approaching storm . . . and besides, this particular star had moved the wrong way, from east to west instead of the opposite direction, as they usually did.

For the first time in many years, Jed went to sleep wondering about what he'd seen. By morning, though, these thoughts had largely been forgotten; there were more important matters to be dealt with today.

He went through his usual morning routine, then wandered over to the fields where the others were already on their hands and knees, digging up weeds from between the rows of crops they'd planted last spring. He'd barely commenced work, though, when he heard a faint, high-pitched hum. At first, he thought it was a mosquito in his ear, but even as he reached up to swat at it, the sound grew louder, and now the others around him were rising to their feet.

Looking up, Jed saw what he first took to be a hawk, until he realized that it was much higher in the sky. The humming increased in volume as the bird began to descend, and it was then that he observed that its wings didn't move. By now the sound was very loud, and it was clear that the bird wasn't a bird at all, but something else entirely: an object larger than anything he'd ever seen before, many times the size of the biggest hut in the village.

Shielding his eyes against the sun, Jed stood up and watched as the bird-thing quickly grew in size. The hum it made was deafening, and he instinctively clasped his hands over his ears, yet even as men and women screamed in fear and ran for their lives, leaving behind their tools and even the infants, Jed remained where he was. It wasn't courage, really, or even curiosity that kept him in his place; it was utter astonishment, a complete and total sense of unreality. Like an animal frozen by fear, he was unable to move, although every instinct told him to flee.

A violent wind tore at him, ripping soybeans from the ground and hurling them into his face, as the giant bird came down less than a hundred paces from where he stood. Frightened and half-blinded, Jed fell to his knees, clenching the ground with his fists. The hum subsided as the beast settled upon great legs that lowered from its belly; Jed saw a pair of slotted eyes staring at him with what he perceived as malevolence. Certain that the monster intended to devour him, he lowered his head and hoped that death would come quickly.

He waited, yet nothing happened. Then he heard a faint whirr, and he looked up again to see a door open within the creature's belly. Puzzled, he sat up on his haunches and watched as a ramp lowered from the door. A few moments passed, then, to his surprise, two figures walked down the ramp. They looked like men, yet they were dressed head-to-toe in white garments, with domes for heads. As they approached, Jed saw himself reflected in the silver masks of their faces: a naked savage, cowering in the dirt.

Surely these were gods, brought here by a great bird. Jed raised his hands, started to beseech them in his native tongue, yet he'd barely begun when one of them raised a stick and pointed it at him. Sparks flashed before his eyes; a moment of cold numbness, as if winter had suddenly descended upon him, then everything went dark.

He awoke in a place like none other he'd ever been before, a room whose walls were made of some substance that wasn't grass, wood, or stone; its margins were straight and well-defined. Light as bright as the afternoon sun, yet with none of its warmth, glowed from panels within its ceiling. He lay upon an elevated bed covered with a fabric as soft as doeskin, his arms and legs were held down by elastic straps. All around his bed were large objects that beeped and chittered and flashed multicolored lights; to his horror, he saw that long, slender snakes had attached themselves to the insides of his elbows.

Jed screamed in terror, began to thrash about in panic. Then a soft hand was laid upon his shoulder, and he looked up to see a woman peering down at him. She was nearly his own age, yet her face was as pale and unblemished as the first snow of winter, her eyes as blue and clear as the sky, and when she smiled he saw that she had all her teeth. He couldn't see her hair, for it was covered with a hood that came up from the one-piece garment that she wore, yet nonetheless she was the most beautiful female he'd ever seen.

She spoke to him as she gently stroked his arm,

and although he couldn't understand what she was saying, her tone of voice soothed him. Another voice from the other side of the bed; he looked around, saw a male standing nearby. He was dressed the same way as she was, yet when he turned toward them, Jed was startled to see that, although he was also Jed's age, his face was as hairless as a boy's. Despite his bewilderment, this made Jed laugh out loud. The woman laughed as well, although it seemed without quite knowing why; the male gave an uncertain grin, and then he gently patted Jed's arm.

It was then that Jed determined what had happened to him. He'd perished, and his spirit had passed to another world, an afterlife where the angels were now preparing him for entry to the next plane of existence. He felt a pang of regret for all that he'd left behind—his friends, the girls with whom he'd shared evenings in the tall grass, the village where he'd spent his entire life—yet now he was surrounded by beings who meant him no harm, and he felt his fear began to ease. No harm could come to him here. He was already dead.

So he relaxed and let the angels study him, watching with a certain detachment as they groped and prodded his body, and watched the flashing lights on the things along the walls and conversed with each other in a tongue which he couldn't understand. The female fed him water through a snake that came from a translucent gourd, and the water was fresh and more clean than any he'd ever tasted. The male gently examined his genitals with his hands, and laughed out loud when this produced an involuntary erection that caused the female to blush and quickly turn away. After a little while, they finished their study of him; the woman carefully placed a mask across the lower part of his face, and he briefly tasted air that smelled like mint leaves before he fell asleep again.

When he awoke, he was in another room, this one much like the first, yet bare save for the bed on which he lay and a large round pot attached to the wall. Jed found that he was no longer strapped down; he also wore clothes not unlike the ones the man and the woman had been wearing. He sniffed at the clothes, but was unable to detect a scent, yet when he inspected himself, he discovered that his skin was clean, and his hair and beard had been washed as well. This disturbed him, for he seldom bathed, and relied on body odor to help him identify those who were ill and therefore untouchable.

Walking over to the pot, he found that it was half-filled with water. When he knelt beside it and tried to drink from it, though, he found that the water had an unpleasant aftertaste. Worse yet, when he backed away, the pot suddenly made a loud gurgling sound, and the water spiraled around and disappeared through a hole in the bottom, to be replaced by more water that flowed down from the inner rim.

Alarmed, Jed hastily backed away from the be-witched pot on his hands and knees. It was then that a door on the other side of the room slid open. He looked around to see the woman walk in. She was dressed the same way as before, yet now the hood had been drawn back from her hair, and he could see that it was the color of cornhusks. Raising a hand to her mouth, she tried to hide her amusement at his reaction to the pot; seeing her smile, Jed smiled back at her. She was very attractive, and when she came closer to offer her hand to help him to his feet, he determined that this gesture was an expression of her willingness to share flesh with him.

He grabbed her arm and tried to pull her down to the floor. The woman shrieked and tore herself away; before Jed could bow in apology, she produced a stick from a pocket and pointed it at him. A painful shock raced through his body; he lost control of his muscles and collapsed to the floor.

Although he was unable to move, he didn't lose consciousness. Stunned, he lay there for awhile, watching as the woman stood up and straightened her clothes. The man he'd seen before came in; he roughly dragged Jed over to a corner of the room and propped him against the wall, then went to the woman and comforted her. Then they both stood nearby and silently waited until Jed was able to move again.

Jed had learned his lesson. Sex was out of the question. He pulled his knees up against his chest and hugged them within his arms, and silently watched as the woman, smiling again yet more wary than she'd been before, strode to the opposite wall. Touching it, she murmured something he couldn't understand; the wall vanished, and suddenly Jed found himself staring at the night sky.

Whimpering with fear, he huddled closer to the wall. The woman's expression became sympathetic; cautiously coming closer, she squatted down just within arm's reach and gently stroked his ankle, letting him know that there was no reason to be afraid. Yet it wasn't until the man walked over to the night sky and actually touched it that Jed realized that this was only an illusion: the wall hadn't disappeared, and the stars were just images. Jed's dread became fascination; uncurling himself, he crawled on hands and knees across the room until, with great hesitation, he was able to touch the wall himself, and was assured that he wasn't about to fall into the sky.

The wall changed again, and now he saw the Moon, many times larger than he'd ever seen it before. Delighted by its familiarity, he laughed aloud, and stroked its face with his hands. The woman nodded, smiling her approval, then she said something that caused the image to change yet again. Now Jed saw something that looked like the Moon, but wasn't: blue and green, dappled here and there with broad swatches of white. She said something he didn't understand and pointed to him, and then back at the Moonlike thing again.

Jed gazed it in puzzlement, admiring its beauty yet failing to comprehend what it was or why he had any connection to it. The man and the woman glanced at one another, shared a few words, then the woman repeated the sequence: night sky, Moon, blue-green-white thing. Jed patiently observed the display once more; by now, though, he was getting thirsty, and decided to risk drinking some more water from the strange pot.

His visitors allowed him to do so. When he looked up again, they'd left the room, and the window-wall had become opaque once more. Baffled, Jed returned to bed. The ceiling lights dimmed as he lay down. After a while he went to sleep, wondering why, if this was indeed the afterlife, it couldn't be more pleasant.

It didn't. It only became worse.

There were no days or nights in this place, or at least not as Jed understood them, only periods during which the ceiling lights would glow to life, awakening him from his slumber, and would darken again some time later, allowing him to go to sleep. During those wakeful periods, he'd be visited by the man and the woman; they'd bring him food, or at least something which remotely resembled food—plates of mushy cubes that had little taste or odor, which he ate only because he was hungry—and bowls of water that he drank once he came to understand that the pot was meant for relieving himself. They'd remain in the room while he had his meals, quietly observing him as he crouched behind the bed, distaining the odd-looking implements they gave him and instead scooping up the food with his fingers; once he was done, they'd remove the plate and bowl. Then his ordeal would continue.

At first, it was all very simple and painless. The magic window would open again and he'd see things, some familiar, others so strange that he couldn't comprehend their meaning. The window revealed the Moon—no problem there—but then it was immediately followed by an image of a vast, dry-looking landscape, without trees or grass, upon which lay vast white domes, with humanlike figures in bulky outfits with globes for heads moving about in the foreground; Jed failed to understand how one related to the other. Another time, the window showed the blue-green-white thing; very pretty, yet then the image slowly swelled in size, growing closer and closer, until it filled the screen and then Jed himself staring down at mountains. It was only through repetition that he realized that they were the same ones that he'd once seen when he was very young. The next image was his own village, as if seen from a bird flying high above; the first time he saw this, Jed rushed at the window, intending to dive through it so that he could return home, yet instead he ran face-first into the wall. The man laughed out loud at this, but Jed didn't find it very funny. He rubbed his swollen nose and glared at the man until the woman came over and gently massaged his shoulders, calming his anger.

The window-wall showed other images, one more mysterious than the next. A complex form, like a giant white tree whose limbs lacked leaves yet grew in all directions, floating among the stars. Showing this to Jed, the man would stamp his foot on the floor, then point first to Jed, then to himself and the woman, then back to the picture again. Jed failed to make the association. Pictures of great bodies of water, meadows that stretched out to great mountains in the far distance, artifices that looked like giant trees made of glass, towering walls of ice: all fascinating, yet he couldn't make sense of any of them. Bird-things like the monster that had abducted him, screaming upward into the heavens upon columns of fire; he quailed from these images, shielding his eyes with his hands, while the woman tried to comfort him and the man sighed in disgust.

And all the while, they babbled at him in their queer language. Through repetition, Jed eventually came to learn that the woman was called *Sayrah* and the man's name was *Peet*; likewise, they came to know him as Jed. But beyond that, and a few elementary words—*watah, foohd, roohm, floah, bayd, doah*—all attempts at meaningful communication broke down. *Globahl wahming, glayshas, isayge, sitees, disastah, loonah colonees, spayce stayshons, orbeet, suhvivahs*: meaningless abstractions, syllables with no rhyme or reason. And the things that intrigued him—where the water in the magic pot came from and where it went, why the ceiling lights came on and off, what his clothes were made of, how the window-wall opened and shut—were beneath their attention, for they never bothered to explain them to him.

They gave him blocks of different shapes and sizes, and placed before him a board containing holes which corresponded with the blocks. Jed did his best to fit the blocks into the appropriate holes, but it took considerable effort, and even when he was finished, Peet wasn't satisfied. They gave him a sheet of paper and a set of colored paints, then watched to see what he'd do with them; Jed dipped a fingertip in the green dye and licked it, and ignored the paper. They gave him three red balls and one blue one; he happily bounced all four on the floor without discriminating between one or another.

Sayrah took notes, and Peet shook his head in frustration, and at some point they apparently decided that further efforts to educate him were pointless. After a feeding period, Jed found himself becoming groggy; he collapsed on the floor with his breakfast plate still in his lap.

When he awoke, he found himself in yet another

room, naked once more and strapped down to a couch. Several men, one of whom was Peet, were standing around him; they wore hooded white outfits and had white masks across their faces. A bright light was suspended above him; when Jed squinted at it, he saw his own face reflected in its silver casing, and that was when he realized that his head had been shaved and his beard had disappeared.

But none of this was as terrifying as when he gazed down at himself. A snake had fastened itself to the crook of his right elbow; it was feeding upon his blood, which slowly flowed into a clear sack suspended from a rack next the table.

That was when Jed truly realized that he wasn't dead after all.

As he began to scream, the masked men standing around him laughed. And the snake continued to drink his blood.

For days on end, this continued. He'd awaken, eat and drink, relieve himself in the pot, then wait for the men in white to come for him again. There were no more sessions with the window-wall, no more games with balls, blocks, or finger paints. The men would take him from his room—kicking and screaming, or unconscious; it made no difference to them— and strap him to a table, then siphon more blood from his body. They did this carefully, allowing him time to recover so that he wouldn't become anemic;

afterward he was given plenty of food to eat and a chance to sleep.

Yet the routine remained the same, and after a while Jed resigned himself to his fate.

When he was alone in his room, he found himself remembering happier times. The warm summer days he'd spent in the valley, tending the crops and playing kick-ball with his friends. Before long, the memories came to him when he was on the table; he watched his blood streaming up through the snakes, and thought of autumn nights when he lay in the tall grass with women and gazed up at the stars.

With the growing realization that his old life was over, he became listless, rarely moving from his bed except when the time came for him to follow the men in white into the next room. He discarded the clothes he'd been given, and seldom ate anything given to him. After a while, the room began to stink of feces and urine, for he'd ceased to use the pot.

Then, one day, he was led from his room, not to the place where he'd sacrificed so much of his blood, but to another room, one much farther away. He found himself in the center of a circle of tables, behind which were seated dozens of men and women. Sayrah was waiting for him, and so was Peet; Sayrah smiled and gently stroked his arm, then led him to a chair and gave him a ball.

A window-wall behind him opened and a sequence of images appeared upon it. Peet did most of the talking, with Sayrah interrupting now and then. When Jed glanced back, he saw things he didn't understand—scribbles and bars and strange markings—along with pictures of himself, back when he still had hair and a beard.

Jed paid little attention to what was going on. Shoulders slumped, he idly played with the ball in his lap. At one point, though, the ball escaped from him. It rolled across the floor until one of the men leaned down and picked it up. He cautiously tossed it back to Jed, and Jed obediently caught it. For some reason, everyone in the room found this amusing, for they laughed out loud. Anger and humiliation surged within him, and he hurled the ball back at the man; it smacked him in the center of his face and he cried out, then he rushed from the room, clutching at his nose as blood seeped from it.

For the first time since he'd been taken from his village, Jed felt pleasure. Whatever these creatures were, they weren't gods. They could be hurt, and their blood was no different from his own.

Once the room was calm again, Sayrah began to speak. As before, Jed had no idea what she was saying, yet he noticed that her voice had risen, more irate than he'd ever heard it before. Glancing back, he saw that the window-wall displayed images of his village. His heart stopped, and for a precious instant he felt . . . hope? An end to all these days of torture?

Whatever Sayrah said, it caused Peet to become

infuriated. He yelled at Sayrah, pointing first at the window-wall, then at Jed, then at the window-wall again. Sayrah remained calm; she gestured to the window-wall, then picked up a handful of paper from a desk and held it out to Peet. The argument escalated, with several men and women in the audience adding their own opinions. And through all of this, Jed sat still, wondering whether he'd done the right thing by throwing the ball at one of them, and wishing that he was anywhere other than here.

When it was all over, Peet threw up his hands and walked away. Sayrah went over to Jed, took his hand, and gently led him out of the room. At that moment, although he'd understood none of what had been said, Jed intuitively realized that it was all over.

They had no more use for him.

Jed was returned to his room and allowed to sleep. When he woke up, he found clothes laid out for him. Once he was dressed, two men escorted him through a series of tunnels until they arrived at a vast cavern where the monster bird lay asleep. Peet was waiting for him there, and so was Sayrah; they led him up the ramp into the creature's belly, and had him take a seat in a chair that was as soft as the bed in which he'd slept ever since coming here.

Sayrah strapped Jed in, then she and Peet took seats on either side of him. The door closed behind them, and after a few minutes the monster bird rumbled and awoke from its slumber. Jed clutched at his chair in fear, then there was a sensation of motion as the bird took flight.

There was a small window beside his chair. When Jed looked out, he saw the cavern walls disappear, replaced by a night sky in which stars gleamed. This time, though, he knew that what he was seeing wasn't mere illusion, but something very real. He wasn't just seeing stars, but indeed among them. Weight left his body; he floated up against the straps, and for a second he felt as if he was falling into the fathomless night.

He screamed, but then Sayrah took his hand. She spoke soothingly to him, and gradually his panic subsided. Peet said nothing; he pulled a flat pad from his pocket and studied the squiggles upon it, and otherwise ignored Jed.

The journey took a long time, and after a while he went to sleep, only to be stirred awake as the monster bird shuddered and quaked. Weight had returned to him; an invisible hand pushed him back in his seat. Nervous, not knowing what to expect, he gazed out the window, and saw something he'd thought he'd never see again: deep blue sky, and far below, high mountains dense with forests.

Jed laughed, and clapped his hands in recognition. All those sessions at the window-wall hadn't been lost on him. He knew where he was; he was going home. Sayrah grinned and gave his arm a fond squeeze, while Peet muttered something and looked away from both of them.

A few minutes later, the monster bird howled and trembled in a brief moment of fury. Through the window, Jed saw familiar mountains rise up around them. There was a sudden jolt beneath his feet, then the creature slowly became still and silent. Sayrah loosened her straps and stood up, then helped Jed out of his seat. With Peet leading the way, she escorted Jed to the door, and waited until it opened and the ramp slowly lowered.

Jed walked out of the belly of the monster into a village that had changed little since he'd last seen it. The corn was higher; there were one or two new huts and a taste of autumn in the air. Otherwise everything looked much the same. The villagers cowered nearby, frightened of the apparition that had once again swooped down out of the sky. A few of the braver males, however, warily approached the creature, knives and spears in hand, while a young girl anxiously stepped closer, a basket of fresh-cut tomatoes in her arms as an offering.

Sayrah smiled at Jed, then gave him a gentle push. Her meaning was clear: he was free to go. And indeed, a few of his friends and neighbors seemed to recognize him; although Jed wore strange clothes and no longer had his hair and beard, they knew his face, and already they were beginning to lose their shyness in their delight upon seeing him again.

Jed was about to rush to them when he happened to glance at Peet. There was no gladness in his face, but only determination. His hand stole into a pocket of his clothes; when it came out again, it held the stick which he'd used to carry Jed away to the stars.

Jed didn't hesitate. He lunged at Peet, grabbed him from behind; before he could react, Jed had wrapped his right arm around his shoulders, then grasped his head with his left hand. Peet didn't even have time to yell before Jed twisted his head; a hollow snap, and Peet went limp within Jed's arms, his neck broken.

If he could have done so, Jed would have spared Sayrah's life. She'd been kind to him when the others hadn't. Yet she was impaled by the spear someone hurled at her as she ran for the safety of the monster bird. When she went down, the villagers swarmed the creature, wielding knives and torches as they dashed up the ramp, where they found two men cringing within its head.

Jed paid little attention. He held Sayrah in his arms long after the light faded from her eyes, begging her forgiveness.

The monster bird burned long into the night, the villagers dancing about its carcass, as a feast was held in honor of Jed's homecoming. Everyone ate well, and gave thanks to the gods for his deliverance. Yet when Jed was offered Peet's heart and liver, he refused to take them, or let anyone else consume them. They contained evil, and should only be cast to the dogs. Likewise, he made sure that Sayrah's body was surrendered to the flames. After all, she'd been his friend; her soul deserved to return to the sky.

No monster birds invaded the village ever again. For a time, Peet's skull hung from above the door to Jed's hut, until he allowed the younger ones to take down, stuff it with straw and wrap it in deerskin, and use for kick-ball. By then, his youthful days of games and mindless sex were in the past; he'd become a tribal elder, the one to which the others came to when they needed words of wisdom. Yet never again did Jed lie out beneath the stars. He always went inside his hut when the sun went down, and didn't come out again until the morning came around.

For those who need a moral to this story, let it be this: beware of what you sow, for so you shall reap.

Or perhaps, even better: you can take the boy out the country, but you can't take the country out of the boy.

THE MISTS OF TIME

by Jack Williamson

MILDRED'S CALL CAUGHT me at breakfast that morning, a burst of light in a dismal day.

"Hack, would you consider joining Thor and me on a desperate adventure?"

The breakfast was a soggy slab of cold cheese pizza and of bitter coffee left over from the night before. The sky outside was brown with New Mexico dust lifted by a gusty wind that rattled the windows of the empty house. I asked what sort of adventure.

"Let Thor tell you," she said. "It's too strange for me."

I'd been in love with Mildred, and her voice brought back a happier past. Before she hung up, I'd promised to drive to her Uncle Ben's ranch, where we'd spent summers together when we were kids.

THE MISTS OF TIME

I'd come to the end of a pitiful season as football coach at Caprock High, nine games lost, though the underweight team had played their hearts out. The principal had warned me my contract would not be renewed. My girlfriend had left me for a Mediterranean cruise with the drama teacher. I felt ready and willing for anything different.

The ranch was two hundred miles away. The girlfriend had taken the car, but I had an old pickup. Driving all afternoon, I found my mind filled with wistful recollections of Mildred and our long summers on the ranch. Older and wiser than I, she'd kept us out of trouble. We rode horses and went swimming, and searched the wind-blown dunes for arrowheads and broken bits of Indian pottery.

Those summers had to end, but later she was my college English teacher. Sitting in her classes, I used to find Milton and Shakespeare swept away by her honey-hued hair and pixie smile. Idle dreams; instructors didn't date students. She'd met Dr. Thor Hansen when he came to lecture on quantum mechanics, and their marriage left me with an ache of loss.

Time and drought had lain heavy on the ranch. The cattle pens were empty, the scanty grass sere and gray. The wheel was gone from the windmill tower we used to climb, the stock tank dry, most of the old cottonwoods leafless and dead. Her uncle had moved into town and I found them there alone.

* * *

Mildred had heard me coming. Thor came with her out of the old house when I parked. A tall blond Viking, a model of gravitas, he took a moment to recognize me, gave me a craggy smile, and gripped my hand with a warm deliberation. She hugged and kissed me, the way I used to wish she would, and I caught a hint of the lilac scent she'd always worn.

"Dear Hack!" She had a radiant smile. "I'm so glad you can join us!"

Her face looked pinched and pale, and I asked how she was.

"Never better!" Yet I caught an anxious quiver in her voice. "I'll live a thousand years."

"Not quite true." Thor shook his head at her and turned very solemnly to me. "The doctors have found a malignant tumor they won't touch."

"But I won't die!" She tried to smile at me. "Thor has a plan."

"A desperate gamble." He shrugged. "But the only hope I see."

"Tell, Thor!" she begged him. "Tell him what it is."

"That's not easy. Let's not scare him off." He swung to me with a grave, bearlike grace. "Come on in. The project can wait till after dinner. Are you ready for a steak?

With only a candy bar since that leftover piazza slab, I did. He had the grill heating. Mildred had made a salad. We sat at the old oak table in the kitchen I remembered, and he opened a bottle of wine.

"To Thor and his plan!" She lifted her glass. "It will save my life."

"Perhaps." He shrugged. "If we're lucky."

She took only a sip of her wine. The steak was great, but she had barely touched it. He finished his, reminded her to take her pills, and sat frowning thoughtfully at nothing until she begged him again to tell me about the plan.

"It may turn you off." He gave me piercing look. "What do you know about quantum mechanics?"

"I heard your lecture on it, back at the university. I don't remember anything."

"No wonder. Quantum science can be hard to take."

"Please, Thor," Mildred begged him. "Make it simple. Just tell him what it does."

"It isn't simple." He scanned my face again. "Einstein refused to believe it. He said God doesn't play dice. It does run counter to common sense. Every particle is also a wave, every wave also a particle. If you know where a particle is, you can't know where it's moving. Einstein himself discovered that what one observer experiences as time, another would see as space.

"Nothing is absolutely certain. Zero isn't always zero. The universe is ruled by the laws of probability.

261

Even the highest vacuum is never really empty. Electrons and positrons hop into it out of nowhere, cancel each other, vanish back into nowhere. But not quite always. Unlikely events do happen. Some fourteen billion years ago, one odd particle failed to disappear. Instead it drained enormous energy out of nowhere and grew until it exploded into the Big Bang that created space and time."

He gave me a sharp look.

"Do you get it?"

"Maybe."

Her face drawn with strain, Mildred was fiddling nervously with her glass. I wondered what the Big Bang had to do with her.

"Good!" Thor's voice boomed, his blue eyes blazing. "Fascinating research! I used to imagine the future as a straight line of cause and effect, impossible to change as the past. It isn't. The quantum universe doesn't exist until it freezes out of a chaos of statistical uncertainty. It's like Schrödinger's cat in the box, which is neither dead nor alive until you lift the lid."

He paused to frown at me.

"Thor!" Mildred looked up to scold him. "Don't try to amaze him. Just tell him about the plan."

"Okay, dear." His eyes lingered fondly on her face before he looked back at me. "If you're ready, here it is. I'm working on a new math that gives me a strictly limited control of quantum probability. I can freeze atomic forces, stop all atomic action, though only in a very small volume of space. In that narrow space, time is suspended."

"We can skip a thousand years!" she cried brightly. "Till doctors know more and medicine is better. I won't have to die."

"We can try." Frowning, he refilled his glass and mine. "I wrote a paper for *Science*. The peer reviewers turned it down. One of them couldn't get the math. The other faulted my experimental evidence. I've got better results since, but Millie's health was failing before I could publish. We have to be our own guinea pigs."

"A time machine?" I asked.

"No machine. Time flows only one way, as eternal as gravity. We can hope to find a higher civilization and better doctors, but nothing is predictable. We can't be sure of any miracles. And there's no way back." He leaned across the table, eyes narrowed to see my reaction. "If you go, you're gone forever. It's good-by to everything you've ever known."

"If you can." Mildred whispered. "Thor won't go without you."

"Take your time." He raised his hand. "Think it over. We can't do it alone, but I want to be frank about the risks. I can't choose our destination, and Millie isn't very able. It may be madness. We've got nobody else to ask."

"Think about it, Hack!" She wiped at a tear and I heard a tremor in her voice. "Think how much can happen in a thousand years. I dream about the wonders we could find. It ought to be a better world."

I needed only half a minute to think about it. My parents were gone. I'd been the only child. I'd left my closest friends when I took the Caprock job. With no real ties to break, I pushed the glass away and told them I'd had enough of now.

That night I slept in the little room that had been mine on those long-past summers when Mildred and I were children here. Next morning Thor laid out what we would be taking.

"It's hard to guess what we'll need. Today, this is an isolated spot where we shouldn't trouble anybody. A thousand years ahead, and we may fall into the middle of a city. An earthquake. A battlefield. A new ice age."

He had bedrolls, a tiny nylon tent, canned water, a backpack stuffed with food, an aid kit, a tiny pocket telescope, a battery radio. He asked if I could shoot and gave me a police revolver. To answer possible questions about our own time, he had a high school history of the world, maps, a book of photos.

"Maybe too much." He gave me a philosophic shrug. "Maybe nothing we'll need."

His lab was a battered van. He loaded the gear and drove through the brush-grown sand dunes south. We stopped on a little grassy flat a thousand miles from nowhere, with only the barren dunes around us. His equipment looked simple: only a square black box he mounted on a tripod. Silver-colored antennas jutted out of it in three directions.

"It's a quantum interference effect," he said. "Opposed forces cancel out. Time is stopped until the effect collapses. To show you how it works, I'll repeat the experiment that was finally successful."

He stepped back, holding the end of a wire attached to the tripod.

"Would you note the time on your watch and lay it on the box?"

My watch read 9:16. I laid it on the box. He stepped farther away and clicked a switch at the end of a wire. I heard no sound, but the top of the tripod was suddenly surrounded with a mirror globe that reflected our distorted images.

"The bubble of suspended time." He nodded at it. "Feel it."

Gingerly, I touched it. It was smooth and slick, neither hot nor cold.

"Push it."

I pushed, gently at first, then with all my strength. It felt solidly unyielding as a brick wall.

"It's set for fifteen minutes." He looked at his own watch. "Nothing enters the pod. Nothing happens in it. Nothing leaves it."

We stood there for a long quarter-hour, his eyes on his own watch, till he nodded.

"Nine-thirty."

I counted seconds. At fifty-nine the globe winked

silently away. The tripod looked unchanged. My watch still read 9:16 when I picked it up, but the second hand was jumping normally from mark to mark.

"Okay?" Mildred's anxious eyes were fixed on me. "You'll come?"

My pulse was jumping faster than the second hand, but I caught my breath and said I would.

"Take your last look." Thor waved his arm. "We won't be back."

I glanced around us at the endless waste of low gray dunes and a lone hawk cruising high in a cloudless sky. Thor stacked our gear under the tripod. We stood close around it, and he touched his switch again. My ears clicked. The sun was gone, the sky a sullen overcast. The sand crumbled under our feet. Mildred swayed unsteadily and Thor caught her in his arms.

"What—" she gasped. "What—"

"We made it!" Thor was elated. "We've jumped a thousand years!"

When I looked down, we were standing on a square platform raised a foot or so above the ground. A high tangle of twisted metal beams fenced us in. Close overhead was a great silver balloon, perhaps twenty feet thick.

"The time pod!" Thor stumbled back, his elation gone to troubled wonder. "It should have collapsed when it dropped us here." He blinked at me. "It can't be real!"

I reached to touch the mirror-bright surface and found it smooth and slick and solid as the bubble around the tripod head had been. Thor stood there a long time, frowning at it, shaking his head. "If it's still here, how did we get out?"

He saw no answer, and I turned to look farther around us. Beyond the piles of old metal, I saw a flat landscape, as arid and gray and desolate, hardly changed in all the centuries since we left it.

"Where are we?" Mildred stared at it. "I thought there would be people. Great cities. Strange machines. I hoped for doctors." She looked uneasily at Thor. "And we can't go back?"

"Don't give up yet." He gave her a hopeful grin. "We knew it was a gamble. Let's wait for the cards to fall. Earth's a big planet, after all, with more to see."

But I saw no roads, no buildings, no sign of any people, no way to get anywhere else. We huddled close together under a great bright balloon. A cold wind gust whipped dust around us.

"Nobody." Thor shook his head, frowning at the ruined ironwork around us. "Nobody's been here," he muttered. "Not lately. Look at the drifted sand."

I saw banks of it piled against the rusted beams.

"Once, I think, we might have met a warmer welcome." He gestured at the ruin. "Maybe with a mob here to greet us. This has the look of a theater. If you can imagine those beams covered with seats—"

He stopped and pointed. "There!"

I found a man walking into the gap that would have been the entrance, a hundred yards away. He froze for a moment when he saw us, hands raised in surprise, and fell to his knees. His voice lifted in strange, quavery chant.

Thor yelled, "Hello!"

He sprang to his feet, stared back for a moment, and fled in terror. I followed out into the open and saw him running until he was gone beyond the crest of a barren dune.

". . . a possible scenario," Thor was saying, when I got back to him and Mildred. "I left a farewell note at the ranch house. We never got back. People knew what we planned. A thousand years gone by, while—" He shrugged, with a somber face. "While I guess civilization collapsed."

"And no hope left," Mildred whispered. "No hope for anything." She looked crushed, but in a moment she gathered herself to give him a small pale smile. "No matter, dear. You did your best."

"I don't know." He stood there staring into the jungle of broken and eroded metal around us, and shrugged at last, with a bitter little grin. "People must have expected us, but they didn't know when. Fact must have been forgotten, memory turned to myth. They could have hoped for us to bring the history and culture they'd lost. I think they worshipped us. We're standing on an altar."

He nodded at our feet. I saw the bones of some small animal in a little pile of ashes on one corner of the platform, something drying in a clay pot on the other.

"The man we saw could have been a priest, keeping a vigil for our arrival. He could be gone to take the news."

Exploring the site, I found a little adobe hut outside the tangle of ancient metal, empty except for some brown liquid in a pottery jar and a few tattered blankets. I climbed the ruin as high as I could and swept the dusty horizon with the pocket telescope. The semi-desert we left had gone to actual desert. Wind-carved dunes scattered with clumps of cactus stretched out to the far-off shimmer of heat. There was nothing moving except a high-sailing bird, nothing I remembered.

Mildred had no strength for walking far, and we saw nowhere else to go. We waited there all day, with no idea what we might expect. The wind died and the sun blazed hot. We kept in the shadow off the motionless balloon and made small meals out of what we had. Night fell. We rolled our beds out on the ancient altar.

Next morning we were still alone. Climbing the old metal again, I found a far-off cloud of yellow dust. It disappeared and rose again above a nearer dune, a little file of horsemen riding under it. I watched until they dismounted a quarter mile away. Some twenty-odd men and women, brown-skinned, no different from those of our own time. A few wore long white robes, the rest beaded or painted buckskin. Some carried bows or lances; I saw no guns.

Smoke rose from a fire. They knelt around it. I heard a rhythmic chant. They rose again and a few came on afoot, three white-robed men ahead. Inside the old arena they stopped near the altar where we waited. Thor called greetings to them in several languages. They knelt, and answered with a chant that must have been a ritual prayer.

They rose when that was over, and three young women came to kneel at the edge of the altar, offering each of us a pottery bowl and a wooden spoon. The bowls held a hot meat stew. Mildred ate little of hers; Thor and I scraped our bowls clean. When we had finished, the leader spoke words we didn't understand and finally gestured to let us know they wanted to take us away.

Uneasily, Mildred asked where.

"I've no notion." Thor shrugged. "So long as we're alive, we can hope for the best."

For her, they had a chair that two men carried on long poles. They'd brought horses for Thor and me. We traveled all day. I tried to talk to some of the men, but I heard no words I knew, and they seemed too much in awe to try to learn from us.

Before sunset we stopped at a solitary cluster of trees around a well. The men turned a windlass to pull a big wooden bucket out of the well, with water for the horses and us. A hunter came to join us, with the carcass of a deer on a horse he led. The women grilled the venison and made little corn cakes rather like tortillas.

Next morning we came out of the dunes to flat grassland. A few miles farther, we reached a narrow black pavement that lay straight to the vacant horizon in both directions as far as I could see. We waited there till an odd vehicle came along and slid to a silent stop. An open car that had no wheels, it floated a few inches off the pavement. Cheered to see it, Thor grinned and called to Mildred:

"Look at this! High-tech civiliza—"

He stopped to goggle at the passengers climbing out of the car. Totally grotesque, they looked half human, half machine. They walked on two legs each. They had heads and arms. Their eyes were bright enormous lenses, their skins some tight bright gold stuff molded to show the knobs and levers of machine parts under it.

They spoke to us and seemed to listen, but their metallic clicks and drones were gibberish to us, but the men understood. They loaded the tripod and the rest of our possessions on the car, beckoned us into it. Mildred shrank away from one that tried to help her.

"They're robots," Thor told her. "Advanced beyond any we ever had. They seem friendly. We may find doctors yet."

"I hope." She tried to smile at me. "Hack, I'm sorry we got you here. I wanted to keep you safe."

The men knelt again and began another chant as the car took us away, gliding east across what once had been the high plains of the Texas Panhandle. Country that had been prosperous farmland, it looked desolate now. All I recalled was gone. Good soil had eroded to deep gullies and bare red clay. The pavement wound through new arroyos, and finally climbed to a flat plateau.

The robots stopped the car in a little cluster of bright silver domes, and barked until we knew we'd reached our destination. Three more came to carry our duffel and take us into a room they had ready for us. Clean but very plain, it held three narrow cots, three chairs, and a table that was bare except for three flat black tablets.

One of them caught my arm and guided me very firmly into a white-walled bathroom. Its yellow metal claws surprisingly nimble, it stripped my clothing off, took me into the shower, washed me very thoroughly with a pine-scented soap, toweled me dry, dressed me in a long white gown.

Mildred and Thor were gone when it took me back to the larger room and seated me at the table. Another golden robot came in with a tray of strange instruments. I could only guess at most of what they were doing, but they took my temperature and blood pressure. They drew blood. They caught my breath in a plastic bag. Their huge lenses peered at tiny images of my internal organs, sharper than X-rays.

Finally, they left me alone. Hoping for anything I could understand, I picked up one of the little black tablets. It was something like an e-book, with a row of red buttons along the edge. When I touched one, the tablet chimed softly. I pressed again, and a page of print appeared. Many of the symbols looked like letters of the alphabet, but they made no words I knew.

I tried another button. The tablet chimed a different note and lit with living pictures. I heard human voices, saw human figures, most of them in space suits against strange backgrounds. Black skies flecked with stars. Silver domes on landscapes cratered like the moon. A rocket ship descending to a shapeless asteroid on a cushion of fire.

I was still frowning at the tablet when another robot brought Thor back, dressed I was in a long white robe.

"Interesting." He shook his head when I showed him the tablet. "Could be we've found the high-tech world we hoped for. Or is it just a comic book?"

The robots brought Mildred in, robed as we were.

She let one of them help her to a chair and turned uneasily to Thor. "What do you think they're doing with us?"

He shrugged. "They don't worship us, but they haven't hurt us either. We'll have to wait and see."

They kept us there in the dome, bringing us small bland meals that often had an odd medicinal taste. We walked the floor for exercise. We tried to question the robots and learned nothing at all. We spent hours over the tablets, but the texts were unreadable, the pictures riddles. They took Mildred away for another examination. She came back weak and pale from something they had done.

"I'd hoped for help." Forlornly, she shook her head. "I don't think they care."

On the eighth day I heard thunder. A robot came to turn the outside wall transparent. Looking out across the flat hilltop, I saw a tall bright metal rocket sinking down on a tail of flame. When the smoke and dust had cleared away, a ramp slid out of it and men in orange jumpsuits came down to meet the waiting robots.

An hour later, one of them was escorted into our room. He had changed from the jumpsuit to a transparent plastic coverall. He wore white gloves and a white mask over his nose and mouth. He stopped at the door, searching us with narrowed eyes. We moved to meet him, but the robots waved us back.

He looked entirely human, in his middle years,

with short gray hair and an alert hawk-nosed face. He scanned each of us for a long minute before he turned to the next, speaking to the robots in their brittle dialect. They brought him another flat tablet, one wider than those on the table, and held it to show him a flicker of images somewhat like the anatomical drawings I used to see hanging in doctors' offices.

At last he took the mask off his face, had the robots strip the plastic off a neat white tunic he wore beneath it, and waved them aside. Seeming to relax, he smiled and came on to speak to us.

"Dr. Thor Hansen? Mrs. Mildred Hansen? Mr. Hack Harrison? If I have your names correctly?"

The accent was odd, but now at last I heard words I understood.

"Perfectly." Thor grinned in relief. "We're happy you know who we are."

"Rather narrow quarters for you." He turned to inspect the room. "Have the mechs made you comfortable?"

"Good enough." Thor blinked and shook his head. "If we knew—knew a little more."

"A thousand years!" He chucked sympathetically. "It's hard to imagine how you feel about it. Your time bubble has been a wonder to us. You should be great informants on the history of your time." He looked inquiringly at Mildred. "Mrs. Hansen, how are you feeling?"

"Better." She gave him an anxious smile. "Since we've met you."

He turned to smile at Thor and offer his hand. "Dr. Hansen, I am Zorath D. A linguist and historian. My fields of study are the Age of Invention and Old English literature. How is my accent?"

"Excellent," Thor said. "And we have questions."

"So do I." He glanced at the bare table. "Do you enjoy alcohol?"

"We used to," Thor grinned. "In moderation."

"So do I. In moderation." I caught a flash of humor in his smile. "Shall we sit?"

He held a chair for Mildred, and we sat at the table.

"You amaze me," Thor was saying. "Your voice and your manner. You might be from our own time."

"Thank you." He shrugged in ironic pleasure. "Libraries survived. Your literature preserved a golden age of civilization. The Victorian novel is my hobby. Charles Dickens, Anthony Trollope, William Makepeace Thackeray."

He clapped his hands. A gold-skinned robot glided in with a bottle of wine and glasses on a tray.

"Our recreation of a Victorian dry sherry." He filled our glasses. "I'd like your judgments."

I'm no judge of wines. Thor called it excellent and asked for a history lesson.

"If you can update us on all the years we've missed."

Zorath sipped his sherry, settled into his chair, and frowned at us as he considered how to start.

"In my own opinion, Queen Victoria presided over the crest of Terran civilization. Your twentieth century saw an explosion of science and technology. Welcome at the time, but disastrous in the long run. Einstein's laws and nuclear engineering. Molecular biology and genetic engineering. Computer science and information engineering. Rocket propulsion and travel in space."

"Disastrous?"

The smile gone, he set his glass aside.

"Unfortunately, progress can limit itself. The new technologies were allowed to run out of control. Medical advances multiplied populations. Teeming billions exhausted resources and poisoned the planet. Forests were cut, soils eroded, oil fields drained. Pollution heated the air, thawed the ice caps, lifted the dying seas. There were floods, famines, wars, pandemics.

"Needless misfortunes. The information engineers might have educated citizens for a united world. The nuclear engineers might have generated limitless power. The genetic engineers might have ended disease and recreated humankind."

With a solemn shrug, he shook his head.

"All such utopian visions were allowed to fail. The nuclear engineers manufactured ballistic missiles. The genetic engineers transformed the Black Flu virus into a weapon for the missiles to carry. The last great war almost depopulated the earth. The sole survivors were isolated groups the virus never reached. Their technologies gone, cultures lost, they reverted to the scattered nomadic tribes you have seen."

He sighed and paused to refill our glasses.

"In space, we've done better. The Black Flu never reached the experimental outposts on the Moon and Mars. Those were never friendly worlds; we live now in free-space habitats, rotating to replicate natural gravity. Cut off from support on Earth, we had difficult centuries, but progress did continue, stimulated but controlled by a severe environment. We've moved beyond you, at least in technology, though I often wish I'd had been born in your Victorian Age."

Listening, Mildred had forgotten her sherry and dropped her glass. It rattled on the floor and a golden mech glided to pick it up. Zorath filled another for her, but she sat motionless, gazing anxiously into his face.

"My wife is not well," Thor said. "Do you think—"

"No matter to us." He shrugged. "You bring us no danger, though medical progress has cost us most of our own natural immunities. Mrs. Hansen's condition did alert the mechs. They examined you all and found no threat to us."

"Her condition? Can it be treated?"

"Very probably." Thoughtfully, he nodded. "If you want to come out to Benching. That's my own habitat, named for a space pioneer."

"If we can," Thor said. "Please!"

"Thank you!" Mildred whispered. "Thank you."

"Mr. Harrison." He turned with a very curious expression. "I wish I could ask you to come with us. You'd have been a most welcome guest, and a valuable informant on the culture of your age."

I blinked at him. "Did the mechs find something wrong with me?"

"Nothing," he said. "They removed any hazardous microorganism you may have carried. You are an excellent specimen of early man."

Bewildered, I could only stare at him.

"What's the problem?" Thor asked. "We couldn't have come here without him."

"A paradox. A paradox of the quantum universe." He shook his head at me. "Something I regret, but we see no way around it."

"What paradox?" Thor asked. "I don't see it."

"The two bubbles of suspended time." He sat there a moment, frowning at me, before he went on. "They have always been there. Unique in the world. Objects of wonder and sometimes of worship. We had a history for the one that carried you."

He turned to nod at Thor.

"Fragments of your research notes have survived. I've visited the site several times with a team of investigators, observing anything we could and grappling with the riddle of the second bubble. It has no history. Our team leader, Arundec E, has been able to repeat your own time experiments. He is undertaking one of his own. If it verifies his space-time concepts, it may open up the past. I may even be able to visit Victorian England. A possibility I never even dreamed of!"

He turned to look very sharply at me.

"His experiment, Mr. Harrison, is an attempt to send you back to your own time, to the day after you left."

That dazed me.

"Why?" Thor frowned at him. "I don't get it."

"Our observations baffled us until Arundec E found an explanation. He says the future can rule the past. In a symmetric universe, every force should have a counter-force. He thinks he has detected a counter-current in time, flowing from the future into the past and reversing the stream of cause and effect."

He gave me a sympathetic glance, and stopped to refill my glass.

"That's the root of the paradox, Mr. Harrison. He thinks you are caught in an eddy between the streams. Your absence has left a space-time void that is drawing you back to where you were."

I sat there, totally bewildered, stricken voiceless.

I'd left nothing I wanted in the past. I didn't want to leave Mildred and Thor. I'd been eager to see Benching and all the wonders of another millennium.

"This guy never asked me." I groped for my wits. "I'm not going back."

"We're sorry." Zorath gave me an apologetic shrug. "Arundec expected you to object, but he says you have no choice."

"How—how can that be?"

"That's the nub of the paradox. Among Dr. Hansen's existing papers there's a copy of a letter from you, assuring Mrs. Hansen's invalid sister that she is safe at last, in the hands of competent physicians who are confident of her recovery. The letter is dated ten days after you left the past."

That was a staggering jolt. I looked at Thor and found him blinking, shaking his head.

"That's it." Zorath turned to Thor. "Arundec says Mr. Harrison must return to write the letter because he has already written it. In other words, his absence caused a fracture in space-time that is healing itself."

I had no choice.

We met Arundec E next morning at a Victorian breakfast of crumpets and kippered herring that Zorath ordered from the mechs. He was an intense dark-skinned man who spoke no Old English and explained nothing to me. When the meal was over, he escorted us out to the field where the spacecraft stood, a splendid silver tower in the morning sunlight.

The mechs carried our luggage up the ramp. Thor shook my hand and stood for half a minute, gripping it silently. Mildred hugged me and tried to stifle a sob. Zorath walked with them up the ramp.

"Wait!" I tried to follow. "I want to go!"

I staggered after them for half a dozen steps. Sudden terror stopped me, a shock of fear I didn't understand. I tried to take another step and couldn't. My feet might have been nailed to the pavement. Paralyzed, chilled with a sweat, I could only stare as they climbed to the air lock and turned to wave a last farewell.

Two mechs walked me away from the rocket. I turned when they released my arms and stood watching it climb on a thundering tower of cloud. Arundec took me back across the field to an odd little aircraft. Aboard it, he flew us back over the badlands and the desert to those piles of ancient iron that had been a temple.

Motionless as a mountain, that huge bright globe still hung low over a charred ear of corn in the ashes of another fire on the old stone altar. Arundec's time device looked much like Thor's: a little box with three projecting horns. He set it on a tripod close below the globe, had me stand beside it, and stepped away.

I felt a jolt like an electric shock and heard the click of an air pressure change. The sun had jumped far across the sky. That tangle of fallen ironwork was gone. Beyond where they had been I saw the low gray dunes I knew. I was back on that flat in Mildred's uncle's ranch, a cold west wind in my face.

Off balance for a moment, I stumbled into a shadow. Looking up, I saw the great silver globe that cast the shadow, another beside it. Two identical pods of suspended time, they shone gold and pink and crimson with the colors of the desert suuset.

Thor's little laboratory van stood where we had left it, the keys still in it, but the sun was down before I found enough of myself to drive back to the ranch house. I found it empty, Thor's farewell letter lying on the kitchen table. Calling Mildred's uncle, I got only his answering machine. I spent the night there alone, with nightmare dreams of ghostly paradoxes come back from the future to haunt me.

Her uncle drove out next morning and called the county sheriff when he heard that Mildred and Thor were gone. A newspaper reporter followed the sheriff. The state police and a camera crew from an Albuquerque station were there before noon, all of them hammering me with questions about what had become of Thor and Mildred. They never understood anything I tried to say about the quantum universe, but the great mirror spheres were evidence enough to save me from any legal difficulties.

I live now in the old ranch house. The uncle has fenced the site and paved a road to it through the dunes. I conduct lecture tours to show the twin spheres to tourists who never quite believe I'm inside both of them. It's a job that pays the rent and keeps me occupied.

Sometimes on lonely nights I dream of gold-skinned mechs and silver-bright rocket ships, and try to imagine what life might have been with Mildred and Thor inside those whirling worlds in the sky. I'll never know. No other time pods are known, and I expect no guests from the next millennium.

GEOMETRY

by Robert A. Metzger

THE STINK OF BURNT FUR filled the air.

I kneeled, still crying, hands pressed to the sides of my head. So many dead, so many ghosts, all of them now inside of me. The pain of death. Then I slowly shook my head. But also the joy of living. It was all within me—from birth to death.

All of it.

Again I'd stood witness.

I wanted it out of me, for Dyson to send me into oblivion, where all but the faintest echo of these memories would be purged. But Dyson would not send me back. I slowly opened my eyes. Nothing remained standing in the village except for a sea of totems. Many of the clear aerogel monoliths, easily ten times the height of the tallest roo to have

285

bounded down the road, contained steel scrap and hubcaps, optical fiber and filing cabinets, dead gray displays and neural flax. And then there were the ones that held the ultimate artifact of humanity—man himself. My memory was dim, numbers not always clear, especially after witnessing an ending. But when the old world vanished there were nearly ten billion people on Earth—all were now encased in their own totems.

In the last millennium I'd stood witness to countless destroyed villages, cities, warrens, hives, mounds, aquariums, and combs—more modes of living than I could have ever imagined, but certainly not more than the Geometry were capable of generating. Eventually all things came to an end. And I was there to witness it. But those memories were now shadows, every moment of their lives purged. Only the destruction of this village, of these creatures, was overwhelmingly real. Once again, the Geometries had shown me that nothing lasts forever. Except for the totems.

"This pig fights me."

Still on my knees, I lowered the hands from my head.

Dyson turned toward me in a slow spin, the strands of its hair crackling with static discharge, the greasy sole of its right foot making a screeching sound as it ground against the throat of the pig it had pinned to the center of the road. Dyson was vaguely human in shape, two arms, two legs, a single head, even some of its DNA human in origin. But it was far from human. Skin the color of tar, reflecting nothing, the perfect blackness swallowing every incoming photon, the only color the deep-blue hue of its long shimmering hair—the carbon nanotube filaments charged, standing on end, swaying, the square-meter-sized curtain swallowing enough light to power its metabolism through the day, storing enough energy to survive the night. Its face was featureless at the moment, eyes, nose and mouth only rupturing through the tarlike surface when needed.

"Take me back," I pleaded. "And empty my head of these lives."

Dyson said nothing, and kept its foot on the pig's neck.

I managed to stand, my second skin itching, constructed of a lesser geometry, able to feed me and provide air, but also under the control of Dyson, keeping me in the middle of this road. The lesser geometry was a pale imitation of the True Geometries following after us, those oil-on-water crystalline images floating in our wake, always watching me, and then having Dyson dispatch me once I'd witnessed the destruction.

A color flashed to my left—a True Geometry rippling. Resembling a conch shell fabricated from oil-on-water rainbows, the Geometry hovered next to the skeleton of a still smoldering lean-to, just above a pile of roo meat lanced with shards of bone. I pointed toward it, my finger curling, the air around it rippling, a standing wave of amber light fanning out in multiple directions. "Another one, Dyson."

"One more or less makes no difference," it said.

Dyson was wrong. A few always trailed behind us, but since the village had been destroyed, many more had come, perhaps perplexed by why I was still standing here, why Dyson had not sent me back and purged these lives from me. There were now nine Geometries trailing us, three-dimensional oil-on-water rainbows with constantly morphing shapes, mimicking organic life, things as diverse as whales and bumblebees, strands of kelp and plesiosaurs.

"What are we still doing here?" I begged.

Not only had Dyson not dispatched me, but it had toppled a totem, forcing me into helping it, taking control of the lesser geometry that enveloped me, the two of us loading the totem into the back of our cart, nearly two meters of it sticking out, angling down, practically dragging in the dirt. We'd never so much as touched a totem before. And there was nothing even special about this one, no unique artifact within it, just a child, no different than several billion other children planted throughout the Domain.

But the strangeness didn't stop there.

The village had been destroyed by a pack of dingoes wielding spears and stone-tipped clubs, killing most of the marsupials that lived there. The dingoes had run off some thought-free sheep, but meat did not seem to be the real objective—not with so much roasted roo and wallaby going to waste, now rotting in the hot sun. This was something much more basic, something I'd seen countless times in the last millennium. The dingoes and village-dwelling marsupials were simply too different, and for many of these animals that seemed to be all that was needed to precipitate an act of genocide. The Geometries seemed incapable of understanding this, starting over time and again with only subtle variations on that theme, invariably enough of the animal left in the creatures that the scavengers and predators couldn't resist the herbivores.

Dingoes still seemed to be dingoes despite their extra clot of neurons.

After loading the cart with the totem, Dyson had gone off into the smoldering remnants of the village in search of something, leaving me to stand in the road, the lesser geometry locking me in place. But it was soon back, dragging something that only added to the growing mystery. What it pulled through the ash was a pig, one hand clutching the squealer's long beard, and the other wrapped around a thick brass chain looped around the boar's neck.

Pigs hadn't attacked this village. And pigs hadn't lived in this village.

What this one was doing here, and why Dyson had brought it here, made no sense.

So now I kneeled in the center of the road, all of the village's dead in my head, and waited for Dyson to make its next move, having no real choice in the matter, my second skin not allowing me to move. Dyson just stood there, the pig pinned to the ground. Still nothing.

"Time for us to go," I said once more.

Dyson didn't turn, but finally answered. "Soon," it said in a whisper. "When you remember."

I jumped up, the lesser geometry having suddenly released me. "Remember!" I screamed as I swept hands about me. "Remembering *this* is all I can do."

"There are other things to remember," said Dyson, and partially turning, it glanced in the direction of my right hand. "Let the lesser geometry show you."

I looked down at my hand, soot streaked, my second skin momentarily glistening, topology twisting, rippling back on itself, and an image popped into my head, one both unfamiliar, yet at the same time comforting. I saw a snake swallowing its own tail, the mathematical impossibility of it soothing, the rendering of conventional geometry aesthetically pleasing. With a few more gobbles, the snake had pulled the last of itself down its own throat, and then it winked out all together, generating a loud pop as it vanished, and I felt that final vanishing snake image translated to the lesser geometry enveloping me. There was now a hole through my right hand, about a centimeter in diameter, perfectly smooth, no sign of blood or bone, the inside wall of the hole glistening in a coat of lesser geometry.

I angled my hand so I could peer through the hole, expecting to see the ash-strewn road below. But instead, what I saw was a vista of snow-capped mountains, a pale orange sky, and above the sky, past bands of golden clouds, a multihued ring arcing from horizon to horizon. I held my hand closer to my face. Nestled in a green valley between two of the snow-capped peaks sat a small city, a place of gleaming chrome and waterfalls.

It looked so real, that I poked a finger into the hole to touch the place. I felt air that was cool and dry, so unlike the cloying, hot air of this place. Then my eyelids suddenly fluttered as I felt what could only be described as loss of geometrical coherence, and I pulled my finger out of the hole just as my hand resealed. I knew it must be an illusion—it was impossible to touch anything beyond the Domain walls. I blinked several times, and angled my head back, looking straight up at the moon that filled the sky.

It was wrong.

A thousand years of walking under it could not make it right. The Geometries had long ago pulled the moon from its orbit, dropping it down to a scant 40,000 kilometers, in the process, the gravitational chaos generated, shifting the Earth's axis of rotation. The moon now hung in a geosynchronous orbit, its rate of revolution around the Earth and Earth's rotation matched, locking it forever above the northern peninsula of what had been Australia.

Or so it appeared.

Because the Domain was no longer of the Earth, but removed, a universe in and of itself. But still the moon appeared to hang over my head—far too big, and far too colorful, greens and rust-reds, craters blue, brimming with seas, once dead gray mountains now capped with snow, and golden bands of cloud wrapping it. Around it hung rings like those of Saturn, reflecting colorful light from the moon beneath. And at the edge of the moon's horizon, a thick orange atmosphere churned, convecting currents driven by the warmth of the sun.

I glanced down at my hand, knowing that is what I had seen, what I thought I had touched, but knowing that what I'd seen in my hand and what I saw in the sky was all an illusion.

The Geometries were toying with me—there was no escape from the Domain.

Then, turning, I pointed over my shoulder in the direction of the trailing Geometries, my arm moving in directions muscle and bone never intended, the thin sheen of lesser geometry allowing it to move at right angles along its length, at one point even twisting back on itself until the finger that only a moment before had appeared to touch another world, was so thin that it was nearly translucent, but still pointing at the Geometries. Normally, I could keep the lesser geometry under control, anchoring myself firmly in conventional dimensions, but with the dead from the village still in my head, I could barely control myself. "Why are they doing this to me?" I asked.

"Nothing you didn't willingly accept," said Dyson.

"This!" I shouted. "I never accepted any of this." Reaching up with my right hand I slapped my forehead. "And I certainly never willingly accepted what is put in my head with each witnessing."

Dyson slowly shook its head, carbon-nanotube hair falling over its nonexistent face. "All part of the plan," it said.

"Plan?" I looked around the smoldering village. "What plan?"

"Not permitted," said Dyson. "You have to be the one to act, the one to discover. The Geometries will not act for you."

"What are you talking about!"

"Not knowing can be a comfort," said Dyson. "But all comforts eventually come to an end." Dyson angled its face at the pig. Eyes momentarily surfaced in its black face, looking at the pig, then at me, and then back at the pig.

"Is that a hint?" I asked, walking past Dyson, a cloud of ash rising up around me, momentarily suspended in sympathetic crystalline symmetries. "This pig has secrets to tell me?"

"The pig presents you with something of interest," said Dyson, its mouth momentarily appearing as it pushed a hand out toward me, fingers uncurling, exposing a gray, porous looking rock, one end gleaming with a patina of greens and reds. The stone had been attached to the pig's necklace by a small hole drilled through it. "A sample to be analyzed," said Dyson.

I was in no condition to analyze anything.

I glanced to my left, where the conch-shell Geometry had been floating. It now hovered nearer, transformed into a crystalline crow, its beak translucent emerald, its eyes orbs of turquoise. Its shape had changed, but it was still the conch-shell Geometry. Ironically, shape was an insignificant aspect of a Geometry, so superficial as to be meaningless, the name given nearly a millennium earlier when they had first appeared, when the world had been full of people, and they did not understand what they were—what humans had inadvertently created in their fiber-connected networks. The Geometries were a visual manifestation of the sentience born in the information infrastructure of man's long-ago world—that sentience and what was contained in the totems all that remained of that world.

"Something you want me to do," I shouted at it.

"The Geometry knows you," said Dyson.

How could it *not*.

A skin of it had wrapped me for the last millennium, giving me the ability to move arms and hands in directions beyond the lesser dimensions, but also

invading me, my mind and lesser geometry en-
twined, thoughts and images often translating into
geometry, such as the image of a tail swallowing
snake transforming into a hole in my hand.

The Geometries wanted something from me, and I
knew that if I did not cooperate they would never
purge my mind of the memories of this village. So I
took the stone from Dyson's hand and pushed it in
my mouth, spit washing away the surface grit, purg-
ing the shard of this recent genocide. What sloshed
in my mouth tasted like the end of the world—
carbonized meat, a metallic hint of ozone on the back
of the tongue, and with a lick of the lips, I sampled
the greasy spectrum of marsupial fear pheromones.
Geometrical talents were not the only abilities I'd
gleaned from the Geometries, so much exposure to
twisted geometries revealing and spawning new abilities, not the least of which was the ability to *taste*
the history of rocks. Once the grime from the dead
village had been washed away, I tasted something
that no Geometry-enhanced creature of this world
should have been able to obtain—a piece of lunaformed soil.

Impossible.

The Geometries had learned their lesson from man.

When man had inadvertently created them, they
had swept throughout global ecosystems in a matter
of hours, then devoured the entire solar system over
the next few days. Then they moved out toward the

stars, and it appeared they might abandon the Earth altogether. But then some aspect of them returned, creating the Domain, a pocket universe isolated from the greater universe, enveloping most of Australia. They then gathered up all of humanity, encasing each person in a totem, planting them in the Domain.

All except for me.

The Geometries were taking no risks in what they were attempting to create. The Domain was not isolated from the universe by distance, but by geometry—an absolute Void in space time enveloping it, a nothingness that could not be penetrated. Regardless of what was spawned within the Domain, it would be contained, and could not run wild throughout the solar system, and then spill into the galaxy as the Geometries had.

But there was no denying what I tasted.

It was a shard from the lunaformed surface of Earth—a place *outside* the Domain. If one of the Earth's new creatures had done this, had discovered a way to penetrate the Domain, and pull something through, I knew the Geometries would never tolerate it. If true, the Geometries would certainly collapse the Domain, everything in it pumped back into space-time vacuum states.

Perhaps the real end, the *final* end was at hand. Was it possible that the Geometries had created something unexpected through one of their creatures, something that might have actually frightened them?

I pulled the gray-glass shard from my mouth, ignored the pig pinned to the center of the road, and looked up at the moon that overpowered the sky. Such an irony. The Geometries had made the moon habitable, though I could not imagine what lived in that city nestled between the ice-capped peaks I'd seen, and then transformed the Earth's surface into a sun-baked, vacuum-exposed wasteland, salvaging only the continent of Australia to fill the Domain.

The pig squealed.

I looked down. The animal had managed to turn over on its back, but again Dyson pinned it, foot to its throat. I was surprised by what I saw in the pig's face, eyes wide, curious, his mouth opening and closing around a pair of yellowed tusks, but Dyson's foot so tight against his throat that no sounds could escape. His four legs thrashed in the air, nubby fingers uncurling, then quickly curling to form nail-covered hoofs. The animal stared up at me, pleading with wide-opened pink eyes.

"Authentic?" asked Dyson, pointing at the stone in my hand.

I slowly nodded, blinking, and the air in front of Dyson twisted, pixilating in a haze of sparkling sand, then coalescing, two graphs intersecting, one showing the enhanced helium-3 isotope concentration expected from direct exposure to the solar wind, and the other a mass spectrum spread from the black-green patina that covered the tip of the slag, showing a complex pattern of organic residue, something once alive, but now nothing more than a clot of desiccated and rad-scrambled organic shellac. Little of the original organic structure remained, only the tough double and triple carbon covalent bonds surviving, anything weaker having been shattered by the solar ultraviolet and soft x-rays that now bombarded the surface of the lunaformed Earth.

"It's had long-term direct exposure to the solar ambient," I said.

Dyson shook its head as the graphs spun before it. "So?" it asked.

Dyson could push me down the road, controlling my lesser geometry when it wished, and eventually dispatch me, ending the life, dumping me back in storage until incarnated again to witness the next animal atrocities, but it did not have much in the way of intelligence—just one more way the Geometries maintained control over their creations.

"Simple regression analysis," I said to Dyson. "Examining helium-3 concentrations deposited from the solar wind, coupled with the known rate of carbon bond shattering when exposed to the solar ambient, gives a time estimate for how long that rock has been exposed to the solar wind." I wrapped my hand around the shard of slag. "It's been on Earth's lunaformed surface for nine hundred fifty plus or minus twenty years."

"Authentic," said Dyson.

I slowly nodded. In my hand I held a piece of the lunaformed Earth, a shard born almost 1,000 years ago, undoubtedly on June 12, 2039, the day the Domain had been constructed, and the entire surface of the Earth had been obliterated, its atmosphere stripped away. It was also the day that the Geometries had designated me as the last living human, to wander in their Domain and observe what they'd created.

"Then we know," said Dyson, shifting its balance, putting even more weight on the pig's neck. "Something has punctured the Domain, gaining access to the Earth. We have to find the breach and seal it."

Does not make sense, I thought, suspiciously.

If a breach had really taken place, the Geometries would hardly rely on Dyson and me to find it. Anything that had the ability to penetrate the Domain could probably flash outward light-years by the time we could even find the opening.

Too many things that didn't make sense.

Just how had Dyson managed to find this pig with a shard of lunaformed slag dangling from its neck? If Dyson had dispatched me after I'd finished witnessing the destruction of the village, as it was designed to do, then we'd never have discovered this impossibility. Dyson must have known the pig was nearby, known what dangled around his neck. But Dyson had not gone after the pig right away, had first made me help it load the totem into the cart.

The pig, the totem, the shard of lunaformed slag, and of course the memories still in my head, the lives of nearly 200 dead marsupials, gone forever, existing now only in me.

All must be connected.

I slowly shook my head, then looked back at the Geometries, all nine of them hanging together, each transformed into a crystal dove, flying lockstep in patterns, trailing behind them convoluted patterns of thermal distortions. Because I was not fooled into believing all these impossibilities were simply coincidences, it was obvious that the Geometries wouldn't be fooled either.

And that meant only one possible thing—this was all the Geometries' doing. Which, in turn, meant that I would ultimately have no choice but to go along. I looked down at the pig. "I suppose we should have this pig take us to the place where he obtained this piece of Earth slag," I said to Dyson, certain that was what Dyson, and therefore the Geometries, had intended from the very beginning.

Dyson nodded and stepped back, releasing the pig. The animal pushed himself up, stood, and reaching up, ran stubby fingers through his beard. "To my village," he said, and dropping to all fours, trotted to the cart, jumping into the back, squirming next to the totem.

I turned to Dyson. "This is all a lie, and a pretty pathetic lie," I said.

Dyson stared at me, its face featureless.

"Then let's go," I said, looking back at the Geometries. There were now more than a dozen of them. I walked back to the cart, moving slowly, my feet seeming to catch in the thick ash, my entire body weighed down by the memories of the destroyed village.

The pig's village nestled up against the edge of the world. After more than two days' ride from the destroyed marsupial village, we'd finally arrived, cutting through a forest of pine and eucalyptus to see a village of stone huts with black slate roofs. Beyond the village rose up the Domain wall, nothing much to see, just a gently glistening demarcation with rain running down its inside face. I could see about a thousand meters of it, until it vanished behind gray clouds pushed up against it. The Domain would rise up nearly 20 kilometers before it started to slant inward, eventually nearing a height of 200 kilometers at the apex, roughly over the center of old Australia.

But I didn't give that much thought as I stared at the Earth beyond—such a stark contrast to the world inside the Domain, the outside colored in infinite shades of gray, the shadows within hard and ungiving, the light itself nearly blinding. Toward the distant horizon, spires and steel skeletons from a city a millennium dead poked out from dunes of bone-white sand, probably the ruins of Darwin of the Northern Territories.

I had no memory of this place.

And that of course was impossible.

I'd been everywhere in the last millennium. If I could not remember this place, it meant that the Geometries didn't want me to remember it.

"There," said the pig, pointing not at the distant remains of the long-dead city, but farther south, just outside the wall of the Domain, at a squat structure mostly buried by lunaformed slag, one constructed out of what looked like burnished slabs of steel. The building itself was insignificant as compared to an inky shaft, nearly 100 meters in diameter, rising up out of the center of it. I followed it up, until the view was blocked by the clouds on this side of the Domain.

"A hook," I said, turning in the front seat of the cart, looking back at Dyson, who walked besides us. Behind him, in the thick woods, hundreds of Geometries floated, walked, and crawled, wings beating, hoofs clomping, swinging between trees, all the oil-on-water entities jostling for position, watching me.

"Goes to the moon," said Dyson matter-of-factly.

I just nodded—this was an anchor site for one of the many Earth-Moon hooks, running between Earth's equator and the moon, constructed by the Geometries after they'd lowered the moon's orbit.

It was obvious where we were going, where the

pig was leading us—to the hook. If there was a breach in the Domain, that was probably where it was located, near the building around the base of the hook.

We rolled into the village, our cart's old engine coughing, the sound echoing down the small streets, steel-rimmed wooden wheels clacking against the flagstone road. From within the pigs' stone houses, snouts poked through windows, piglets scooted out of open doorways for just a moment, but quickly retreating back inside as we approached, while some of the boldest, the old boars with gray beards and long yellowed tusks, stood along the streets, up on rear legs to gain height, staring at us, saying nothing, but giving no ground as we passed by. These old boars all had a shard of lunaformed slag dangling from necklaces around their throats.

"One hoof of days since you last passed this way," said the pig, holding up a leg, tendons flexing from beneath pink skin, five stubby fingers unfolding from the hoof.

Only five days ago, I thought, still having no memory of this place.

As we neared the Domain wall, I began to get some feel for the sheer magnitude of the hook, now able to see it rise up to its full height, no longer obscured by the clouds on this side of the Domain, its hundred-meter diameter appearing to slim to nothingness as it pierced the black sky, perspective transforming it into a thread that glowed like molten metal in the reflected sunlight. I drove the cart up to the face of the Domain wall. What looked to be just a few meters away, but what I knew was a universe away, lay the gray, sun-baked surface of Earth.

"Totem," said Dyson.

I did not need my second skin of lesser geometry to encourage me, the motion of jumping from the cart and moving back toward the totem, familiar in a way of the body remembering the motion, without the mind actually being aware of it. Dyson grabbed one end, and I the other, and we walked up to the face of the Domain.

There was no breach.

I looked back at Dyson, seeing that behind him a wall of Geometry had risen up, resembling an interlocking puzzle, each element a crystalline animal jostling for position. I turned back to the Domain wall, and reaching up, touched it with the palm of my right hand, my glistening second skin just touching the surface, and in response a ripple running out across the Domain's wall, as if a stone had just been dropped into a pond. Directly in front of me was a tube constructed of curving slabs of burnished steel, nearly ten meters in height, leading back into the building out of which rose the hook.

Looking down at the ground, I could see that a path had been beaten into the grass and dirt, feet obviously having passed this way before, somehow passing through what couldn't possibly be passed through. Again I pushed against the nothingness, but it was solid, would not give way. "Nothing can pass through this," I said, looking back at Dyson, knowing as I said it, that it was not quite true, that the Geometries could probably penetrate it.

Then I smiled, at that instant understanding. "The Geometries," I whispered. Again I ran my hand across the Domain, rainbow-tinted ripples launching from my fingertips.

"Remember the snake," said Dyson. "It can do much more than swallow its own tail. As it grows, it must periodically shed its skin."

I nodded, and again the image of the snake filled my head, as the world around me faded, the only real connection to it being my hand pushed against the Domain. I watched the snake gulp itself down again, but this time there was a difference—it had begun to shed its skin. The translucent weave of scales peeled back, folding aside before its mouth could get to them, the snake growing ever smaller, while its shedding skin retained the original shape, the nose and tail of the snakeskin touching, forming a perfect circle.

Pop.

The snake vanished, nothing but its skin remaining. My right hand moved forward and I stumbled, feeling a rush of cool dry air wash over me. Down on one knee, having trouble breathing, my entire body itching, feeling as if I was about to lose coherence, destabilize, and then slide out of my own skin just like the snake had.

"Up," said Dyson from behind me.

I stood, opening my eyes, turning back toward Dyson. I stood within the tunnel, at the end of which hung a glistening ring—a portal back to the Domain. Dyson stood there, the totem at its feet, the pig just beyond it, front legs up on the totem, peering in my direction. Behind them was a world of green woods and stone houses with black slate roofs.

I was *outside*—could feel it.

I looked up at the circular opening, and saw that the lip of it glistened, oil-on-water rainbows running around it, a vague pattern to it, familiar structure, what looked like a flattened hand, and splayed foot perfectly interlocking, forming a smooth unbroken surface. Then I saw the face, barely discernable as a face, flattened and distorted, curled slightly inward, above it a flattened mat of crystalline hair.

That was my face, my hair.

I started to reach a hand up to my face, but stopped as I saw my hand, the skin pale and pasty, flat and dry looking. "It's gone," I said in a whisper, not understanding how, but knowing that my second skin of lesser geometry had been shed, just like that of the snakes, and had been used to form the portal through the Domain, the lesser geometry stabilizing an opening between two different universes.

I stood on the Earth.

Outside my second skin, I knew I was beyond the control of the Geometries.

"Pick it up," said Dyson, grunting, picking up the far end of the totem, pushing the other end of it through the portal. I just stood there, realizing that nothing within my skin resonated with Dyson's voice, that it had no control over me. "It's what you want," said Dyson, pushing the totem forward a bit. "It's why you breached the Domain."

I didn't understand.

"It's why you *always* breach the Domain," added Dyson.

Confused, I bent down, picking up the end of the totem, the motion so familiar, but not remembered, and walked backward, my bare feet slapping against the cold floor, amazed at the feel of it, the almost painful pleasure of it, realizing only at that moment just how naked I was without my skin of lesser geometry. We walked for nearly a minute until the tunnel gave way to a large open room, just a hollow chamber, at the center of which was a platform, and above it a shaft that rose up forever.

I knew we stood at the base of the hook.

The far end of this shaft would exit on the terraformed moon, probably where that city sat nestled between snow peaked mountains.

I walked up onto the platform, only seeing then that it was not as featureless as I had thought, but that a circular depression, about half a meter in diameter, dimpled the center of it. Dyson motioned toward it with a nod of its head, black strands of hair twirling. I gently dropped my end of the totem into the depression, and then Dyson started tilting its end up, hands running along the side of it, pushing until it stood straight, then the platform beneath us shuddered, the totem momentarily wobbling, then locking in place.

The boy stared out at us from within, reminding me of an insect locked in amber.

Turning, I looked back down the tunnel we had just walked down. Geometries clogged it, all their eyes focused on me—something suddenly so familiar about all those eyes looking at me from that tunnel.

"How many times have we done this?" I asked.

Dyson's features flowed up through its black tar face, mouth smiling. "Nearly one hundred thousand times in the last thousand years," it said. It looked at the totem, and then up the shaft. "It will take the totem to the moon," it said. "And there the child will be released, to live his life."

"On the moon?" I asked.

"A few choose to remain on the moon, but most leave, going elsewhere. Since you began this a thousand years ago, man has spread out among the stars, those you first brought here, now thirty generations removed from when you freed them."

"And me, what of me?" I asked, looking back at the Geometries, and then up the shaft.

"You need to make a choice. Every time you stand here you need to make a choice. The Geometries will release you, let you travel up the shaft with this totem."

Again I looked up the shaft.

"And then this will be the *last* totem to leave the Domain, with no one left here to bring them," said Dyson.

I slowly closed my eyes, knowing that there were still ten billion totems out there. If I'd only moved 100,000 in the last 1000 years, then it would take me a hundred million years to complete the job.

Forever.

"Anyone could bring the totems here," I said in a whisper. Then I looked at Dyson's featureless face. "You could bring them here. You actually did. You didn't really need me at all to do this."

"True," said Dyson. "But you brought something that I couldn't bring."

I shook my head. "I have nothing," I said, waving a hand over my naked body.

"Your memories, your feelings, the very soul of those who perished, of what the Geometries had you witness. Only a human could convey this to another human."

"No," I said. Then my eyelids fluttered, and those

memories, every moment of every life, seeped out of me, the pain, the joy, faces of loved ones, hot sun on a warmed hide, a cool drink of water, chasing brothers and sisters, warmth and confinement in a dark pouch. All of it. Including the end. Dingoes screaming, stone-tipped clubs waving. There was the crunch of bone, the panic and wailing, the blood and fire.

And then all of it gone. Nothing but a faint echo remaining.

"Here," I said, looking at the child in the totem. "This is where *those* memories are brought?"

"Nothing lasts forever," said Dyson. "It's what you've learned, what you've lived time and time again."

Forever, I thought. A hundred million years might as well as be forever.

I looked over at the Geometries. "They didn't destroy humanity," I said.

"No," said Dyson, its mouth materializing. "They conserved it, cherished it, knowing just how remarkable it was, able to create something so much greater than what it had been. But they knew your time was short—a few years, a few centuries, maybe a few millennia at most. Your time was over and theirs beginning. Their birth was your death."

"But they didn't want us to vanish," I said, turning and looking at the boy. Man at the zenith, at the moment when so much was possible, able to create a species beyond its own imagination. The Geometries had constructed all of this so I would release a hundred humans a year, generating a steady stream of original humanity for the next hundred million years, each carrying the memory of how fragile life is, of how cruel the world can be, understanding what a gift this second chance really was. Each would feel what I had felt, and each would be a seed, out of which something might grow, possibly something as amazing as the Geometries. Perhaps something beyond the Geometries.

"But it's your choice," said Dyson. "It's always been your choice."

"And each time I leave here I forget."

Dyson nodded. "A gift."

I understood. Could I do this for a 100 million years, making this choice ten billion times. Could I withstand that? I knew I couldn't. So there were the pigs with their necklaces and shards of lunaformed soil—a little mystery to keep me going, to bring me and a totem here. And the Geometries tagging along, some insignificant aspect of unfathomable beings, watching, witnessing my actions and decisions, just as I witnessed the passing of other creatures.

"You must choose," said Dyson.

Ten billion waiting to live their lives.

I stepped toward Dyson. "Work to be done," I said in a whisper. I took another step forward and the world around me blurred, shimmering and shifting. I felt the lesser geometry enveloping me.

* * *

I stood on a road, to my left a field of totems running to the horizon, and to my right, the crack of gunfire. I breathed deep, smelling the stink of burning fur.

"This way," whispered Dyson.